RANDOM HOUSE
HOUSE

LARGE
PRINT

SLEEPING WITH FEAR

Also by Kay Hooper
available from Random House Large Print

Chill of Fear

KAY HOOPER

SLEEPING WITH FEAR

RANDOM HOUSE
LARGE PRINT

Published in the United States of America by Random House Large Print in association with Bantam Dell, New York.
Distributed by Random House, Inc., New York.

Library of Congress Cataloging-in-Publication Data
Hooper, Kay.
Sleeping with fear / by Kay Hooper.—1st large print ed.
p.   cm.
ISBN-13: 978-0-7393-2648-0
ISBN-10: 0-7393-2648-1
1. Government investigators—Fiction. 2. Psychics—Fiction. 3. Occult crime investigation—Fiction.
4. South Carolina—Fiction. 5. Large type books.
I. Title.
PS3558.O587S55 2006b
813'.54—dc22
2006017842

www.randomlargeprint.com

FIRST LARGE PRINT EDITION

10 9 8 7 6 5 4 3 2 1

This Large Print edition published in accord with the standards of the N.A.V.H.

For my sister Linda,
because the title worked so well

SLEEPING WITH FEAR

Even before she opened her eyes, Riley Crane was aware of two things. Her pounding head, and the smell of blood.

Neither was all that unusual.

Instinct and training made her lie perfectly still, eyes closed, until she was reasonably sure she was fully awake. She was on her stomach and probably on a bed, she thought. Possibly her own bed. On top of the covers, or at least not covered up.

Alone.

She opened her eyes a slit, just enough to see. Rumpled covers, pillows. Her rumpled covers and pillows, she decided. Her bed. The nightstand, holding the usual nightstand accessories of lamp, an untidy stack of books, and an alarm clock.

The red numbers announced that it was 2:00 P.M.

Okay, that **was** unusual. She never slept late, and she never took naps. Plus, while either a headache or the smell of blood was not uncommon in her life, the two together were setting off alarm bells in her mind.

Riley concentrated on listening, her unease growing when she realized that she could hear only on the "normal" level. The faint hum of the air-conditioning. The muffled rumble and crash of the surf out on the beach. A gull screaming as it flew past the house. The sort of stuff the usual everyday sense of hearing could glean automatically without any added concentration or focus.

But nothing else. Try as she might, she couldn't hear the underlying pulse of the house that was made up of things like the water in the plumbing and electricity humming in the lines and the all-but-imperceptible shifting and creaking of seemingly solid wood and stone as wind blew off the ocean and pressed against the building.

She couldn't hear any of it. And that was bad.

Taking the chance, Riley pushed herself up on her elbows and then slid her right hand underneath the pillows. Ahhh . . . at least it was there, right where it was supposed to be. Her hand closed over the reassuring grip of her weapon, and she pulled it out, giving it a quick visual scan.

Clip in, safety on, no round in the chamber. She automatically ejected the clip, checked that it was full, and slid it back into place, then chambered a round, the action quick and smooth after so many years of practice. The gun in her hand felt comfortable. That was right.

But something else was very wrong.

She could see the blood now as well as smell it. It was on her.

Riley rolled and sat up in a single motion, her gaze darting around the bedroom warily. Her bedroom, something she recognized with a sense of familiarity, the reassurance of being where she should be. And it was empty except for her.

Her head was pounding even harder from the quick movements, but she ignored it as she looked down at herself. The hand holding the gun was smeared with dried blood, and when she shifted the weapon to her other hand, she saw that it was as well. On her palms, on the backs of her hands, her forearms, even, she saw, underneath her fingernails.

As far as she could tell, there was no blood on the covers, the pillows. Which meant all the blood on her had dried before she had apparently fallen across the bed fully dressed and gone to sleep. Or passed out. Either way . . .

Jesus Christ.

Blood on her hands. Blood on her light-colored T-shirt. Blood on her faded jeans.

A lot of blood.

Was she hurt? She didn't feel any pain, apart from the throbbing headache. But she did feel a cold, growing fear, because waking up covered with blood could not, by any stretch of the imagination, possibly be a good thing.

She got herself off the bed, a little stiff and more than a little shaky, and moved on bare feet out of the bedroom. Quickly but cautiously, she checked her surroundings to reassure herself that she was alone, that no immediate threat existed here. The second bedroom was neat as a pin and looked as though it hadn't been used recently, which was probably the case; Riley seldom had the sort of guests that required an extra bedroom.

Checking out the remainder of the house was

quick work, since most of it consisted of a large open area that was kitchen, dining area, and living room. Clean, but slightly untidy, with books, magazines, newspapers, CDs, and DVDs stacked here and there. The usual clutter of everyday life.

It looked like she'd been using the small dining table as a work surface, since place mats were pushed aside and her laptop carrying case was on one of the chairs. The computer wasn't out, which told her only that she probably hadn't been working on it recently.

The doors were closed and locked. The windows were also closed—it was **hot** in summer along the South Carolina coast—and locked.

She was alone.

Nevertheless, Riley took her weapon along when she went into her bathroom and checked behind the shower curtain before she locked herself in the relatively small room. Then she suffered another shock when she looked into the mirror above the vanity.

More dried blood was on her face, smeared across her cheek, and some appeared to be matted in her pale hair. Thickly matted.

"Shit."

Her stomach churned, and she stood there

for a moment, eyes closed, until the nausea passed. Then she laid her weapon on the vanity and stripped to the skin.

She checked every inch of herself and found nothing. No injury, not even a scratch. It wasn't her blood.

That should have been reassuring. It wasn't. She was covered with blood, and it wasn't hers. Which left her with a hell of a lot of unsettling, potentially terrifying, questions.

What—or who—had bled all over her? What had happened? And why couldn't she remember?

Riley looked down at the crumpled clothing on the floor, then at herself, pale gold with her summer tan, her skin unmarked except for the dried blood on her hands and forearms.

Forearms. Somehow or other, she'd literally been up to her elbows in blood. Jesus.

Ignoring all the training that insisted she call the local authorities before doing another thing, Riley got into the shower. She made the water as hot as she could stand and used plenty of soap, scrubbing away the dried blood. She used a nailbrush to reach the dark slivers of dried blood underneath her fingernails and shampooed her short hair at least twice. Even after it was clean, after she was clean, she stood under the hot water, letting it beat against her shoulders, her neck, her still-sickly pounding head.

What had happened?

She didn't have the faintest clue, that was the hell of it. She had absolutely no memory of how she'd gotten herself covered with blood.

She remembered lots of other things. Almost all the important stuff, really. "Your name is Riley Crane," she muttered aloud, trying to reassure herself that something wasn't terribly wrong. "You're thirty-two years old, single, and a federal agent assigned, these last three years, to the Special Crimes Unit."

Name, rank, serial number—more or less. Knowledge she was certain of.

No amnesia there. She knew who she was. An army brat with four older brothers, she'd grown up all over the world, had a rich and varied education, a wide range of training of a kind few women could claim, and had been able to take care of herself from a very young age. And she knew where she belonged, in the FBI, in the SCU. All that she remembered.

As for her recent life . . .

Christ, what **was** the last thing she remembered? She vaguely remembered renting the cottage, sort of remembered settling in. Carrying boxes and bags from the car. Putting things away. Walking on the beach. Sitting out on the deck in the darkness at night, feeling the warm ocean breeze on her face and—

Not alone. Somebody out there with her. The vague, fuzzy memory of quiet voices. Hushed laughter. A touch she felt, for a fleeting second, so strongly that she looked down at her hand in bemusement.

And then it was gone.

Try as she might, Riley couldn't remember anything else clearly. It became a confusing jumble in her head. Just flashes, most of which made no sense to her. Faces that were unfamiliar, places she didn't remember being, random snatches of conversations she didn't understand.

Flashes punctuated by jabs of pain in her head.

Blaming the headache for the huge blank space that was her recent past, Riley got out of the shower and dried off. It was just the headache, of course. She'd swallow a few aspirin and get some food into her system, some caffeine into her veins, and then she'd remember. Surely. She wrapped a towel around her and, picking up her weapon again, returned to the bedroom to find fresh clothing.

It struck her, as she opened drawers and checked the closet, that she had been here awhile. She really was settled in, far more so than was her habit. This wasn't her usual living-out-of-a-suitcase jumble. Her clothing was fairly neat in the drawers, hanging in the closet. And it was more than beach vacation clothing.

Casual stuff, yes, but several dressy things as well, from nice slacks and silk blouses to dresses. Even heels and hose.

So, okay. She was here to work, that had to be it. The problem was, she couldn't seem to remember what the job was.

Riley opened one drawer and pulled out an extremely pretty, lacy, sexy bra-and-panty set, and felt her eyebrows rising. Not her usual stuff **at all,** obviously new, and there was more in the drawer. What the hell kind of job was she here to do, anyway?

That question echoed even stronger in her mind when she also discovered a garter belt.

A **garter belt,** for crying out loud.

"Jesus, Bishop, what've you got me doing this time?"

3 Years Previously

"I need somebody like you on my team." Noah Bishop, Chief of the FBI Special Crimes Unit, could be persuasive when he wanted to. And he definitely wanted to.

Riley Crane eyed him, her doubt and her wariness obvious. Knowing her background, he understood and had expected both.

She was interesting, he thought. Physically not at all what he'd expected: A bit below average height and petite, almost fragile in appearance, she didn't look as if she could throw a man more than twice her size over her shoulder with little apparent effort. Large gray eyes that were deceptively childlike, gazing innocently out of an elfin face that was quirky and intriguing and infinitely memorable without being in any way beautiful.

Fascinating that such a face belonged to a chameleon.

"Why me?" she demanded, straight to the point.

Bishop appreciated the directness, and answered matter-of-factly. "Aside from the necessary skills as an investigator, you possess two unique abilities I expect will prove highly useful in our work. You can fit yourself into any situation and be anyone you choose to be at any given time, and you're clairvoyant."

Riley didn't bother to protest. She merely

said, "I like playing dress-up. Playing Let's Pretend. When you live in your imagination as a kid, you get good at stuff like that. As for the other, since I haven't gone out of my way to advertise—just the opposite, in fact—how did you find out?"

"I keep my ear to the ground," Bishop replied with a shrug.

"Not good enough."

"I'm building a unit around agents with paranormal abilities, and I've spent a great deal of time these last few years . . . casting out lines. Quietly alerting people I trust, within law enforcement and outside it, as to the sort of potential agents I'm looking for."

"Psychics."

"Not just any psychics. I need exceptionally strong people who can handle both their abilities and the emotional and psychological hardships of the work we do." He nodded to the scene just past her. "It seems fairly obvious that you can handle the sort of extreme stress I'm talking about."

Riley glanced back over her shoulder, where the rest of her team was working in the rubble of what might or might not have been a deliberate explosion. The victims had been located and carried—on stretchers or in body bags—from the scene hours ago; now the army investigators were searching for evidence.

"I haven't been doing this particular sort of thing for long," Riley said. "I tend toward investigative work, sure, but my last job dealt with base security. I go wherever I'm sent."

"So your CO told me."

"You spoke to him?"

Bishop hesitated only long enough to make it obvious, then said, "He's the one who got in touch with me."

"So he's one of those trusted people you mentioned?"

"He is. The friend of a friend, more or less. And open-minded to the possibilities of the paranormal, a trait not terribly common in the military. No offense intended, obviously."

"None taken. Obviously. What did he tell you?"

"He seems to feel that your talents are being wasted and that he can't offer you the kind of challenges he believes you need."

"He said that?"

"Words to the effect. You're on short time, I take it, with a few weeks left before you re-up. Or not."

"I'm career military," she said.

"Or not," Bishop said.

Riley shook her head slightly, and said, "Offhand, Agent Bishop, I can't think of a single reason why I'd want to exchange the military life for one with the FBI—however **specialized** your unit is. Besides, even if I do get an occasional hunch, it never makes a difference in the outcome of any given situation."

"Doesn't it?"

"No."

"We can help you learn how to channel and focus your abilities, how to use them constructively. You might be surprised at just how much of a difference that can make—in any given situation."

Without waiting for a response from her, Bishop opened the briefcase he carried and extracted a large, thick manila envelope. "Take a look at this when you get the chance," he said, handing it to her. "Tonight, tomorrow. After that, if you're interested, give me a call. My number's inside."

"And if I'm not interested?"

"Everything in there is a copy. If you're not interested, destroy it and forget about it. But I'm betting you'll be interested. So I'll stick around for a few days, Major. Just in case."

Riley stood gazing after him for a long moment, tapping the envelope against her hand thoughtfully. Then she locked it in her vehicle and got back to work.

It wasn't until much later that evening, alone in her small off-base apartment, that she discovered Bishop hadn't been entirely truthful. One thing in the envelope wasn't a copy.

She had half-consciously steeled herself before opening the envelope, partly because common sense told her the sort of thing she was likely to find and partly because her extra sense was tingling a warning as well—and had been from the moment she'd first touched it. But years of disciplined living, particularly in the military, had taught her a fair amount about concentration and focus, so that she was usually able to damp down those distracting feelings until she needed them.

Until she was ready to focus on what she saw when she upended the envelope onto her desk.

Copies, yeah. Copies of hell. Autopsy reports—and autopsy photos. Crime-scene photos. Not just one crime, but half a dozen. Murders of what appeared to be healthy young men. Brutal murders, cruel and bloody and savage.

Without looking through the autopsy reports, Riley nevertheless knew the murders had taken place in different cities and towns. She knew all the victims had known their killer. She knew only one killer was responsible.

She also knew what Bishop intended to do in order to catch that killer.

"So that's why me," she said to herself. A challenge? Oh, yes, definitely. The challenge of a lifetime. A deadly test of her skills. All of them.

She reached out slowly and picked up the single object from the envelope that was not a copy. It was a coin, a half-dollar. Nothing, apparently, unusual about it at all. Except that when she touched it, Riley knew one thing more.

She knew what would happen if she refused Bishop's invitation.

In the end, there wasn't a great deal to think about. Riley found the card with his cell number on it and placed the call. She didn't bother with pleasantries when he answered.

"You don't play fair," she said.

"I don't play," he replied.

"Something I should remember, for future reference?"

"You tell me."

Riley closed her fingers over the coin in her hand, and sighed. "Where do I sign up?"

Present Day

It didn't take Riley long to get dressed. She avoided the lacy underwear and pulled on the plainer and more practical—and more comfortable—stuff she usually wore, then found jeans and a cotton tank top. She didn't bother to dry her short hair, just finger-combed it and left it to dry on its own.

Barefoot, she went to the kitchen and set up the coffeemaker, then rummaged around until she found some aspirin. She swallowed them dry with a grimace, belatedly discovering orange juice in the fridge to wash down the bitter aftertaste.

The fridge was well-stocked, which again raised Riley's brows. Generally speaking, she was a take-out girl, not much given to cooking more than eggs and toast or the occasional steak.

Her stomach rumbled, telling her she hadn't eaten in a while. That was something of a relief, actually, because it also offered a possible reason why her senses were so muffled: There was no

fuel in her physical furnace, an absolute neces-
sity for her to function at peak efficiency.

It was her own individual quirk; most of the
SCU agents could claim at least one such
oddity.

Riley fixed herself a large bowl of cereal and
ate it leaning against the work island in the
kitchen.

Her weapon was never out of reach.

By the time she'd finished her meal, the coffee was ready. She carried her first cup with her
as she went over to the ocean-side windows and
the glass doors leading out to the deck. She
didn't go out but opened the blinds and stood
drinking the coffee as she scanned the grayish
Atlantic, the dunes and beach.

Not a lot of activity to be seen, and what was
there was scattered. A few people stretched out
on towels or beach loungers, soaking up the
sun. A couple of kids near one sunning couple
building a peculiar-looking structure out of
sand. One couple strolling along the waterline
as small waves broke around their ankles.

The beach between Riley's small house and
the water was empty; people here tended to respect the boundaries of public/private beach
access, especially at this less-populated end of
this particular small island, and if you paid the

higher bucks for oceanfront you generally had your little piece of the sand to yourself.

Riley returned to the kitchen for her second cup of coffee, frowning because her head was still pounding despite aspirin, food, and caffeine. And because she still couldn't remember what had happened to leave her covered in dried blood.

"Dammit," she muttered, reluctant to do what she knew she had to. As with most agents in the SCU, control was a big issue with Riley, and she hated having to admit to anyone that a situation was out of her control. But this one, inarguably, was.

At least for the moment.

Leaving her coffee cup in the kitchen but still carrying her weapon, she searched for her cell phone, finding it eventually in a casual shoulder bag. One glance told her the cell was dead as a doornail, something she accepted with a resigned sigh. She found the charger plugged in and waiting near one end of the kitchen counter and set the cell into it.

There was a land-line phone on the same end of the counter, and Riley stared at it, biting her lip in brief indecision.

Shit. Nothing else she could do, really.

She finished her second cup of coffee, perfectly aware that she was stalling, then finally placed the call.

When he answered with a brief "Bishop," she worked hard to make her own voice calm and matter-of-fact.

"Hey, it's Riley. I seem to have a bit of a situation here."

There was a long silence, and then Bishop, his voice now curiously rough, said, "We gathered that much. What the hell is going on, Riley? You missed your last two check-ins."

A chill shivered down her spine. "What do you mean?" She never missed check-ins. Never.

"I mean we haven't heard a word from you in over two weeks."

2

Riley said the only thing she could think of. "I'm . . . surprised you didn't send in the cavalry by now."

Grimly, Bishop said, "I wanted to, believe me. But aside from the fact that all the teams were out and hip-deep in investigations they absolutely couldn't leave, you had insisted you could handle the situation alone and that I shouldn't be concerned if you were out of touch for a while. Any of us going in blind didn't seem like the best of ideas. You're one of the most capable and self-sufficient people I know, Riley; I had to trust you knew what you were doing."

Almost absently, she said, "I wasn't criticizing

you for not riding to the rescue, just sort of surprised you hadn't." Which told her that he himself was undoubtedly "hip-deep" in a case he
was unable to leave; whatever she'd told him,
Bishop tended to keep a close eye on his people
and was rarely out of touch for more than a day
or two during an ongoing investigation.

Then again, he also likely would have sensed
it if she had been in actual, physical danger.
Or at any rate had certainly done so more than
once in the past. He was like that with some of
his agents, though not by any means all of them.

"And, anyway, I'm all right," she said. "At
least . . ."

"What? Riley, what the hell is going on down
there?"

His question made her grimace half-
consciously, because if **Bishop** didn't know
what was going on here, she was most likely in
very big trouble.

How on earth had she managed to end up in
a situation deadly enough to cover her in blood
and apparently trigger a short-term memory
loss and yet still manage to conceal what was
happening from the formidable telepathic
awareness of the SCU chief?

Perhaps the memory loss had something to
do with that? Or maybe the same thing that had

triggered the memory loss had thrown up some kind of block or shield? She didn't know.

Dammit, she just didn't **know.**

"Riley? You didn't believe there was a risk of violence, at least according to what you said when you did check in. No suspicious deaths, no one reported missing. I got the impression you were half-convinced it was just a series of pranks. Has something happened to change that?"

Avoiding the direct question, she asked one of her own. "Listen, what else did I say?"

For a moment she didn't think he was going to answer, but finally he did.

"Since you arrived at Opal Island three weeks ago, you've filed only one formal report, and that one was seriously lacking in details. Just that you'd settled in, you had a reliable contact in the Hazard County Sheriff's Department, and that you were confident you could successfully resolve the situation."

Riley drew a breath and said casually, "The situation being?"

The silence this time was, to say the least, tense.

"Riley?"

"Yeah?"

"Why did you go to Opal Island?"

"I . . . don't exactly remember."

"Have you been injured?"

"No." She decided, somewhat guiltily, not to mention the blood. Not yet, at any rate. She thought she might need that later. "Not so much as a scratch, and no bump on the head."

"Then it's likely to be emotional or psychological trauma. Or psychic trauma."

"Yeah, that was my take."

Being Bishop, he didn't waste time exclaiming. "What **do** you remember?"

"Getting here—vaguely. Renting this house, settling in. After that, just flashes I haven't been able to sort through."

"What about before you left Quantico?"

"I remember everything. Or, at least, everything through the close of the investigation in San Diego. I got back to the office, started in on all the paperwork . . . and that's pretty much it, until I woke up here a couple of hours ago."

"What about your abilities?"

"Spider sense seems to be out of commission, but I woke up starving so that probably doesn't mean anything. I dunno about the clairvoyance yet, but if I had to guess . . ." She knew she had to be honest. "Not exactly firing on all cylinders."

Bishop didn't hesitate. "Go back to Quantico, Riley."

"Without knowing what's happened here? I can't do that."

"I don't want to make it an order."

"And I don't want to disobey one. But I can't just pack up and leave with this—this huge blank place in my life. Don't ask me to do that, Bishop."

"Riley, listen to me. You're down there alone, without backup. You can't remember the last three weeks. You don't even remember what you're there to investigate. And the abilities that could normally help you focus on and sort through undercurrents aren't available to you—either temporarily or permanently. Now, can you give me a single reason why I should ignore all that and allow you to stay there?"

She drew a breath, and gambled. "Yeah. One very big reason. Because when I woke up today, I was fully dressed and covered with dried blood. Whatever happened here, I was up to my elbows in it. One call to the local sheriff and I'd probably be sitting in his jail. So I have to stay here, Bishop. I have to stay until I remember—or figure out—what the hell's going on."

Sue McEntyre wasn't at all happy with the local ordinance that kept dogs off the beach from eight A.M. until eight P.M. It wasn't that she minded getting up early to allow her two Labs a good long run on the beach, it was just that big dogs—hers, at least—would have been happier if they'd been able to get out into the water a few times during the day as well. Especially during a hot summer.

Luckily, there was a big park skirting downtown Castle with an area complete with wading pond where dogs were allowed off-leash anytime during the day, so at least once every day she loaded Pip and Brandy into her Jeep and off they went, across the bridge and onto the mainland.

On this Monday afternoon, she didn't expect it to be crowded; summer visitors tended to be baking on the beach or shopping downtown, so it was mostly locals who used the park, and most of them for the same reason Sue did.

She found a space closer to the dog area than usual and within minutes was throwing a Frisbee for Brandy and a tennis ball for Pip, giving all three of them plenty of exercise as she threw and they happily fetched.

It wasn't until Pip abruptly dropped his ball and shot off into the woods that Sue realized a section of the fence was down and that the bolder and more curious of her two dogs had seized the opportunity presented.

"Damn." She wasn't too worried; he wasn't likely to head toward the streets and traffic. But neither was he at all likely to respond if she called him, especially since he loved exploring the woods even more than running on the beach and had perfected the art of going suddenly and temporarily deaf when his interest was engaged.

Sue called Brandy and clipped a leash to her collar, then set off in pursuit of her other dog.

One would think it would be easy to see a pale gold dog in the shaded woods, but Pip also had the knack of making himself virtually invisible, so Sue had to rely on Brandy's nose to find her brother. Luckily, it was a common enough occurrence that she didn't have to be told what to do and led her owner steadily through the woods.

This patch of woods was fairly uncommon in the area, consisting as it did of towering hardwood trees and fairly dense underbrush rather than the more usual spindly pines in sandy soil. But since it was also less than a mile from downtown Castle, it was hardly what anyone would have called a wilderness.

Sue and her dogs had probably explored every inch in the five years she'd lived on Opal Island.

Even so, she would have avoided the big clearing near the center of the woods had Brandy not been leading her straight for it. She'd heard the talk about what had been found there a week or so ago and didn't like the realization that what had seemed to her just an interesting jumble of boulders providing a seat to pause and enjoy the quiet of the forest now had a possibly more sinister purpose in her mind.

Satanism, that's what people were saying.

Sue had never believed in such things but, still, there was no smoke without fire, hunters weren't allowed in these woods, and why else would somebody kill an animal—

Pip began barking.

Conscious of a sudden chill, Sue picked up her pace, almost running beside Brandy along the twisting path to the clearing.

Anybody who would butcher an animal out in the woods for no good reason, she thought, probably wouldn't hesitate to kill someone's pet, especially if it was in the wrong place at the wrong time.

"Pip!" Not that it would do any good to call him, but she was desperately afraid suddenly, afraid in a way she'd never been before, on a level so deep it was almost primal, and that terror had to be voiced in some kind of cry.

It wasn't until much later that she realized she had probably smelled the blood long before she reached the clearing.

She and Brandy burst into the clearing to find Pip only a couple of yards in, standing still and barking his head off. Not his happy I'm-having-fun bark, but an unfamiliar, nearly hysterical sound that spoke of the same primal fear Sue felt herself.

Holding the whimpering Brandy close to her side, Sue went to Pip and fastened his leash to his collar blindly, her gaze fixed on what was at the center of the clearing.

The seemingly innocent jumble of boulders was there, no longer innocent but splashed with blood, a lot of blood.

Sue paid little attention to the rocks, however, nor even noticed that there had been a fire built near them. Her gaze was only for what hung over them.

Suspended by ropes from a sturdy oak limb, the naked body of a man was only barely recognizable as such. Dozens of shallow cuts all over him had bled a great deal, turning his flesh reddish and, clearly, dripping down onto the boulders.

Dripping for a long time.

The ropes were tied around the wrists, both of them tied together and stretched above . . . above the . . . Except that the wrists weren't stretched above the head.

There was no head.

Sue turned with a choked cry and ran.

It took considerable persuasion, but in the end Riley prevailed.

In a manner of speaking.

Bishop agreed not to recall her, but he wasn't willing to leave that open-ended. It was Monday afternoon; she had until Friday to "stabilize" the situation—by which he meant recover her memories of the last three weeks and/or figure out what was going on here. If she couldn't do that to his satisfaction, she'd be recalled to Quantico.

And she was to report in every day; one missed report, and he'd send in another team member or members with orders to pull her out. That or come himself.

She was also to send the bloodstained clothing she'd awakened wearing to Quantico for testing immediately; Bishop would send a courier within a couple of hours to pick up the package. And if the results showed human blood, all bets were off.

"You think it could be animal blood?" she asked.

"Since you went down there to investigate reports of possible occult rituals, it may be more likely than not." Bishop paused, then went on. "We've had a number of these reports across the Southeast in the last year or so. You remember that much?"

She did. "But nine times out of ten, there's no real evidence of occult activity. Or at least nothing dangerous."

"Nothing satanic," he agreed. "Which is always the idea feeding local hysteria, that devil worshippers are conducting robed rituals out in the woods that involve orgies and sacrificing infants."

"Yeah, when in reality it's almost always either pranks or just somebody jumping to conclusions when they find something on the weird side while out taking their daily constitutional."

"Exactly. But once the gossip gets going, such incidents are blown out of all proportion, and fear can stir up real trouble. Sometimes deadly trouble."

"So I came down here to investigate possible occult activity?" Riley was still struggling to remember and still trying to reconcile the clothing and underwear she'd brought along with what sounded like a perfectly ordinary investigation—for her, at any rate.

She **was** the go-to girl of the SCU when it came to the occult.

"The possible beginnings of occult activity," Bishop said. "A friend and former colleague of yours got in touch. He didn't want us down there openly and, in fact, lacked the authority to ask us to get involved, but he had a very bad feeling that whatever's going on in Castle and on Opal Island is both serious and more than the local sheriff can handle."

"So I'm here unofficially."

"Very unofficially. And on the strength of Gordon Skinner's request and your confidence that his instincts were trustworthy."

"Yeah, Gordon has a rep for hunches that pay off. I always figured him for a latent precog. And he's not a man to jump at shadows." Riley frowned to herself. "I guess he got in his twenty and retired just like he planned. To Opal Island?"

"So you said."

"Okay. Well, Gordon's definitely somebody I can trust. If I'm here because of him, it's a cinch

I've spent time with him over the last three weeks. He can fill me in."

"I hope so. Because you aren't there under-cover, Riley. You haven't hidden the fact that you're an FBI agent. As far as the locals are concerned—including the sheriff, since you checked in with him when you arrived—you're on Opal Island on vacation. Taking some accu-mulated leave time after a particularly tough case."

"Oh," Riley said. "I wonder if that was smart of me. Being here openly, I mean."

"Unfortunately, I have no idea. But it's clearly too late to second-guess that decision."

"Yeah. So I picked the island for a vacation spot because my old army buddy Gordon re-tired here."

"It gave you a legitimate reason to be there."

Riley sighed. "And that's all you know?" His silence spoke volumes, and she hastily added, "Right, right, my fault. Should have reported in. And I'm sure when I remember **why** I didn't report in, there'll be a good reason."

"I hope so."

"Sorry, Bishop."

"Just be careful, will you, please? I know you can take care of yourself, but we both know investigations that turn up genuine black-occult practices or some other variation of evil go south more often than not. Usually in a hurry."

"Yeah. The last one involved a serial killer, didn't it?"

"Don't remind me."

She wasn't all that happy to have reminded herself, because that memory, at least, was quickly all too clear. She had come within a hair of being that particular killer's final victim.

"I don't like any of this, Riley, for the record," Bishop said.

"I know."

"Remember—you report some degree of success by Friday, or I pull the plug."

"Got it. Don't worry. I've got Gordon to watch my back, if necessary, while I figure out what's going on."

"Be careful," he repeated.

"I will." She cradled the receiver and stood there for a minute or so, frowning. Her headache was finally easing off, but although the pounding was somewhat muffled now, so were her senses.

She refilled her coffee cup, then rummaged in the pantry for the high-calorie PowerBars she tended to buy by the case. It was normal for her to carry at least two of them in her purse or

back pockets at all times; if she didn't eat something about every hour or two, she simply
couldn't function at peak efficiency.

Psychic efficiency.

Several of the other SCU members envied her
the high metabolism that enabled her to eat
anything she wanted—and rather astonishing
quantities of it, at that—without gaining an
ounce. But they also understood the downside.
It was not always possible for Riley to eat
enough or often enough during the course of a
busy investigation to continually provide fuel
for her abilities, and at least once it had nearly
cost a life.

Hers.

She ate a PowerBar with her coffee and placed
two more in the shoulder bag she had found.
She checked the contents of the purse, just on
the off chance that something unusual might
trigger her memories, but everything looked
normal.

She tended to travel light, so there wasn't
much. Keys to her rental car and this house. A
small pocket phone/address book. Tube of lip
balm; she wasn't a lipstick kind of girl. Mirrored
compact with pressed powder that was barely
used, because she wasn't a makeup kind of girl
either—unless the situation called for it. Bill-

fold with cash, credit cards in their protective case, and her driver's license; her FBI I.D. folder and badge would be in her nightstand, or should be, since she was technically off duty.

She went and checked, and it was.

Returning to the main living area, Riley turned on the TV to CNN to check the date and find out if she'd missed anything crucial in the way of world news.

July 14. And the last clear, solid memory she could claim was somewhere around June 20, at Quantico. Paperwork at the desk, nothing unusual. Feeling a little drained, which was normal for her following the conclusion of a tough investigation.

And then . . . nothing but flashes. Whispers in her mind, snatches of conversation that made no sense. Faces and places she thought she knew but couldn't put names to. Feelings that were oddly unsettled and even chaotic for a woman who tended to take a reasonable, rational approach to life. . . .

Riley shook that off and frowned at the TV. Okay, so she wasn't doing so hot. How went the world?

One earthquake, two political scandals, a celebrity divorce, and half a dozen violent crimes later, she muted the set and returned to the kitchen for more coffee.

Same old, same old.

"I can't just hide in this house until it all comes back to me," she muttered to herself. For one thing, there was no guarantee it would; short-term memory loss linked to some kind of trauma wasn't all that uncommon, but in a psychic it could also be a symptom of bigger problems.

Bishop hadn't needed to remind her of that.

For another thing, nothing here was sparking her memory. And she needed information, fast. Needed to have some idea of what was going on here. So the most imperative order of business was, clearly, contacting Gordon.

She took the time first to bag the clothing she'd been wearing and managed to find what she needed to construct a decent package for shipment back to Quantico. And she did another search through the house, this time looking intently for anything unusual.

Aside from the sexy underwear, there was nothing she considered unusual. Which meant that she found nothing to either answer any of her questions or raise more.

By the time she was finished with the more

thorough search, she'd also eaten another Power-Bar and her headache was all but gone. But when she attempted to tap into her extra senses, she got nothing. No deeper, more intense connection to her surroundings that was her spider sense.

As for her clairvoyance . . .

She was stronger with people than with objects, so it was difficult for her to be certain that extra sense was out to lunch when she was in the house all alone—

The doorbell rang, and Riley's first reaction was an intense suspicion that came from both training and a lifelong addiction to mystery novels and horror movies.

A visitor just when she needed one was **not** a good sign.

She took her gun with her, held down at her side until she reached the front door. A small clear-glass viewing panel in the solid wood door allowed her to see who was on her porch.

A woman in a sheriff's deputy uniform, no hat. She was a tall redhead, rather beautiful, and—

"I don't know, Riley. We just don't see this sort of thing around here. Peculiar symbols burned into wood or drawn in the sand. An abandoned building and a house under construction both burned to the ground. That

stuff we found out in the woods that you say could indicate someone's been performing—or attempting—some kind of occult ritual—"

"Leah, so far it's just bits and pieces. And weird bits and pieces at that."

"What do you mean?"

"I mean something's not adding up."

The flash of memory vanished as quickly as it had come, but the knowledge it left her with was certain.

Deputy Leah Wells was her "reliable contact" inside the sheriff's department.

Riley stuck her automatic inside the waistband of her jeans at the small of her back, then unlocked and opened the door.

"Hey," she said. "What's up?"

"Nothing good," Leah replied grimly. "Sheriff sent me to get you. There's been a murder, Riley."

3

Do you think it was a good idea to leave your door unlocked?" Leah asked a few minutes later as she drove the sheriff's department Jeep toward the middle of the island and the bridge that would take them to the mainland.

"Like I told you, a courier should arrive in the next hour to pick up that package I left just inside the door." She had made a quick call to Bishop to alert him to the location of the package.

"You could have left the package in your rental car."

"Yeah. But doing that was a bit too . . . visible for my taste."

Leah sent her a glance. "I probably shouldn't ask, but—"

"Did it have anything to do with what's going on here?" Riley shrugged. "Maybe. I'll know more when Quantico reports back. At least, I hope so."

She had debated, but in the end Riley decided against confiding her memory loss to Leah. Not yet, at any rate. She was independent enough that even Bishop had never been able to match her with a permanent partner, and that independence demanded that she keep her current vulnerability to herself as long as possible.

Plus, it was quite simply a reasonable precaution until she could wrap her mind around whatever was going on here.

Leah sent her another look. "You know, you've been awfully secretive the last week or so."

"Have I?" It was more an honest question than a mere response, something Riley hoped the other woman wouldn't pick up on.

"I'd say so. Gordon thinks so too. He thinks you've either found something or figured out something that's making you very uneasy."

"He told you that?"

"Last night in the shower and again this morning at the breakfast table. He's worried about you, Riley."

Of course. Gordon always did love red-heads; that's why I can trust Leah. They're involved, and he vouched for her.

Aloud and somewhat offhandedly, she said, "Gordon's worried about me for years."

Leah grinned faintly. "Yeah, he's mentioned that a few times. Says you keep digging when any rational person would throw away the shovel. That's why he wanted you here—even knowing he'd worry the whole time. And now we've got this murder. I'd say the stakes just went up, and maybe we've **all** got something to worry about."

"Is the sheriff sure it's a murder?"

"**I'm** sure—and I've never seen a murdered body before, not outside the textbooks. Believe me, Riley, it's a murder. The guy's hanging from a tree over that possible altar in the woods. And he didn't hang himself."

"Who's the vic?"

"Well, we don't exactly know yet. And it may take a while to find out. There isn't—he doesn't—his head is gone."

Riley looked at the deputy, conscious of a cold finger gliding up her spine. There was something eerily familiar about this. "And it wasn't found nearby?"

Leah grimaced. "Not so far, when I left. We've been searching, but it's just a little patch of trees, you know that, and I'm guessing that if we haven't found it by now, we won't. Not in those woods anyway."

Nodding, Riley turned her gaze forward again. There was something nagging at the back of her mind, but she had no idea if it was a memory or some bit of pertinent knowledge.

Or something utterly irrelevant and useless, of course, which was what lots of nagging things tended to be.

"Leah, the sheriff still thinks I'm here on vacation, right?"

"Far as I know."

"Then why call me to a crime scene?"

"Apparently he knows you're with the SCU. And he considers this a **special** crime, being as how we haven't had a murder in these parts for, oh, a decade or more. Deaths, sure. Even a killing or three, but not like this, not anything like this."

Riley wasn't very happy about the sheriff's knowledge, although she also wasn't surprised. Of course he had likely checked on her, and any law-enforcement officer at his level could easily learn that she was assigned to the Special Crimes Unit.

That should, however, be all he could learn.

Before she could ask, Leah said, "From the way he talked, I gather he doesn't know what your specialty is. The occult stuff, I mean. Because this one **has** to be occult-related, and he didn't say that was why he wanted you at the scene. Just for your general expertise in investigating crimes. All he knows is that you're an FBI agent working with a unit that uses unorthodox methods to investigate unusual crimes—and this one is definitely unusual."

"He knows I'm psychic?"

"He doesn't believe in psychics. But there's an election coming up in the fall, and Jake Ballard wants to be reelected. What he doesn't want is to be accused by the voters of not taking advantage of any possibly helpful source in investigating a brutal murder. An FBI agent staying in the area has to be counted as an excellent source, no matter which unit she belongs to or what extra senses she claims to have." Leah shook her head. "I assumed you two had talked about stuff like that."

"Why?"

"Well, it is the normal sort of chitchat for two cops on a date."

Oh, shit.

"Then again," Leah continued, clearly oblivious of having delivered a shock, "it seems you ex-army types tend to talk less than the rest of us, at least about your work. I've been sleeping with Gordon for nearly a year now, damn near living with him, and he still won't tell me what wakes him up in a cold sweat some nights."

"He doesn't want you to know the ugly stuff," Riley murmured. "Things he's seen. Done."

"Yeah, I get that. Still feels like he's shutting me out of a very big part of his life."

"Past life. Over and done with. Let it go." Riley forced a smile when the other woman looked at her. "Advice. I know you didn't ask, but I'm offering anyway. The monsters under the bed and in the closet? Leave them be. If he wants to show them to you, he will. But that may not be for a long time. If ever."

"And it isn't about trust?"

Riley shook her head. "It's about scars. And about giving them time to fade. Twenty years of scars aren't going to fade in a hurry."

"If at all."

"Well, good men tend to hold on to their bad memories. I'd be a lot more worried about him if he **didn't** wake up sometimes in a cold sweat."

"You know what he's been through," Leah said.

"Some of it. Not all of it."

"But they're his stories. He has to be the one to tell me."

"That's the way it works. Sorry."

"No, it's okay. I get it."

Riley thought the other woman probably did get it; she was a cop and even in this small coastal town would likely encounter a few horror stories of her own during the course of her career.

Starting, possibly, with what she'd seen today.

A silence fell between the two women. Riley wanted to break it, but there didn't seem to be any good, reasonably casual way to guide the conversation back to her date or dates with the sheriff.

Dates? Jesus, what on earth had possessed her to do **that**?

With a reliable source inside the sheriff's department, it didn't seem likely that she'd gone out with him on a fact-finding mission, especially since he knew who and what she was. What he wouldn't confide professionally he wasn't likely to confide personally, not if he was like most of the cops she'd known.

Was it personal? Had she set aside the training and preferences of a lifetime to go out with a law-enforcement officer while she was investigating occurrences in his town?

Investigating, possibly, him?

What would have compelled her to do something so out of character for her? With her busy life, she barely dated at all, but to date someone during an investigation—

A sudden, uneasy suspicion surfaced in her mind as she abruptly recalled the fleeting memory of quiet voices and a lingering touch out on the deck of her house.

Surely she hadn't . . . surely to God she hadn't gone further than a few casual dates? She hadn't taken a lover. No. No, **that** would be so totally out of character it was unheard-of for her.

But. What if? In a situation so torn by uncertainty, how could she discount the possibility?

And, most important of all, what if neither her memories nor her clairvoyance kicked in when she saw the man again? How was she supposed to fake her way through **that**?

The woods were dense enough that getting a vehicle to the clearing near the center was virtually impossible. So Leah parked her Jeep near the other police vehicles, and they got out.

Riley had another flash of memory, and said, "Somebody's dog found the body, right?"

"Just like one found all that stuff in the clearing last week," Leah confirmed. "Different dog, though."

Riley paused to study the break in the fence, ignoring a bored deputy stationed there to prevent the idly curious from entering the woods at this point. It wasn't a particularly strong fence, meant more as a border delineating the park from the woods than a barrier to hold a determined animal in—or out.

She frowned as she half-turned to look back at the area used for local pet owners. "Odd," she murmured.

"What's odd?" Leah asked.

Riley kept her voice low. "Rituals aren't meant to be public. Especially occult rituals, and even more especially if you mean to sacrifice something or kill somebody. You don't want outsiders watching or even knowing what's going on."

"Makes sense."

"Yeah. So why choose this place? There are patches of woods farther from town and much more private. Forests with a lot more acreage that would offer far greater secrecy. Places where a fire wouldn't be seen. And where local dog owners don't bring their pets every single day."

"Something special about this patch of woods?" Leah guessed. "You did say that group of boulders looked like a natural altar. Or something old that was used a long time ago. Maybe that's it?"

"Maybe." But Riley wasn't convinced. Still, she continued with Leah through the break in the fence and into the woods.

She was trying very hard to focus and concentrate, to settle and ground herself so she could get through what lay ahead without making a fool of herself. Or betraying herself.

Professional, that was the ticket. Cool, detached, and professional. Whatever the reason she'd dated Jake Ballard, he would expect her to behave like a professional at a crime scene, however unofficial her presence.

Riley remembered all that sexy underwear, and winced.

Christ, she hoped he expected an FBI agent and not a lover.

Surely she'd remember if she'd taken a lover in the last couple of weeks.

Surely.

"Grand Central Station," Leah muttered as they reached the clearing.

There was plenty of activity, all right, and Riley was aware of a fleeting, though resigned, wish that she had been able to see the scene before it was trampled by many feet. Trained feet, for the most part, but not specially trained. And it showed.

Rather than join them, Riley stood where she was at the edge of the clearing, her hands in the front pockets of her jeans, and just looked for several minutes. She ignored the uniformed deputies and technicians moving about, ignored the snatches of conversation she heard, closed out everything except the scene of a murder.

Leah had been right: No one could see this and not know they were dealing with murder.

Riley looked at what the killer had left. At the headless body that was still hanging by its wrists, at the blood-spattered rocks below. At the evidence of a fire nearby, which a technician was currently photographing.

It all looked . . . familiar.

"Riley, thanks for coming."

She turned her head at the sound of his voice, holding on to her professional detachment with an effort. It was a nice voice. It was a nice package, of the tall, dark, and handsome variety. With piercing blue eyes thrown in just for gilding.

Okay, so he was gorgeous. Maybe that was why she'd dated him.

Sheriff Jake Ballard wore his uniform with an air that said he knew he looked good in it. He walked with an authority that wasn't quite a swagger. And he had the sort of smile—even here and now—that nature had designed to charm the female of the species.

Riley was hardly immune.

"Hey," she said. "Nice goings-on in such a pretty little town."

"Tell me about it." He shook his head, adding, "Sorry to pull you out of your vacation, but, frankly, I wanted an opinion from someone who probably knows a lot more about this sort of thing than any of us."

"And you thought I might?"

He looked sheepish, and Riley tried not to believe it was because he knew it was a good expression for him.

"Okay, so I checked up on you when you arrived. I didn't mention it later because . . . well, because I thought you'd tell me about it in your own time."

"It?"

"The Special Crimes Unit. It isn't exactly a secret in law-enforcement circles, you know. I made a few calls. And learned a bit more than the standard FBI line of bullshit double-talk."

Taking a chance, Riley said, "You don't believe in the paranormal."

His eyebrows lifted. "Is that a problem?"

"Not for me, no. It's the sort of thing we run into more often than not."

"I imagine you would."

"But if it isn't something you believe in, then how much value can my opinion have?"

"You're an experienced investigator, and your unit deals with murder on a regular basis. Yes?"

"Yeah."

"I believe in that. Your experience. That's enough for me."

Riley looked at him and tried to find a memory, a single memory.

Nothing.

As for her clairvoyant sense, it was as absent as her memory. All she knew was what her usual but slightly dulled senses were telling her. He was gorgeous, he had a nice voice, and he was wearing Polo cologne.

"Riley, I need your help," Jake Ballard said. "Or at least your expertise. I can call your office, make it official so you're on the clock. No need to waste vacation time."

She hesitated, then said, "If you make it official, my boss will probably want to send another agent or two down here. We seldom work alone."

The sheriff grimaced. "That, I'm not so crazy about. A major FBI presence wouldn't sit well with the civic leaders. If we scare away the summer visitors . . ."

He didn't have to complete that sentence. Towns like Castle and Opal Island weren't as dependent on summer dollars as the northern coast areas were; winter this far south was mild and brief, and visitors came year-round. But the summer season still produced the most income through higher rentals and for other area businesses.

Her voice mild, Riley said, "Well, I imagine my boss will be okay if we keep this semiofficial." **Yeah, sure he will. Bishop is not going to be happy that we've got a murder now.** And why the hell hadn't she mentioned that fact when she'd called him back to explain where the package for the courier would be found?

Man, what is wrong with me?

"I can explain the situation," she continued, pushing her way through uncertainty, "and I'd be on the books as an adviser to your office, not an investigator."

"Suits me," he said promptly. "Look, the doc wants to cut down the body—"

"No." She softened that with a smile. "It would really help if you could clear most of your people out for a bit. Not long, just a few minutes. I'd like to wander around, take a closer look at the scene before anything more is changed."

"For the psychic vibes?" His voice wasn't— quite—mocking.

"For whatever I can pick up," she returned pleasantly.

He eyed her for a moment, then shrugged. "Okay, sure. My forensics team has done all they can do, and God knows we've got plenty of shots of the scene. But the people I've got combing the woods aren't done yet."

"No reason to call them in. I just need the immediate area around the body clear."

He nodded and stepped away to begin issuing orders to send his people temporarily back to their vehicles.

Leah, who had stood silently nearby, murmured, "What I can't figure out is if he really wants your help or just wants a reason that Ash can't argue with to keep you close."

"Mmmm," Riley said.

Who the hell is Ash? she wondered.

4

It was one of the bloodier scenes she'd been
called to.

With the deputies and technicians out of
the way and only the sheriff and Leah watching
from the path, Riley moved slowly around the
clearing, concentrating on opening up all her
senses.

It wasn't easy to focus with so many questions
tumbling in her mind, but she gave it her
best shot.

The smell of blood was strongest, and she
needed no enhancement of that particular sense
to tell her so. There was plenty of the stuff, after all, splashed about.

Directly beneath the hanging body were the boulders. Which, if one could feel playful at so gruesome a scene, could have best been described as a chair for a giant. Well, a fairly small giant, anyway. Because the "seat" of that chair, while about four feet wide and three deep, was only as tall as Riley's waist. But the "back" of the chair was close to seven feet tall, as wide as the "seat," and only about a foot thick.

It didn't really look like a natural part of its surroundings, Riley had thought the first time she'd seen it.

Ah—a memory.

She had been here with . . . Gordon. That was it. He'd brought her here not long after she'd arrived on the island, because—

" . . . and the boys thought I'd be the one to show it to, probably because of the stories I'd told 'em about my great-grandma being a voodoo priestess."

"That's bullshit, Gordon."

"Yeah, but they didn't know that. Big black man from Louisiana talking 'bout voodoo, who's gonna call him a liar?"

"I am."

He laughed, a deep, booming sound. "Yeah, but you'd call St. Peter a liar if he introduced himself at the pearly gates, babe."

"Let's not discuss my religious beliefs, Gordon. The boys told you they'd found the bones here? On this rock?"

"Yeah, right here. A circle of bones strung together on fishing line and layin' over an upside-down cross made out of—"

"Riley?"

She blinked and looked at the sheriff. "Hmm?"

"Are you okay?"

She wanted to swear at him for breaking the thread of memory, but all she said, calmly, was, "I'm fine." It was gone, dammit, the scene frozen in her mind as though she'd hit PAUSE on a DVD. And fading by the second.

"You looked sort of spaced-out there for a minute." He sounded concerned.

Standing slightly behind his shoulder, Leah rolled her eyes.

"I'm fine," Riley repeated. She turned her gaze back to the boulder chair. The seat was roughly the right size and height for an altar, she thought, considering it. The back would be an unusual feature for an altar—unless it could be used in some way.

She took another step toward the boulders, closing her mind to the bare and bloody feet dangling above them.

She was no geologist but recognized granite when she saw it. What she wasn't sure of, what was difficult to make out, was whether there were distinct patterns among the spatters of blood on the rocks, especially the relatively flat surface of the tall, upright boulder. Was it sheer carnage, or was there a message?

"Will you give me access to the crime-scene photos?" she asked the sheriff.

"Of course. You see something?"

"Hard to tell with so much blood. Using digital photos and pattern-recognition software might help."

"We have that," he said somewhat uncertainly.

Riley glanced at him. "If not, I have a friend at Quantico who'll take a look, quietly and quickly. No problem e-mailing him the relevant photos."

Jake frowned, but said, "I'd be okay with that."

She nodded and kept her attention on the boulders for another minute or two. It was a bit like one of those trick 3-D pictures, she thought; if you stared at it long enough, you saw—or thought you saw—something hidden within the confusion.

The question was, what was she really looking at?

She turned away from the boulders, still reluctant to concentrate on the body, and walked
out about four feet. There was a faint white line
on the ground. She followed it in a slow circle
around the boulders. All the way around.

An unbroken circle, or had been before many
police feet had trampled the area.

Riley knelt and touched two fingers to the
white line, coming away with fine grains sticking to her skin.

"We're having that analyzed," Jake told her.

She glanced at him, then touched one finger
to her tongue.

"Jesus, Riley—"

"Salt," she said calmly. "Ordinary, everyday
table salt. Or possibly sea salt. It's supposed to
be purer."

Leah said, "You knew what it was."

"I suspected." Riley stood up. "It's sometimes
used in occult rituals. To consecrate the area
inside the circle." An area which included the
boulders, the hanging body, and the fire.

Jake was still frowning. "Consecrate? You
mean make it holy? Because there's nothing
holy about this."

"That depends on your point of view, really."
Without giving him time to respond to that,
Riley added, "A circle of salt is also used as pro-
tection."

"From what?" he demanded.

"A threat or perceived threat. And before you
ask what kind of threat, the answer is, I don't
know. Yet." She smiled faintly. "All this is only
preliminary, you have to understand that. First
thoughts, hunches, instincts."

"And no inside knowledge, huh?"

Riley felt everything inside her go still and
chilled, but she held on to her slight smile and
waited.

"I mean, if the paranormal is your thing, then
you must know more than the rest of us about
this sort of shit."

She didn't let her relief show, and acknowl-
edged to herself that it was extraordinarily
draining to keep up her guard and try to behave
normally when she was constantly digging for
memories, for knowledge, for answers.

And, more often than not, coming up empty.

Still coolly professional, on the outside at
least, she said, "The paranormal as defined by
the SCU has absolutely nothing to do with occult or satanic rites or practices. That is a totally

different thing, not grounded in science but in belief, in faith. Just like any religion."

"Religion?"

"To most practitioners, that's what it is. If you want to understand the occult, that's the first rule: It's a belief system, and not inherently evil in and of itself. The second rule is, it's not a single belief system; there are as many sects within the occult as there are in most religions. Satanism alone has at least a dozen different churches that I know about."

"Churches? Riley—"

She interrupted his indignation to add firmly, "Practitioners of the occult may be nontraditional and their rites and habits blasphemous from the viewpoint of the major religions, but that doesn't make their beliefs any less valid from their own point of view. And believe it or not, Satan is rarely involved—even in Satanism. Nor is any sort of sacrifice, barring the symbolic kind. Most occult groups simply honor and worship—for want of a better term—nature. The earth, the elements. There's nothing paranormal about that."

Usually, at least.

"And the SCU?"

"The SCU is built around people with real

human abilities, abilities that are, however rare and beyond the norm, scientifically definable." If only as possibilities.

He shrugged off the distinction, saying only, "Well, call it whatever you like, you obviously know more about this shit than the rest of us. So you think this is somebody's idea of religion?" He waved a hand back at the carnage behind him. "This?"

"I think it's too early to make assumptions."

Jake gestured again toward the hanging body. "That's not an assumption, it's a murder victim. And if he was killed in some kind of ritual, then, goddammit, Riley, I need to know that."

Still reluctant, she turned her attention at last to that victim.

Riley had seen corpses before. In war and in peace. She'd seen them in the textbooks, in the field, at the body farm. She had seen corpses so mangled they barely looked human anymore, destroyed by explosions or dismembered by an arguably human hand. And she'd seen them on the medical examiner's table, laid open with their organs glistening in the bright, harsh lights.

She had never gotten used to it.

So it demanded even more concentration and focus, even more energy, for her to study that dangling body.

Yet, at the same time, once she [was see]-ing it, she found herself moving [toward] it warily. Absorbing the details.

He was naked and virtually covered in blood. There were numerous shallow cuts all over his torso, front and back, all of which had undoubtedly bled for some time before what looked to her to be the final cut and ultimate cause of death.

Decapitation.

Out loud, slowly, she said, "I'm no M.E., but I think the cuts on the body came first. That he was tortured, maybe over a period of hours. And that his head was hacked off while he was hanging here."

"What makes you sure of that?" Jake asked.

"The amount of blood on the boulders directly below him; it probably came mostly from the shallow cuts, and there's a lot of it. The spray pattern out in front of his body, on the rocks and on the ground, looks arterial to me. His heart was still beating when his throat was cut. I think somebody was behind him, probably standing on the tallest boulder, and grabbed him by the hair. Then—"

Leah made a choked sound and hurried back up the path away from the clearing.

Riley gazed after her, then looked at Jake and

grimaced. "I forget some cops aren't used to this sort of thing."

He was looking a bit queasy himself but didn't budge. "Yeah. Okay, what else can you tell me?" He considered, then added, "If somebody was standing on that tallest rock and had to keep his balance while he—he sawed off a head—he must have held on to something. Or somebody else held on to him."

"It takes some strength to decapitate by sawing or hacking, even with a sharp knife or other tool," she agreed. "Especially with the vic's arms in the way so that he had to reach around them for at least the first part of the job. Keeping his balance would have been tricky." She circled behind the tallest upright boulder and studied the ground intently. "No sign of marks left by a ladder."

"Just don't tell me the guy levitated or something, okay?"

She ignored that. "Your forensics people have been all over this, right?"

"Like I said. Pictures from every angle and samples of everything."

At the side of the larger boulders, a cluster of three smaller ones made it quite easy to climb up onto the seat, and it was likely many a hiker in these woods had done just that over the years.

Riley hesitated only a moment, but since she had picked up absolutely nothing clairvoyantly, she had to conclude that all her psychic senses were AWOL. Touching the blood-spattered boulders was unlikely to change that.

Probably.

She drew a breath and climbed up onto the seat so that she could look at the slightly curved top edge of the back, unwilling to admit to herself that she was glad even the usual five senses seemed to be functioning at less than accustomed norms.

The smell of blood and death would have been overpowering.

It occurred to her only as she was standing there on the blood-spattered rock that she might well be wearing the same shoes—casual running shoes—that she'd likely been wearing the day before. Or the night before. She had awakened barefoot, but there had been no blood on her feet, she remembered that much.

What if there was blood on these shoes?

She hadn't thought to check.

Man, I'm losing my mind as well as my memory. Why the hell didn't I check my shoes?

"Riley?"

Pretending that her stillness and silence hadn't

lasted too long, Riley rose on tiptoe in order to study the top of the tallest boulder. "If he stood up here, it doesn't look like he left any helpful traces."

"Yeah, that's what my people said. No marks from a shoe or any forensic traces at all. Including blood. All the blood went on the flat rock you're standing on or got splashed on the upright part of the taller rock, but not a drop hit the top."

"Odd."

"Is it? That rock's not really close to the body and, as you said, most of the blood on it is from drips that fell straight down."

"Yeah, but that's the thing. He should have struggled. If the body had been moving at all, I'd expect to see at least a few droplets of blood on that top edge."

"Maybe he was drugged."

"That's certainly possible." **But why torture somebody who isn't conscious of what you're doing? Unless maybe the shedding of blood was the point. . . .** "I assume you've requested a tox screen?"

"Definitely. The blood and tissues will be checked six ways from Sunday."

"Good enough."

Riley turned on the seat to study the body

from this closer position, trying not to think about whether her shoes had had blood on them before she'd climbed up here. Because they certainly did now.

Since the body was hanging directly above the front edge of the seat, her position put her roughly at eye level with the small of his back. She studied the distance between the body and the tallest boulder, and said slowly, "Balance had to be a real problem, if the killer was standing up there. He also had to lean forward quite a bit in order to reach the vic."

"He could have pulled him closer," Jake offered. "At least long enough to get the job done."

"But then the vic's head would have been pulled behind the arms, and there's no arterial spray to indicate that happened. All the evidence says his head was forward when his throat was cut, or at least between his arms, not pulled back behind them."

Jake studied the body and boulder for a long moment, then cleared his own throat. "See what you mean. The doc says same as you, by the way—that the head was hacked off, front to back. Of course, by the time the killer was working on severing the spine . . ."

"He probably did have the head pulled back

toward him," Riley finished. "But by then the heart had stopped, so the blood was no longer spraying."

She stood gazing at the body, trying to concentrate, to focus. But it was something other than deliberate thought that made her step forward and lift her arms, not touching the body but stretching upward to measure how high she could have reached.

As she did that, it occurred to her with cold realization that if she had been standing here, reaching up like this, possibly holding this man's body in a better position for his killer to cut his throat, blood would likely have spattered her clothing and hair and covered her hands and forearms.

All the way to her elbows.

The forensics people were back, carefully cutting down the body, by the time the search teams finally called it quits. If the severed head was in these woods, they reported, then it was buried or otherwise well hidden, and where there were signs of fresh digging the searchers had discovered only two beef bones and a rawhide chew toy.

"Oh, Christ," Jake muttered when that news

was relayed to him. "You don't think some-body's dog carried off the head?"

Riley, who had just fished in her shoulder bag to produce a PowerBar, paused in unwrapping it to say, "I doubt it. A feral dog or a very hungry one, maybe, but somebody's pet would hesitate to consume human flesh. As a rule, anyway."

Jake stared at her.

"Cats will," Riley clarified after taking a bite. "Once we're dead, to them we're just meat, apparently. Dogs are different. Maybe because they're domesticated. Cats really aren't. They just want us to believe they are."

Leah laughed under her breath. "Cat person, are you?"

"Actually, I like both." She looked at Jake, who was still staring at her. "What?"

"Talk about jaded. How in the hell can you eat right now?"

"It's for energy." The new voice spoke matter-of-factly. "She has a high metabolism, Jake. No calories, no energy."

"I knew that," Jake said. "What're you doing here, Ash?"

"What do you think? I wanted to see the crime scene while it's still relatively . . . fresh."

Ash. Riley turned her head to watch him approach, again digging for memories and again finding none. Absolutely none.

He was about the same height as the sheriff, which made him around six feet. Dark like the sheriff. But that's where any similarity ended. In comparison to Jake Ballard's polished handsomeness, this man was almost ugly.

He had broad, powerful shoulders that seemed to strain the fabric of the very nice suit he wore, as though the covering were something not quite natural for him. His very dark hair was fairly short and not at all tidy, his chiseled face was deeply tanned, and his nose had been broken, Riley thought, at least twice.

He had high cheekbones, slanted brows that lent him a sardonic expression, and hooded, very, very pale green eyes that threw both danger and something enigmatic into the mix.

And where charm came off Jake Ballard in almost palpable waves, this man was radiating something else entirely. Something almost primal.

When he joined them, standing nearest Riley, he touched her lightly, his large hand sliding down her back to rest near her waist in a gesture that was curiously possessive.

"Hey," he said.

Riley, not a woman to be possessed, would

have protested. Except that the instant he touched her, a hot shiver started somewhere near her toes and spread upward through her entire body in pulsing waves until she felt like she herself was radiating something primal.

Heat. Pure heat. And she recognized the sensation, even if the degree of it was rather astonishing.

Oh. Oh, shit.

She **had** taken a lover. Only it wasn't the sheriff.

"Hey, Ash," she said calmly, and bit into the PowerBar.

She needed energy. She needed all the energy she could get.

"I would have called you," Jake was saying to Ash. "But I knew you had court, so—"

"Postponed," Ash said, looking at the sheriff. "Besides which, murder ranks higher on the list of my priorities than breaking and entering. That case can wait."

He had a beautiful voice, Riley thought. Deep and rich and curiously fluid. Probably handy for a lawyer. Which, she assumed from the conversation, he was.

Jake grunted. "You usually work from reports and crime-scene photographs."

A prosecutor, I'm guessing.

"This is something special. Obviously." He had turned his gaze to the center of the clearing, watching as the headless corpse was zipped into a black body bag. "No idea who he is?"

"Not so far. We fingerprinted him first thing, but his prints aren't in the database."

"And no sign of his head," Riley said, feeling she would be expected to participate in the conversation.

"To delay identification, maybe?" Ash suggested.

Frowning, Jake said, "Take a look around you. If somebody just wanted somebody else dead and not identified, leaving a headless corpse in a ditch or thrown into the ocean makes sense. But left in a fairly public area, strung up and tortured over an altar and inside a circle of salt?"

"Salt?"

"It's used in some occult rituals," Riley said.

Ash looked at her. "Yesterday you seemed pretty sure that whatever's going on around here had nothing to do with the occult."

Oh, shit. Was that a professional opinion, or just pillow talk? And would I have told you the truth, whatever I believed?

Not that she could ask, of course.

Instead, calmly, she said, "Well, that was before this happened. And Jake's right—this is a very public way to leave a murder victim if all the killer wants is to delay identification. Whether or not it's some kind of occult ritual, I can't say. Yet, anyway."

One of his slanted brows rose. "So Jake asked you for help? Officially?"

"Not exactly. Not officially."

"She has resources I don't, Ash," Jake said.

"She's on vacation."

"I'll make sure she doesn't lose vacation days helping with this."

"She'll do just that if she's in this investigation unofficially, on her own time."

"At least you're admitting there's something to investigate."

"A murder, Jake. Whatever all the bells and whistles are, it's just a murder."

"You don't know that. I don't know that. Riley can help find out what it is or isn't."

"If you need help, ask for it officially—through the FBI. Let them send an agent down here."

"They **have** an agent down here."

Riley was suddenly aware that the hand still touching her back was exuding tension and . . .

something else, something more she could feel but not quite get a handle on. Danger? Warning?

She stepped away from that hand abruptly and turned to face the two men, conjuring a pleasant smile. "Still here, boys."

Ash was expressionless, but Jake pulled on his sheepish face.

"Sorry, Riley, but—"

"Don't talk about me as if I weren't," she added gently.

Evenly, Ash said, "You're here on vacation. To rest and relax, remember? After a year of tough cases, you said, the most recent of which nearly got you killed."

"I didn't say it nearly got me killed," she objected, hoping to hell she hadn't. "I said it was rough and it was a close call. But obviously not too close, since I don't have a mark on me."

She offered that deliberately, watching him for the slightest reaction. And—dammit—saw a disquieting gleam in those green eyes.

A familiar gleam.

The shower stall was full of steam—the whole damn bathroom, in fact—by the time they turned the water off and made it to the bed.

"We're getting the sheets wet," she murmured.

"Do you care?" His mouth trailed down her throat and between her breasts. "Shall I stop?"

His hair was just long enough for her to get a handful and force his head up so she could gaze into those green, green eyes.

"Stop and I'll shoot you," she said huskily.

He laughed and covered her mouth with his, and that glorious heat began to burn. . . .

"No," he said. "You don't have a mark on you. Still, you came here on vacation."

Damn memories, rearing their heads at the most inconvenient moments. Riley cleared her throat and forged ahead. "I've had almost three weeks, good food, lots of rest and walks on the beach. I'm fine, Ash."

"And I need her help," Jake said flatly. "I'm not too proud to ask, Ash, whether you are or not."

"It's got nothing to do with being too proud." He kept his gaze on Riley.

Half under his breath, but loud enough for them all to hear, Jake muttered, "I know what it's got to do with."

Riley jumped in before the tension she could

feel in Ash made him say something he might later regret.

"Look, I've said I'll help if I can. And I will. So there's nothing more to be said about it. Right?"

"Right," Jake said immediately.

Ash took a moment longer, holding her gaze with those vivid eyes, then smiled. "Sure," he said. "I think the three of us can work together. Professionally."

Riley smiled back. "I'm sure we can."

Gordon rubbed a big hand across his bald head and stared at Riley. "Say what?"

"My memory of the last three weeks resembles Swiss cheese. Lots and lots of holes."

"The other part."

"Oh, that. I woke up this afternoon with dried blood all over me."

"Human blood?"

"Dunno yet. Probably hear from Quantico tomorrow."

"And you can't remember how you got blood all over you."

"One of the holes, yeah. And it's really bothering me, especially since we have this tortured and mangled body, which was apparently tortured and mangled in about the right time frame."

"I can see how that'd be a worry," he agreed.

They stared at each other, Gordon leaning back against the side of his boat and Riley sitting on the bench across from him. The boat was tied up at the dock behind the small house Gordon owned on the mainland side of Opal Island; he kept himself busy as well as made extra money taking fishing parties out onto the Atlantic.

"Not that I think for one minute that you're capable of doing that to somebody for no good reason," he said.

Wryly appreciative of the qualifier, she said, "But what if I had a good reason?"

"Out of the war zone?" He shook his head. "Nah. Not your style. You might get pissed and come out swingin', but nothing more, not back here in the world."

"I am an FBI agent," she reminded him.

"Yeah, so you'd shoot somebody. Maybe. If you didn't have another choice. We both know you're capable of that. But torture and decapitation?" Gordon pursed his lips, his broad brown face considering. "You know, I don't see you doing that even in wartime. It takes a certain cruelty, not to mention cold-blooded ruthlessness, and you never had either."

Riley was reassured, if only partly. Gordon knew her, probably, as well as anyone did, and if he said killing someone like that was not in her nature, then he was very likely right. She didn't think she was capable of it either.

But.

"Okay, so if I didn't do that to the guy, then why did I wake up covered in blood?"

"You don't know it was his blood."

"But what if?"

"Could be you tried to help him at some point. Went to try to cut him down before you realized it was too late."

"And then just went home and fell asleep, fully dressed and still covered with blood?"

"No, that doesn't sound likely, does it? Not for you. Not if you were in your right mind, anyway. Something must have happened in between. A shock of some kind, maybe. You sure you didn't get a bump on the head, something like that?"

"No lumps or bruises that I could find. Woke up with a hell of a headache, though. You know what that usually means."

He nodded. "Your version of a hangover, minus the booze. You'd been using the spooky senses."

"Apparently." He'd known about her clairvoyance for years, believed in it utterly because he'd seen again and again what she could do, and had kept her secret.

"But you don't remember what they told you?"

"Nope. If they told me anything."

"Must have been something bad. Bad enough to take away your memory, maybe?"

"I don't know, Gordon. I've seen some pretty lousy things. Horrible, sick things. It never affected my memory before. What could have been so bad, so totally shocking, that I couldn't bear to remember it?"

"Maybe you saw what happened out there in the woods. Hell, maybe you saw somebody conjure up the devil."

"I don't believe in the devil. Not like that, anyway."

"And maybe that's why you don't remember."

Riley considered that, but shook her head. "In addition to some lousy things, I've also seen some incredibly weird things, especially in the last few years. Off-the-chart scary things. I don't **believe** any occult ritual would actually conjure a flesh-and-blood devil complete with horns and a pitchfork—but I don't know that I'd be all that shocked if it happened right in front of me."

Gordon grinned. "Come to think of it, you'd probably just wonder how they managed to get the guy in the rubber suit so fast."

"Probably. It **is** mostly smoke and mirrors, you know, the seemingly supernatural occult stuff. Usually."

"So you've told me. Okay. So you saw the murder out there, and something about it caused the amnesia. That's the most likely explanation, right?"

She had to agree. "Yeah, I guess. Which makes it imperative for me to recover those memories ASAP."

"Think the killer might know you saw something?"

"I think I have to assume that until I have proof to the contrary. And finding that proof is not going to be a lot of fun, since I don't have a clue who the killer might be. Worse yet, the spooky senses seem to be out of commission, at least for the moment."

"No shit?"

Riley shook her head. "No shit. I should have been able to tap into something at the crime scene; that sort of situation, with everybody tense and upset, is always where I'm strongest. Or always have been. This time, nothing. Not a damn thing, even when I touched those rocks."

"So you're hunting a killer in the dark."

"Pretty much, yeah."

Gordon brooded. "A killer who might know, or at least believe, that you saw something out there. But if he **does** know you saw something, or even suspects you did, why let you run around loose? I mean, he's killed pretty brutally already. Why let you live?"

"I don't know. Unless he had damn good reason to be sure I wouldn't be a threat."

"Like, maybe, he knew you wouldn't remember whatever it was that you'd seen?"

"How could he know that? Amnesia isn't something you can deliberately cause, at least not as far as I know. And the SCU **has** studied this sort of thing, for years now. Traumatic injuries, especially head injuries, have all sorts of consequences, but amnesia other than very short-term isn't especially high on the list. Besides which—no bumps or bruises, let alone anything severe enough to be termed a head injury."

"Very short-term amnesia?"

"It's fairly common after a traumatic injury to not remember the events immediately before it occurred. But that almost always means a gap of hours, not days—and almost never weeks."

"Okay." Gordon brooded some more. "Long shot, maybe, but what about another psychic?"

Riley winced. "Christ, I hope not."

"But it's possible another psychic could be affecting you?"

"Just about anything is possible, you know that as well as I do. Another psychic might have picked up on the amnesia, or even known about it in advance. Hell, maybe caused it. Or at the very least be taking advantage of it." She drew a breath and let it out slowly. "I can tell you this much. If there is another psychic in this, he or she has the upper hand, at least until the fog in my head clears and I can use my own abilities."

If I can. If I can.

"Don't much like the sound of that, babe," Gordon offered.

"No. Me either." It was Riley's turn to brood. "Leah said you two thought I had been unusually secretive lately." The deputy had dropped Riley off and then returned to the sheriff's department, since she was on duty for another hour.

"Well, more than I liked. It was me brought you down here, after all. I been feeling responsible."

"Don't."

He rolled his eyes, a characteristic gesture Leah had probably picked up from him. "Yeah, yeah."

"I mean it. And, by the way, I haven't told Leah about the memory loss. I trust her, it's just . . ."

"I know what it's just," he responded. And he did know. Fellow soldiers understood the need to guard vulnerabilities in a way few civilians ever could. "I'll keep the secret if you want, but I think she can probably help. 'Specially if—"

Riley eyed him, seeing in that suddenly impassive face a lot more than most would have seen. "Especially if I don't remember my obviously hot social life these last weeks," she finished.

"So you don't, huh?"

"Not much of it, no. I gather I dated Jake Ballard, at least for a while. And that I'm currently involved with Ash. Ash what, by the way? I haven't heard his surname used." The very question struck her as almost comical.

Almost.

Gordon's brows climbed into his nonexistent hairline. "Prescott. Ash Prescott. District Attorney for Hazard County."

"Jesus. What was I thinking?"

"One of the things you didn't share," Gordon informed her politely. "Mind you, I wasn't surprised when Jake talked you into going out with him. He's got the knack. Far as I could tell, though, it was just a couple dates—and then you met Ash. You and him surprised me."

"Why? Because of me, or because of him?"

Gordon gave the question serious consideration. "Well, it's not what I'd call normal for you to bed down with a man you've known no more than a few days."

Riley winced. "That fast? Christ. We weren't subtle about it, I gather."

"Subtle?" He laughed. "In case you didn't see it today, the man usually drives a Hummer, Riley. A bright yellow one. Pretty damn obvious parked outside your place overnight. And people on this island do love to talk."

"Great." She sighed, debated briefly, and decided not to ask Gordon if he was privy to any more particulars of the intimate nature of her relationship with Ash Prescott; that was something she'd need to find out for herself. Instead, she said, "But he surprised you?"

"Gettin' involved with you so fast? Yep."

"Why?"

"Hard to say, exactly. He's not a man to let much show, but I wouldn't have said he was all that susceptible to a pretty woman, 'specially living in a beach community with plenty of flesh on parade most of the time. I mean, you're a fox, any man with eyes can see that, and hot as hell when you put your mind to it, but I doubt that was it."

Riley ignored the blunt assessment of her charms, which she had heard before from Gordon and other army buddies, to ask, "Did I do that? Put my mind to it?" She had to ask, in light of all the sexy underwear she'd discovered among her clothing.

"I saw you a few times dressed up a bit more than usual, but like I said, I don't think it was looks that got to him. And I'd say he was the one went after what he wanted. Didn't need any encouragement at all, far as I could tell. And he has the rep for gettin' what he wants. Still, I've only lived here a couple years, but I can't remember Ash ever gettin' involved with a summer visitor before. So visibly, anyway."

"Maybe he was in the mood for a fling."

Gordon shook his head. "If you was to ask me, I'd say he wasn't the type for a fling. Neither are you, if I have to remind you."

"Well, apparently that's what I'm doing," she muttered. "Flinging. With a man whose last name I couldn't remember."

Gordon pursed his lips in another characteristic gesture. "You didn't remember him or Jake, huh?"

"No. At least . . . I had a flash of memory after Ash joined us at the crime scene. But do I remember meeting him or Jake? Dating them? No. There are faces in my mind, but neither of theirs showed up until they did."

"And you don't remember anything you might have found out investigating the situation here?"

"I don't remember the **situation.** Or, at least, I'm having to piece together what I do—did—know."

"That is definitely not good."

"Tell me about it." She sighed, then straightened and added, "And I mean that, Gordon. Tell me about it all. Everything, starting with why you called me down here, what's been happening here, and what I've told you since I got here."

"Filling in the pieces. Hoping something will wake up your memory?"

"I'm counting on it. Because Bishop will expect a report every day—and if I can't convince him I've got a grip on things here, he'll pull me by Friday. Maybe sooner, considering there's been a murder now."

With another sigh, Riley added, "Besides all that, apparently I have another date with Ash in about two hours. Dinner. It would be nice if I could remember what we've talked about so far, so I don't repeat myself. Also nice if I could remember why I started sleeping with the man, since from the little I do remember, I doubt he'll be content with a good-night kiss at the door."

"I gather you don't want to either confide in him or raise his suspicions by suddenly goin' coy?"

"No to the first because . . . because I don't know where he fits in all this, not yet. As for the other part, playing coy wouldn't exactly be in character for me, now, would it? Unless— I wasn't being somebody else here, was I, Gordon?"

"No, you didn't see the need. Just being your-self and on vacation, picking this place to visit an old army buddy, seemed to be the best choice. You were here openly, an FBI agent, so why dress it up and make it look more fancy than it was?"

"Makes sense. Keep it simple whenever possible."

"Which is what you did. No, babe, you were just being you, and playing coy is definitely not your style."

She nodded. "So I get to feel my way—you should pardon the pun—through a relationship I don't remember starting."

Gordon eyed her. "And?"

He knew her too well. "And I can't rely on any of my senses. Any of them, not just the spooky ones. Everything's gone . . . distant and blurry. For the first time in my life, I don't have any kind of an edge. And it's scaring the hell out of me."

Given her druthers, it certainly wouldn't have been Riley's choice to keep a dinner date with Ash that evening. She **had** suggested that helping investigate a grisly murder should probably take precedence over her social life, but as Ash had calmly reminded her, there wasn't a lot she could do until the body was autopsied and forensic evidence tested—neither of which was a specialty of hers.

Jake had suggested they brainstorm at the sheriff's department, but Riley had been forced reluctantly to agree with Ash that endlessly speculating wouldn't be very productive without facts and evidence in hand.

Best to get a fresh start early tomorrow.

Which meant, of course, that she had to get through tonight, feeling her way semiblindly through the nuances of a relationship that had been one of lovers, apparently, for the better part of two weeks.

Passionate lovers, if her physical reaction to Ash and her single flash of memory were anything to go by.

As she got ready for Ash to pick her up just before eight, Riley wasn't all that worried about her ability to behave as he would expect her to during the date. That was the easy part, at least for her. She'd always been able to fit herself into any situation, to look and act as though she belonged no matter what was going on inside.

In this case, what was going on inside was more at odds than usual with her composed exterior.

Butterflies.

Big butterflies. With claws.

The entire situation made her profoundly uneasy, because it really wasn't in character for her to get personally involved with anyone in the course of an investigation, far less tumble into bed with a man when she hadn't had time, surely, to judge his character.

"Just tell me he isn't evil, Gordon."

"He's a prosecutor, Riley, in a small Southern beach community. How evil could he be?"

"Oh, man, don't ask that question. The worst serial killers I've ever known operated out of small towns."

"Maybe so, but I doubt Ash is a serial killer. Mind you, I'm not sayin' the man doesn't have a few rough edges. And talk is, he raised some hell as a kid. But he's respected around here, I know that much."

"The last serial killer I knew was respected. Before everybody found out what was in his basement."

"You been around way too many serial killers, babe."

Probably true, that.

In any case, what Riley had admitted to Gordon was also true. She was scared. Despite the cool and confident exterior she was adept at showing, there was a very large part of her that wanted to crawl into bed and pull the covers over her head, hoping to wake and find all this just a nightmare. Or to run back to Quantico, her safe haven.

Not that she could do either, of course.

Nope, not Riley Crane, sensible, rational, trustworthy professional that she was. She'd stay and see it through, finish the job she'd started, soldier on—and all the other clichés. Because it simply wasn't in her nature to crawl into bed and pull the covers over her head.

No matter how bad things got.

So when the doorbell rang just after seven-thirty, she drew a deep breath and went to greet Ash with a smile and total serenity.

"Hey," she said.

"Hey," he responded. And wrapped both arms around her, lifting her off her feet to kiss her. Right there in the open doorway, for God and all of Opal Island to see.

So much for privacy. So much for serenity.

Riley suspected that all her bones were melting. She also suspected that she didn't much care.

When he raised his head at last and lowered her back to her feet, Ash said a bit roughly, "I've been wanting to do that all day. Just for the record, you seem to have become a habit with me. I didn't sleep at all last night after you kicked me out."

I kicked you out? Why on earth **would I do that?**

"I didn't kick you out," she murmured, reasonably sure she wouldn't have.

"Maybe not literally, but the result was the same. Instead of spending the night in a warm bed with a warm woman, I ended up alone with whiskey and an old movie. I thought we'd gotten beyond that, Riley."

She took a chance. "Beyond what?"

"You know what I'm talking about. If all I wanted was a dinner companion and an hour of sex afterward, there are willing women in my life a lot less complicated than you are." The statement was utterly matter-of-fact and without conceit.

Hmmm. Wonder which complications he's referring to? Wonder who those other women are? And maybe I'm not a fling?

She didn't know how she felt about that. Hell, she didn't know how she felt about any of this.

Ash went on, "Look, I respect this need of yours for space and time to yourself. I get that, I really do. We both know I'm a prickly bastard and pretty much a loner myself. All I'm saying is the next time you decide you want to sleep alone, a little more warning would be appreciated."

I must have had someplace else I needed to

be later last night. Note to self: obviously something last-minute, or else I would have headed Ash off long before bedtime. Wonder what it was? Did I know there was someone in danger? That something bad was going to happen? And if I did . . .

Why didn't I confide in you about it, lover?

"Sorry. And noted, for future reference," Riley said, wondering when her own arms had wound themselves around his neck. Since they were already there, she didn't bother to remove them. "I missed you too, by the way."

"I'm glad to hear it." He kissed her again, briefly but with just as much intensity. "We could skip dinner."

"Not unless you prefer your women nearly comatose," she said, feeling on safe ground here. "I'm starving."

He laughed. "Then we definitely need to get you fed, and I'm not in the mood to cook tonight. Ready to go?"

Guess that explains my well-stocked kitchen. He's been cooking here.

She didn't know how she felt about that either.

"I'm ready," she said.

6

Five minutes later, they were in his very large, very yellow Hummer heading toward the bridge to the mainland, and Riley had to agree with Gordon's assessment of the highly visible appearance of Ash's highly visible ride. Plus, the very low speed limit on the island allowed people sitting on their porches and decks or strolling the walkways beside the road to not only get a good look at the vehicle but recognize who was riding in it.

People waved. And called out hellos to both her and Ash. He didn't stop the truck at any point, which at least allowed Riley to merely smile and wave in response to those greetings from strangers.

Well, at least there was never anything se-cretive about the relationship. Points for that, I guess.

But there had been secrets **in** the relationship, obviously, since she hadn't told him the truth about why she'd needed him to leave early the previous night. Unless he **had** known and was lying about that . . .

Don't borrow trouble, goddammit. He doesn't know you've lost your memory. So he isn't lying. About that, anyway. But some-thing else is going on here. Because appar-ently you didn't tell him the truth about why you asked him to leave early, and you don't know why you failed to do that.

Then again, perhaps she really had only wanted time to herself, and the fact that some-thing had obviously happened later on had been sheer coincidence.

Nah. She really didn't believe in coincidence.

"You're very quiet," Ash said.

"That scene in the woods today." Riley shrugged, ruefully aware that "shop" talk was what sprang most readily to her mind whenever she needed something to fill the silences or the blanks. "I've seen a lot worse, but . . . it never gets easier."

"I was hoping I'd never see anything like it again," Ash said. "I got more than my fill of murder scenes in Atlanta."

Which told Riley that he had, clearly, lived and worked in a large city. Most likely, of course, as an attorney of some kind. Interesting that he was here now. Career setback, or a deliberate choice?

"Murder happens everywhere. Unfortunately."

"True enough. But this kind of murder? You seriously think we could have some kind of occult nonsense going on here? A ritual murder?"

"I think that's what it looks like. At first glance."

Ash frowned. "You still have doubts, don't you? Despite what you said today."

Riley hesitated, then spoke slowly, trying to weigh each word and wondering if she was making a huge mistake in confiding anything at all to this man, even if he was her lover.

Maybe **because** he was her lover.

"I think—I know—that true occult rituals, especially those ending in murder or any other kind of actual sacrifice, are very, very rare. Especially the sacrifice part. A lot more rare than some of the media would like people to believe. Rare as in virtually nonexistent."

Ash nodded, frowning. "I remember. The vast majority of occult groups are completely harmless, you said."

So we have **talked about this. Good. I think.**

"Right. Their rites and practices are merely the . . . trappings of their religious faith. Most such rituals are completely benign, designed to celebrate life and nature."

"But those that aren't benign?"

"Are very rare."

"I get that. And?"

"And involve actual worship of Satan and the belief in magic, the belief that a specific ritual or rituals can cause supernatural forces to grant the wishes or desires of the practitioner. But even those rarely involve physical sacrifice or murder."

"So I gather nobody dies. Usually."

"I'm serious, Ash."

"Okay. So occult rituals, offensive though they may be to the mainstream, are both rare and mostly benign."

"Yeah. What's a lot more common—though still pretty damn rare—is for someone to borrow the trappings, the ceremonies and rituals.

To do his own thing within the framework of the occult. He may or may not possess occult beliefs. He may feel that he believes but not fully understand the rituals he's trying to command. Or it may have nothing to do with faith or belief and be simply window dressing. He may stage a murder scene implicating Satanism or other forms of the occult to confuse or mislead an investigation. He may deliberately use what he knows will frighten and panic his neighbors."

"To cover his tracks."

"It's been done before."

"I think I'd believe that before I'd believe in a cult of Satan worshippers conducting a blood sacrifice in the woods a mile from town."

"It does sound unlikely, doesn't it?" Riley brooded. "That bothers me as much as anything, the proximity to people, choosing a place where dogs are allowed to run and often do. Where people walk most every day. How long would anyone expect their supposed secret to stay that way?"

"Not all groups are secretive," Ash noted. "There's one just up the beach from you, as a matter of fact."

Purely from his tone, Riley gathered somewhat hesitantly that this wasn't something he expected her to already know, so she risked asking questions.

"What, a cult? A coven?"

"They aren't calling themselves either, as far as I know. Just a group of like-minded friends renting the Pearson place for the rest of the summer. But they've applied for and been granted permission to build a beach bonfire on Friday night—the full moon—and they've been asking questions, strongly implying they believe there's occult activity in the area, and they've let it be known that they practice an . . . alternative religion."

"Were they more specific about that? 'Alternative' covers a lot these days."

"Not that I've heard. So far, anyway. But people are talking, of course, especially given what's been happening this summer."

Jesus, I wish I could remember how much of this we've already discussed.

"Can't stop people talking," she ventured.

He sent her another glance, dark brows lifting. "When the talk is bordering on panic, it's time to try. Or, at least, time to offer them a rational explanation to discuss. I thought we'd agreed about that, Riley."

"Yeah," she said. "I remember."

Except that I don't.

The cold, queasy feeling in the pit of her stomach got worse, and it wasn't because she needed food.

"Calls are already coming in," Ash said. "No media yet, but that's probably only because their attention is on all the shit happening in Charleston."

What the hell's happening in Charleston?

Riley scrambled for yet another elusive memory or bit of knowledge and again came up empty. She had absolutely no idea what was going on in the nearest city of any size to Castle.

"Still, I'm bound to be asked for an official statement of some kind soon," he went on. "Especially after today. What do you suggest I say—on the record?"

"That . . . a murder is being investigated."

"It won't stop the talk."

"No. But I can't offer anything else, Ash, not yet. I need time. Time to get a better grip on what's going on here."

"I don't like the idea of you working alone on this."

"Jake and his people—"

"Are out of their depth. We both know that. Why don't you want to be on the official clock,

Riley? Why not call your boss, have him send down some help?"

"The unit's spread really thin right now," Riley answered truthfully. "Besides, Jake said an official FBI presence would stand out around here, and he's right. It may be no secret I'm with the Bureau, but at least I won't be flashing my badge or gun and interrogating people. That makes a difference, Ash; it changes how people respond to even a casual question, much less a pointed one. If I can keep my presence low-key, I'm more likely to find out . . . something."

"Yes," he said. "That's what I'm afraid of."

It was a Monday evening, but it was also in-season for the beach community and surrounding areas, so the restaurant Ash had chosen on the outskirts of Castle was doing brisk business. The good news, as far as Riley was concerned, was that the majority of that business consisted of summer visitors, most of whom didn't know one another.

Knowledge or memory?

She wasn't sure. Dammit.

In any case, if the restaurant's customers on this night even knew a body had been found only a couple of miles away, it didn't appear to be hampering their enjoyment of the quiet music and excellent seafood.

Riley did, however, catch at least a couple of glances and smiles aimed toward them as she and Ash were seated in a semisecluded back corner booth and left alone with their menus, and she murmured, "Nobody looks too panicked."

"Yet," he said. "But you can bet word of what was found this afternoon is spreading. By morning the summer visitors will be uneasy, some to the point of packing up early. The locals will be worried and demanding answers. More calls to my office, that's for sure. But I don't envy Jake, since he and his people will get the brunt of it."

"Part of the job."

"Probably not what he signed on for, though. Not in Hazard County."

"You either, I guess."

"No," Ash said after a moment. "I didn't sign on for it either."

Riley was looking at her menu but not really studying it. Something else was nagging at her. "Jake said nobody'd been reported missing."

"Yeah. You think who the victim is—or was—might be more important than how he was found?"

"At least **as** important, surely."

"No random sacrificial victim?"

"I'll have to do some research," she said, hedging her bets since she couldn't remember just what Ash knew of her background, "but offhand I can't think of any sort of black-occult ritual centering around the sacrifice of a victim chosen at random or just because he happened to be in the right place at the wrong time. Rituals tend to be very controlled, very specific. **Especially** when they involve anything as extreme as a blood sacrifice."

"So I take it all the urban legends about homeless people disappearing, to be used in satanic rites or as part of a black market for organs, are just that. Urban legends."

It was at least half a question, and Riley nodded in response as she met his intent gaze. "The vast majority of stories like that are about as real as leprechauns. The Bureau conducted an exhaustive investigation years ago, when half the country seemed convinced there were devil worshippers on every corner, and didn't find a shred of evidence to support all the scary claims of ritual human sacrifices during black sabbats."

"Yet there are genuine satanic rites practiced."

"Even genuine satanic rites don't involve

murder. You have to get beyond . . . conventional . . . Satanism and really out on the fringes to find that sort of thing."

"Seriously? There are fringes beyond Satanism?"

"You'd be surprised." He really did have the most amazing eyes. She hadn't known eyes **came** in such a pale shade of green. Not human eyes, at any rate.

"So **if** we have occult activity here that involved a ritual murder, it isn't likely those responsible are satanists?"

"Some fringe groups call themselves satanists. So it's still possible. Or it's some other group calling themselves something else. Or it's window dressing to hide a murder." Riley sighed. "And then there's rumor, and speculation, and people with their own agendas who keep fanning the flames, who do their best to take a spark of truth and build it into a bonfire of trouble."

"For instance?"

She shook her head. "I once opened my front door to find a young woman who was attempting to raise money for her church. The spiel was that our children were being threatened by devil worshippers and her church needed money to fight this evil army. She was deadly serious about it. It was in a sweet little town where the worst I ever saw happen was egging a few houses at Halloween, and that poor woman was jumping at shadows and imagining that demons straight out of hell were a breath away from grabbing her babies."

"People will believe in the damnedest things."

"Especially if the authority figures in their lives tell them something is real."

"Which is why," Ash said, "I still believe our best bet is to treat all this as a series of bizarre hoaxes."

"Even the murder?"

"You said the killer could be using all the occult trappings just to throw us off the scent."

"I said it was possible. And it is. But until we know who that victim was, we can't know who might have wanted him dead."

"Are you going to suggest that to Jake?"

Riley once again had the vague sense of undercurrents, of some kind of long-simmering tension between Ash and the sheriff, but couldn't bring it into focus enough to even be sure whether it was professional or personal.

Something there, though. Definitely something there. And strong, if she was aware of it even with all her senses out of whack.

Mildly, she said, "I imagine Jake's cop enough

to know the basics without needing to be re-minded."

Ash returned his gaze to his menu. "Jake's a politician."

"I can't tell him how to do his job, Ash."

"No, I suppose not."

His tension was still there. She could feel it. Barely.

Where's my clairvoyance when I need it? Hell, where are any **of my senses?**

They were still dulled, blurred, as if she saw and heard and touched and smelled her sur-roundings through some kind of wispy veil. It felt weird and cold and scary, this sensation of being distanced from the world.

Being unconnected.

She was alone, that much she **could** sense.

Even stranger, her head was hurting again, but not in any way that was familiar to her. Not a dull ache of tension or weariness, nor the rare "hangover" head-in-a-vise agony of having pushed herself way beyond her limits, but sharp little bursts of pain every few seconds, one after the other, in random spots from just above her eyes over the top of her head and back to the nape of her neck.

Riley'd had a tooth go bad once; it was that sort of pain, like a nerve or nerves pulsing.

In her tooth, the nerve had been dying.

She was afraid to even think about what might be happening inside her brain.

And here she was, in the middle of a tangled situation she didn't remember or understand, painfully aware that a killer or killers on the loose almost certainly knew a hell of a lot more about what was going on than she did.

As independent and self-reliant as she was, Riley had never felt so unsure of herself. She was adept at role-playing—it was one of her strengths—but this? This was a very, very dangerous game of blind man's bluff, and the one wearing the blindfold—her—had cotton in her ears and a clothespin on her nose as well.

With the exception of Gordon, she didn't know who to trust, and he could offer little more than moral support since, if she had even reached any conclusions or formed any theories since arriving here, she had not confided them to him.

As for the other man she was intimately close to . . .

"Riley? Ready to order?"

She looked across the top of her menu at this pale-eyed stranger whose bed she apparently shared, and ignored the cold knot in the pit of her belly to say calmly, "I'm ready."

It was the second time she'd said that in the last couple of hours. She only hoped it was true.

3 Years Previously

"You realize what this will mean?" Bishop said.

A little amused, Riley said, "You're a telepath; you know I realize what it will mean."

"I'm serious, Riley."

"Are you ever anything else?" She got a sudden flash of a strikingly beautiful face and electric blue eyes, understood in an instant who the woman was and what she meant to Bishop, and her question suddenly didn't seem so funny anymore.

"Never mind," he said. "We all have our ghosts. And not many secrets between a telepath and a clairvoyant."

"You really must believe we can do some good," she said slowly. "To . . . willingly expose yourself to so many of us."

Deadpan, he said, "I didn't think it through."

Riley had to laugh, but she shook her head and got the conversation back on its original track. "I do understand what you're asking of me. I know it could take months. Will, probably."

"And you'll have to work alone, at least to all appearances."

"Well, if you're right about how this killer chooses his victims, and right that the first sign of a task force or police focus is what causes him to change towns, then the only way to track him is alone and off the official books. Assuming I can do that."

"I believe you can. I believe you're the best-equipped of anyone in the unit to track him. And to make sure he's caught. But, Riley, you don't get too close. Understand?"

"He only kills men."

"So far. But a cornered animal can kill whatever's threatening it. And he's smart. He's very, very smart."

"Which is why I hide in plain sight. And don't threaten him."

"Exactly."

"That's what I do best," Riley said.

Present Day

In the small part of her mind not occupied with the strain of pretending everything was normal, Riley had struggled to come up with some reasonable excuse for ending up, at the conclusion of this date, in her beach house alone. Short of telling Ash the truth—which she still wasn't ready to do—nothing seemed likely to work without rousing either his suspicion or his anger.

Her senses might be AWOL, but that earlier brief flash of memory plus her instincts as a woman told her he had every reason to expect to spend the night with her—and, despite his calm and almost detached manner during their date, quite definitely the desire to do so. Still, right up to the moment they walked inside the house and he closed the door behind them, Riley believed she might yet come up with a reasonable, acceptable excuse.

She was going to offer coffee or a drink but never got the chance.

Ash picked her up and carried her to the bedroom.

The sheer suddenness of the action, never mind its high-handedness, should have roused some sort of negative reaction in Riley. She was almost sure it should have. Instead, what she felt was an overwhelming sense of familiarity and the first flush of sensual heat sweeping her body.

There was, she realized dimly, something incredibly seductive in the certain knowledge that a man not only wanted you but wanted you **now,** with no patience for small talk or any of the other social niceties. He wasn't interested in coffee or conversation, he was interested in her, and she was left in absolutely no doubt of that fact.

He was just a little bit rough, more than a little bit urgent, and Riley found the combination impossible to resist.

So she didn't try.

And she didn't try to pretend a response to him, because she didn't have to. Whatever else he was or might be, Ash Prescott was a skilled lover, and her body remembered his touch even if her mind didn't.

She'd left a lamp burning low on her nightstand but kept her eyes closed because the only senses that mattered were the ones he was bringing to life. For the first time since waking up in the afternoon, there was no veil, no distance—and no questions.

Not about this.

Their clothing seemed to just vanish; set on her feet by the bed, Riley almost instantly felt the erotic shock of flesh on flesh, and then the cool smoothness of the sheet beneath her. She had no idea which of them had thrown back the covers and didn't care.

His body was amazingly hard, with the packed

muscle of a man who was very athletic, genetically blessed, or both. His skin was smooth and hot beneath her fingers, and the thick, springy hair on his chest teased her breasts with a raw sensuality that only intensified the heat building inside her.

His mouth on hers fed that fire, as hard as his body, as urgently demanding as the hands stroking her flesh. That mouth-to-mouth connection was more than a kiss, more like a melding, a merging, and she had the dim understanding that this was why she had tumbled into bed with a relative stranger.

Because he wasn't. Because they weren't.

Their bodies strained together to be closer than they were, closer than they could be, and she heard herself make a wild sound that would have astonished her if she'd been able to think about it. But there was no time to think or wonder about anything, there was only pleasure that built to an incredible peak and a stunning wave of emotion she'd never known before and couldn't begin to define.

When it was over, Riley felt both exhausted and curiously shaken. What had just happened? It was more than sex, or at least more than she knew sex to be. And she wasn't at all sure she'd be able to pretend otherwise. But she gave it her best shot.

When he pushed himself up on an elbow beside her, she finally opened her eyes and murmured, "Wow. Good thing I had that second dessert."

Ash laughed. "You never say the expected, do you?"

"Probably not. Is that a bad thing?"

"Not as far as I'm concerned." He reached across her to draw the sheet over their cooling bodies, pausing to briefly nuzzle the curve of her neck.

Riley felt her eyes starting to cross at that pleasurable caress, and hastily closed them. "Mmmm."

"If you go to sleep, I'll just wake you up," he warned.

Her laugh ended on a sigh. "You have only yourself to blame."

"Open your eyes and talk to me."

"I thought men always wanted to sleep after," she complained mildly, opening her eyes.

He was smiling faintly. "You should know by now not to lump me in with a group. Neither one of us runs with the crowd."

Now, what in the world does he mean by that?

She couldn't ask, of course.

Instead, she said, "Well, **you** should know by now that I either sleep after—or grab a snack. Fuel, remember? The tank's empty here, pal."

"Okay. I promise you a midnight omelet. How's that?"

Riley turned her head to look at the alarm clock on the bedside table. "That's more than an hour away." She allowed her voice to fade pathetically. "I may not make it."

Before she could turn her head back, she felt his fingers at the nape of her neck.

"What's this?"

It was a sore spot; she realized that when he touched it.

"What does it look like?" she asked, holding on to the sleepy murmur even though she was, now, wide-awake.

He rubbed very gently. "A burn, maybe?"

Just at the hairline at the base of her skull, an area normally covered by her short hair. An area she hadn't checked visually when she examined herself that afternoon. And a sore spot that would have been both hidden by her hair and masked by the headache she'd had almost continually since waking.

7

Riley fought not to react in any way he'd
notice, fought not to reveal the sudden
questions and fears tumbling through
her mind.

"I'm all thumbs with a curling iron," she said
casually. "It happens so often I forget about it,
usually."

"Have you considered maybe **not** using a
curling iron?" Ash inquired dryly.

She turned her head back and met his gaze,
smiling. "From time to time. But it's a girl
thing, you see, and I clung to those when I was
in the army."

"What, you were afraid of ending up butch?"

"That is not a politically correct term. And—yes."

Ash grinned at her. "Not a chance in hell. You are utterly and completely female, my love, from the top of your head down to the tips of your toes. It practically oozes from your pores."

Riley ignored the lurch inside her at the unexpected endearment and pulled on a considering frown. "I'm not at all sure that's a compliment."

"It's disarming, that's what it is. Dandy camouflage for the razor-sharp mind behind those big eyes."

"Mmm. But you weren't disarmed, huh?"

"I wasn't fooled," Ash said. "Not like Jake was."

A little surprised and very curious, she said, "You think he was fooled?"

"I think he's badly underestimating you. And I think if he hadn't done that from the moment he met you, he might be here with you instead of me."

Wry now, she said, "I really stepped in something between you two, didn't I?"

"Maybe." He shifted position to lie more fully on his side, his head propped up on one hand and the other resting warmly on her stomach. "But it had to happen eventually."

"Why?"

Ash's shoulders moved in a faint shrug. "Because letting Jake have what he wanted most of our lives was easy for me. Until what he wanted was something I wanted more."

Riley thought about that. "Me?" she half-guessed.

"If you have to ask," he said, "you haven't been paying attention."

She managed a laugh. "Oh, I was paying attention. Just trying not to feel like a trophy between two jocks."

"You know better than that." He leaned over to kiss her, the caress a lingering one. "At least as far as I'm concerned. This is not about Jake. This is about you and me."

Riley was trying her best to think straight despite the lips playing with hers. "Mmm. But if all Jake sees . . . is that trophy . . . he might still want it."

"Then he'll have to learn a lesson I probably should have taught him when we were kids." Ash pushed the sheet back down so his seeking hand could find bare flesh. "He doesn't always get what he wants."

Riley had thought she was completely exhausted, but her body was coming to life, and as her arms lifted to wrap themselves around his neck, she decided that she just might have the strength for this. . . .

As it turned out, she also had the strength left for a shower with Ash afterward, but by then her energy reserves were seriously low and they both knew it.

"I'll go get started on those omelets," he said, knotting a towel around his lean waist.

"I'll get my hair dry and meet you in the kitchen. Sorry to be so high-maintenance," she said.

He tipped her chin up with a finger to kiss her. "You aren't," he said, and left her alone in the steamy bathroom.

Riley finished wrapping herself in a towel, then held her hands out and watched them shake for a moment. Damn. Between the mental and emotional demands of a Swiss cheese memory and the physical demands of a relationship with Ash, she was using up energy at a rate far faster than normal even for her.

Something was badly wrong, and she knew it.

Shaking off yet another worry, she rummaged in the vanity drawers for a hand mirror and wiped off the steamy mirror over the sink so she could check out the back of her neck. It took a bit of maneuvering, and she ended up sitting on the vanity with her back to the big mirror while she held the hand mirror with one hand and pushed her hair completely off her neck with the other hand.

It looked like a burn, as Ash had said. Like two burns, actually, very close together, just below the hairline at the base of her skull.

Even in the warm, steamy room, the chill that swept her body left gooseflesh in its wake. She had to concentrate fiercely in order to hold the hand mirror steady long enough to study the marks until she was certain of what she already knew.

They were the marks of a stun gun, a Taser.

And what they very clearly showed was that someone had held the gun to the back of her neck and discharged an electrical current directly into her body.

Into the base of her brain.

It took less than ten minutes to blow-dry her short hair, and that didn't allow Riley enough time to think much past the numb realization that in all likelihood a killer had stood over her twitching body and emptied into it from a

weapon meant to incapacitate a target a potentially deadly amount of electricity.

Riley had used a Taser. She had also been
Tasered herself. She knew what the weapon
was capable of, and what its normal aftereffects
were. There was nothing normal about this.

The marks on her neck indicated sustained
contact, with both voltage and amperage con-
siderably higher than the manufacturer had ever
intended for the device.

The question was, had her attacker deliberately used an amped-up stun gun knowing it
could be a lethal weapon? And, if so, was she
alive by design or only by accident?

Either way, the attack could explain her head-
aches and the memory loss, and the dulled—or
absent—senses. It could even explain her unusually frequent need for more fuel.

An electrical jolt to the brain could scramble
a lot of things in the human body.

It could also cause a hell of a lot of problems,
some worse than those she was coping with
now. And the fact that those problems hadn't
yet manifested themselves didn't mean they
wouldn't.

**Great. That's just great. Somebody tried to
fry my brain, probably tried to kill me, and**

**he's still out there running around loose—
with a big advantage.**

He knew who she was.

And she didn't have a clue who he was.

With her hair dry and no more excuses to linger in the bathroom, Riley went into the bedroom to put on one of her customary sleepshirts. She took a moment to sort through their scattered clothing and lay Ash's more neatly over a chair, and despite everything felt a flicker of amusement when she picked up the sexy underwear she had, at the last minute while dressing for their date, chosen to wear.

She doubted he'd even noticed it.

With that wry thought in mind, she chose a football jersey sleep-shirt, exchanged her towel for it, and headed for the kitchen.

You can think about all this later. Figure out what's going on later. Right now you just have to get through tonight. You have to act normal and be Ash Prescott's summer lover.

If that's what she was. Or maybe she was, despite his denial, the trophy he had taken away from his boyhood rival.

There was a cheerful thought. Not.

"Perfect timing," Ash said as she joined him.

He was transferring the two halves of a large omelet onto two plates on the work island. He had already set out silverware and napkins, as well as poured two glasses of wine.

Riley took her place on one of the stools at the breakfast bar and looked at him with lifted brows. "Wine? You know that makes me sleepy." She hoped he knew.

"Yeah, well, I think maybe you need to sleep." Ash put the pan in the sink and brought the plates to the bar.

Riley left her brows raised and waited.

He was frowning just a little, and before she realized what he was going to do, he grasped her wrist and lifted it slightly so they could both see her fingers trembling. "Your tank's not just empty, you're running on fumes. After finishing a sizable meal about three hours ago."

"A gentleman wouldn't talk about how much I eat," she said, keeping her tone light as she reclaimed her hand and took a sip of her wine.

"That's not what this is about, and you know it. Was it the scene in the woods? Is that what took so much out of you?"

"Well . . . scenes like that do, usually." She started eating, hoping the calories would kickstart her sluggish mind.

Oh, I'm in fine shape, I am. If I was half as

responsible as I'm supposed to be, I'd have Bishop recall me to Quantico. Tonight.

"Because of the clairvoyance?"

Riley was only a little surprised he knew about that. It wasn't something she often confided on short acquaintance—or even long acquaintance, in most cases—but the man was in her bed, after all. And at least his knowledge answered one of the questions she'd been asking herself.

One down, at least a dozen more to go.

She nodded. "It takes more energy, yeah. Especially a murder so . . . horrific. Everybody around me is tense, frightened, sickened—and usually worried about their nearest and dearest. Sorting through all that . . ."

"Takes a lot of energy." He was still frowning, still intent. "So this happens whenever you work on a case?"

"To varying degrees. I tried harder than usual today, probably because I wasn't getting anything. That happens sometimes too." Information she hoped would head off at least some of his questions.

Ash picked up his fork and began to eat, but after several bites said, "I had the impression you used your abilities as just another investigative tool."

"Generally. They often give me an edge in an investigation—but not always. This is very good, by the way." She indicated her plate and the omelet, already half-finished. **Sure, keep wolfing down food—that'll solve everything.**

"High-calorie," he said in a tone of sudden amusement. "I put in extra cheese."

Riley had to laugh, albeit without much amusement of her own. "Sorry—I didn't expect to get involved with anyone this summer, much less during a full-blown investigation."

"Stop saying you're sorry. Feeding you is not a problem, believe me." He smiled, then added casually, "So business and pleasure don't mix too well in your world?"

"They both take energy." Riley lifted her glass in a small salute. "One more than the other, sometimes."

"You didn't answer the question."

It was a potential out for her. Maybe. One less pretense she'd have to keep up. If she told him the investigation would demand all her energy, all her attention, then maybe he'd step back out of her personal life for the duration.

Except that she didn't think he would.

Or maybe you just don't want to believe he would.

Finally, she said, "It's never come up for me, so I don't know. We'll find out, I guess."

He gazed at her steadily for a long moment, then smiled again. "I'll order a couple more cases of those PowerBars."

"Good idea," she said.

The wine had its usual effect on her, and she was yawning hugely by the time she crawled into bed a few minutes later. "Probably should have checked the doors," she murmured.

"I did. All locked." Ash got into bed beside her but before turning out the lamp on the nightstand paused to reach into the top drawer. "Here—I know you won't rest easy until this is under the pillow."

Riley blinked at the gun he was holding casually by its barrel, then took it from him. She checked it automatically to make sure the safety was still on, then slid it underneath her pillow.

She always went to sleep on her right side, a habit that made her turn her back to him as she lay down. It was clearly a routine he was accustomed to, since he turned out the lamp and settled down behind her without comment.

Close behind her.

He kissed the nape of her neck just below the burn and said, "Try to sleep past dawn, okay? I think you need to."

"Mmmm. 'Night," she murmured in response.

"'Night, Riley."

Her body relaxed because she told it to. Her breathing was slow and even. Her eyes were closed.

She had never been more wide-awake in her life.

The realization had been slow in coming, but now it took root in her admittedly sluggish mind and began to grow into at least one horrible possibility.

She always slept with her weapon under her pillow. Always. Ever since a very nasty experience with a predawn burglar nearly ten years ago. But very few people knew that.

She had awakened the previous afternoon fully dressed except for her shoes, with her gun under the pillow as always.

There were only two possible routes to that destination, as far as Riley could see. Both of them started with her leaving the house—after telling Ash she wanted time alone—undoubtedly armed, because she certainly would have been. Going to do whatever it was she'd gone to do, and in the process getting surprised or otherwise blindsided by someone with a stun gun. After that . . .

Either she had, after being stunned for God only knew how long, managed to get herself back home and to her bed, too addled to remove her bloodstained clothing but able to kick off her shoes and remember where her gun should go, or . . .

Or her attacker had brought her home. Removed her shoes. And put her gun under her pillow, because he'd known she would expect to find it there whenever she woke up.

Shit.

The field of suspects if that turned out to be the case had suddenly gotten very, very small.

Ash knew where she kept her gun at night. So did Gordon. If anyone else here knew, Riley would be very surprised. But maybe someone else did know. Hell, maybe everyone knew.

Oh, God, what else don't I remember?

Her car had been here, the keys in her bag. Had she driven wherever it was she'd gone last night? **Could** she have driven back here, suffering the aftereffects of near-electrocution? No evidence of blood in her car, but . . . Three miles to the bridge, assuming she'd gone over to the mainland; surely she hadn't walked?

I'm assuming whatever happened didn't happen here on the island. Why am I assuming that?

Because the altar—if that's what it had been used for—was on the mainland. Because a tortured and murdered man's body had been discovered there. And because she found it almost impossible to believe that a second, totally separate violent event had taken place in this small community on the same night.

Rational. Reasonable. Probably right.

Probably.

"Riley?"

Oh, shit. I can't even fake it anymore?

"Hmmm?" she murmured.

"Why are you still awake?" He nuzzled the back of her neck. "I thought you'd go out like a light."

"Just thinking, I guess."

"About what? The murder?"

"Yeah." It wasn't a lie. Exactly. "Occupational hazard."

Without turning her to face him, Ash gathered her into his arms. "Can I talk you into letting it go until tomorrow, or is this something else I should get used to?"

What could she tell him? How much could she tell him?

How far could she trust him?

Riley was conscious of an unfamiliar desperation, and it was a feeling she did not like. Especially when it caused her to blurt, "I'm different. When there's a case."

"So it's not just about using more energy," he said after a moment.

"No. There's that too, but . . . I pretty much live the job. I get obsessed." She tried to put a shrug into her voice. "My boss says it's part of what makes me a good investigator. Other people have . . . indicated that I can be distant or difficult to connect with whenever I'm working on a case."

"Forewarned is forearmed?"

"You have a right to know."

His arms tightened around her. "Riley, I understand how our work can drive us. You know how far mine drove me. All the way back to my childhood home, where being the district attorney is barely a full-time job. You can't allow your job to consume you."

She wished she remembered his story, she really did. She had a feeling it was a vitally important piece of this puzzle she was in. But all she could say was, "A man's dead, Ash. Shouldn't I be bothered by that? Shouldn't you?"

"I'm just saying you won't be any good to the

investigation **or** yourself if you don't get some rest."

"You're right, of course."

His arms tightened around her again, and there was something inexpressibly soothing in his voice when he murmured, "Tomorrow is soon enough to begin to obsess. Go to sleep, Riley."

He hadn't answered her questions, and that bothered her more than she wanted to admit even to herself. At the same time, her body was relaxing against his, for real this time, and she was growing sleepy once again.

Exhaustion, almost certainly. Catching up with her. But it was more than that, and even as her fragmented thoughts began to settle, a last nagging realization followed her into sleep.

Despite everything, even her own doubts, here in this man's arms she felt . . . safe.

And for a woman who had learned a long, long time ago that safety was, at best, an illusion, that was terrifying.

In an unusually grim tone, Gordon said, "Yeah, I'd say this was from a Taser. And a juiced-up one, at that."

Riley smoothed her short hair over the burns

and turned to face him. "I was pretty sure. Just wanted a second opinion."

"Have you reported this to Bishop?"

"Not yet."

"Jesus Christ on a crutch, Riley."

"I know, I know. But I also know what Bishop will say, and I don't want to be recalled. I can't just cut and run, Gordon. Not yet. Look, if whoever attacked me had wanted to kill me, I'd be dead."

"You don't know that. It's more likely he **left** you for dead and that crazy, messed-up brain of yours kept you alive against the odds."

It was a good point, and more than possible. Like all the psychics on the team, her brain had a higher-than-normal amount of electrical activity going on at any given time, so it very well might not have responded as the attacker had expected to an added jolt.

"Maybe." She hesitated, then confessed, "I had a nightmarish scenario running last night where the guy stunned me and then brought me home and put me to bed thinking I'd wake up and not know anything had happened."

"You mean when you woke up covered with blood you wouldn't think anything had happened?"

"I didn't think about that part until this

morning." After about three cups of coffee and a wonderful breakfast courtesy of Ash.

Gordon eyed her consideringly. "You really aren't firing on all cylinders, babe, 'case you didn't know that."

"Why do you men always use car metaphors?" she demanded, even though she'd used the very same one herself in describing her condition to Bishop.

"Don't change the subject."

Riley sighed. "I'll tell Bishop everything when I report in this afternoon. I can't justify keeping any of it to myself, not with a man dead. I'll just have to hope I can convince him to leave me here. But, in the meantime, I'm headed out to the sheriff's department, where I hope there will be statements, photos, and a postmortem report I can take a look at."

"What do you expect to see?"

"I don't know. Probably nothing I couldn't figure out from the crime scene. But maybe I missed something."

Gordon was frowning. "I gather the spooky senses are still AWOL?"

She nodded. "Which makes more sense today than it did yesterday. Now that I at least know what happened to me. Even so, I have a pretty good hunch that Bishop will tell me nobody else on the team has experienced a jolt of electricity straight into the base of the brain. I don't recall reading that in any of the unit's case histories, and I **think** it would have been there. Highlighted. Underlined. With an asterisk."

"Yeah, I get it. Which means—"

"Which means I'm in unexplored territory here and pretty much on my own. God knows what was scrambled or short-circuited inside my head. And what the aftereffects might be."

"Want to tell me again why you aren't going to see a doctor?"

"Because there's nothing a doctor would do except probably run tests. Because I'm functional. I don't even have a headache today, or at least not much of one. Whatever that jolt did to my brain . . . well, let's just say I doubt they have a magic little pill to fix me."

"It could be permanent? The memory loss **and** the damage to your senses?"

"Could be." Riley drew a deep breath and released it slowly. "Hell, that may be more likely than not. If an electrical jolt can trigger latent psychic abilities—and we know it can—then it's reasonable to suppose one could just as easily short-circuit or even destroy them."

"How you feel about that?"

"All my life, I've counted on those extra senses to give me an edge when I needed it. When somebody else was bigger or stronger or smarter or faster—or just meaner. Without them, I don't know if I'm good enough to do my job."

I don't think you have to worry about that," Gordon said. "I've seen you accomplish plenty without the spooky senses."

"Thanks for the vote of confidence. Wish it helped the queasy feeling in the pit of my stomach."

Maybe changing the subject, Gordon asked, "How'd the date go last night?"

She knew he wasn't asking for details, and wouldn't; he just wanted to know if her evening with Ash had changed anything.

It was an answer she didn't have.

"It went . . . it was fine." Riley hesitated, then

said, "Tell me I can trust him, Gordon. Promise me I can trust him."

"Wish I could, babe, but I don't know the man well enough to promise anything. All I know's what I hear, the little bit I've seen for myself, and for what it's worth that's mostly good. I'd want him on my side in a fight. My gut says I could depend on him to watch my back. But we both know that don't mean he couldn't be a bastard to the woman sharing his bed."

"I don't think . . . That isn't what I'm afraid of."

"What, then? Afraid he carved up a living human being out in the woods?"

"I don't think he could do that. But I don't **know** he didn't. Gordon, I'm used to getting a sense of people. Deeper than reading expressions or voices or watching what they do. I know who I can trust and who I can't, almost always, but it's more than that. It's a sense of who they **are,** deep down inside. With Ash, I have the nagging feeling there was something very important I sensed about him. Something I really need to know now. And whatever it was, I can't feel it, can't **know** it anymore. It's gone."

"Maybe not gone for good. Maybe just beyond reach right now."

"Yeah. Yeah, maybe." As well as he knew her, Gordon wasn't psychic, and because he'd never lost a sense he couldn't understand what it really meant to suddenly be without something you had depended on to help you steer your way through an often hostile world.

Riley was only just beginning to realize it herself. The queasy sensation in her stomach intensified.

After a moment, Gordon said, "You got involved with him, and I have a hard time believin' you'd have done that if you'd sensed anything rotten inside him."

"I hope you're right." Riley looked out over the peaceful summertime scenery visible from Gordon's dock and wished fleetingly that she could join the fishing party he was expecting any time now and just sail off for a few mindless hours. That sounded a lot more appealing than looking at autopsy photos.

"Riley?"

She looked at him, then straightened away from the bench she'd been half-leaning against. "I'd better go. Jake expected me at the sheriff's department half an hour ago."

"I got a friend can take this party out."

Grateful for the implicit offer, she nevertheless shook her head. "And we'd tell Jake what?

That I felt threatened enough to bring along an army buddy to watch my back in broad daylight? I'm an FBI agent on vacation and he's asked me to advise on an investigation, all nice and casual. So why would I suddenly feel the need for a bodyguard? Nobody else knows about what happened Sunday night, and I want to keep it that way, at least until I figure out a little more of what's going on around here."

"Whoever attacked you knows what happened. And if he left you for dead, he's going to be mighty surprised if he sees you walkin' around like nothin' happened. Mighty surprised—and mighty worried about how much you know."

"I've been thinking about that, and I'm not so sure he'll be worried at all. Far as I can tell, I never even drew my weapon. Can't be sure about that, but I certainly never fired it. And I was attacked from behind, obviously taken by surprise. Not bragging or anything, but it's not all that easy to take me by surprise."

"I would have said."

"Yeah. So, chances are, I never got so much as a glimpse at whoever was holding the Taser. I think if he—or she, I suppose—believed I'd seen or heard anything that might be a danger to him or her, he or she—Oh, hell. **He** would have made damn sure I was dead."

"That's an awfully big assumption to hang your life on, babe."

"Yeah, well." She gestured to the holstered automatic she wore easily on one hip. "From now on, I'm openly armed most of the time and, as far as most people around here are concerned, officially on duty." A decision she had made after Ash left that morning. "I didn't want it to be this way, because it means some people are going to be less likely to talk to me. But, after thinking about it, I decided the risks of appearing unarmed outweighed the benefits."

"Especially with you being a little bitty thing."

"Yes, I know I don't look very threatening. A gun tends to make people think twice. With my other edge gone, that's one I need."

Gordon pursed his lips. "I'll be happy to spread the word you're hell on wheels in a bare-fisted fight. It's not like it'd be a lie."

"Don't go out of your way." Riley shrugged. "But if the subject comes up, why not? Who-ever the guy is, I want him to get the idea that taking me by surprise a second time won't be so easy." She held up a hand when he would have spoken to say, "Which also means I won't be go-ing out at night by myself, not again."

"Call me," he said. "It was me got you involved in all this, so you'd damn well **better** call me next time."

With some feeling, she said, "Believe me when I say I do **not** want to go up against the bastard's stun gun a second time. If I need to do any investigating at night, I'll call you."

"Any hour."

"I know. Thanks." Riley took a step toward the walkway that would lead her around to the street side of Gordon's house, then paused and looked at him with a frown. "Gordon? What's happening in Charleston?"

He looked blank for a moment, then said, "Oh, you mean the murders?"

"If that's what's happening. Murders?"

"Yeah. They got a serial killer, apparently. A real mean one, leaving his victims pretty much in pieces. Been at it awhile, I gather, but the cops just put it together about a week ago, at least according to the Charleston papers. Bastard's targeting tourists, men only, and everybody's pretty tore up about it all."

"I guess so." Riley felt suddenly cold in the hot July sunshine. **Can't be. Not the same M.O. And there must be a hundred serials operating right now in this country—**

Gordon bent to check a bait bucket, adding, "The papers have been calling 'im The Collector. Seems he's been leavin' a mint-perfect coin on every one of the bodies. Well, not on the bodies. Inside the bodies, after he finishes cutting 'em up. Guess they could just as easily call 'im The Slot Machine Killer, but—Riley? You okay?"

She wondered if the sun had gone behind a cloud, if that's why she felt so cold. Why everything seemed dark all at once and she could barely feel Gordon's big hand on her arm. Except that she knew the sky was cloudless and the sun was hot, that it was a normal summer day.

Normal. That was it, that was the lie.

Because it's not normal. Nothing is normal, not if he's hunting again. A ghost can't hunt, and that's what he's supposed to be. He's dead.

I killed him.

2½ Years Previously

It was an unexpectedly cool night in New Orleans, which suited Riley. She liked heat when she was on the beach or at a pool, but otherwise not so much. Especially at night, and most especially on a night when she might have to move fast.

Being distracted by the sense-assaulting chaos of the French Quarter at night was bad enough without also coping with sticky clothing. What little she was wearing, anyway.

"Hey, honey—how 'bout a date?"

"I'm off duty," she said.

He blinked in surprise and nervously fingered a strand of alien-head Mardi Gras beads that were adding a nicely tacky flourish to his colorful shorts and floral shirt. "Aw, now, don't be like that, honey. I can pay for a room."

"I'm sure you can, champ, but I'm just not interested." She kept her tone bored and her gaze moving; the last thing she needed tonight was to get picked up for solicitation, and she'd been on the watch all evening for cops patrolling the street on foot.

It made the job she was here to do even more difficult, and for at least the tenth time she regretted the skimpy clothing that made her blend right into the festive crowd but also made her a target of unwanted attention.

He'll never notice me, but, dammit, every straight guy between fifteen and sixty-five has. **I could make a bloody fortune. Probably should have picked an outfit closer to tourist and further away from hooker.**

Not that there was much distance between

those two seeming opposites, not with today's skimpy summer fashions. Besides which, she wanted to look more like a native than a tourist and, clearly, had achieved that goal.

Realizing that the hopeful would-be john was still standing there, Riley allowed an edge to creep into her voice. "Look, it's my night off, okay? Find another playmate."

He hesitated, scanning her up and down with clear disappointment, then sighed and moved on.

Riley decided that she obviously looked too available just hovering, so she began to stroll slowly along the sidewalk, allowing the moving crowd to carry her.

It had to be New Orleans. She was certain of it. She had followed the killer from Memphis to Little Rock, a step behind him as she'd been for months, studying the butchered bodies he left for the police to find, trying to climb inside his mind far enough to do more than guess where he'd strike next.

Then, in Little Rock, looking at the bloody scene of his latest murder, something inside her had whispered **Birmingham**. She had hesitated, questioning her instincts, her clairvoyance, whatever it was trying to guide her.

But she had been right; his next victim died

in Birmingham. And Riley had arrived just in time to view yet another scene of butchery.

By then her own anger at being once again too late to help the victim had nearly blocked her, but even through that fury she had heard the whisper. **New Orleans.**

I'll be in New Orleans, little girl. Meet you there.

She hadn't told Bishop that part when she reported it. It had probably been her imagination anyway, that's what she convinced herself. Because she wasn't a telepath and couldn't possibly have heard the killer's voice in her mind. So all she told her boss was that she felt sure New Orleans would be the next stalking ground.

So here she was. A month later.

And so far, nothing.

It was almost impossible to be bored in New Orleans, but Riley knew her patience was wearing thin. This killer had struck at least nine times—Bishop felt there were probably earlier victims not found or not connected, and Bishop was usually right about stuff like that—and all she was sure of after months of exhaustive effort was that her target was a salesman or traveling rep of some kind.

"It makes sense," Bishop agreed. "He knows the cities and towns he visits. So he'd know where to hunt. All the local hangouts. It wouldn't take him more than a few nights to be able to recognize the regulars."

"And pick his target, yeah. But why family men, guys stopping for a beer or two on the way home from work? Jealousy? Because they have what he doesn't?"

"Maybe. Jealousy. Resentment. Envy. Or just rage. Because it's all so unfair. Because they're normal and he's not."

"You think he knows that? Knows he isn't normal?"

"Some part of him knows." Bishop hesitated, then added soberly, "I hope that's the part you're tapping into, Riley. Because the other part of him is black as the inside of hell, pure evil, and that's not a place you ever want to get caught up in."

"I'm not a telepath."

"No, you're an ultrasensitive clairvoyant and you've gotten obsessed with this guy. Which means you're letting his work seep into your mind, your emotions, into your very pores. It's dangerous. I warned you—don't get too close."

"You knew I would," she said, and it wasn't quite an accusation. "When this started. When you recruited me."

"Yeah. I knew."

Hearing or sensing what might have been a touch of regret in him, she said, "It's okay. I knew it too."

"I wish that helped," Bishop said. "Be careful, Riley. Be very, very careful."

Three weeks after that phone conversation, Riley was tense, edgy, and getting a little too familiar with her surroundings. At night on Bourbon Street, it was noisy and colorful and held a particular flavor no other city on earth could match.

People filled the street, some of them lurching or staggering, their eighty-proof laughter scraping along her nerves. The spicy aromas of Cajun cooking mixed uneasily with that of the musty old buildings and cigarette smoke and people. Occasionally the breeze changed, and the muddy smell of the river was added to the rest.

A space had been cleared about halfway down for a juggler to entertain the crowd, his practiced patter loud and cheerful. The music booming from the clubs and strip bars lining the street clashed with the mournful wail of a folk singer, his guitar case open for contributions on the sidewalk before him.

And under the bright lights of the street, the appearance of the crowd ran the gamut from a few garish costumes apparently left over from Mardi Gras to men and women in business suits. In between lay everything from jeans and T-shirts to the brief skirts or shorts and halter tops of the teenagers—and hookers.

Riley was trying to close out all that, trying to focus her mind only on her prey.

You're here, you bastard. The cops don't know it yet, don't know there's a hunter prowling their streets. These people don't know. But I know. I can feel you, like an itch on the back of my neck. Smell you, like the sour stench of cheap cologne and old sweat.

And need. You smell like need. You need to kill tonight, don't you? It's been too long since the last one. Why have you waited so long? You never did before. Three weeks, max, never a whole month. Why wait a month this time?

Is it me? Do you know about me?

Can you feel me the way I can feel you?

A peculiar dizziness swept over Riley, and her step faltered. She blinked at the sea of moving people, then managed to make her way far enough out of the flow to lean a hand against a building.

She realized she was gagging, that there was

an awful metallic taste in her mouth. She put her free hand up to touch her lips and when she looked at it could see blood.

Her probing tongue could find no wound in her mouth, no reason for there to be blood. There was no pain. So why was—

The smell of it was suddenly thick in her nostrils, and for an instant she was sure her hands were slick with the viscous stuff, the knife in her grasp held securely only because he knew what he was doing—

Oh, Christ. It's him.

Riley realized she was moving only when she passed the police cars blocking off the end of Bourbon Street as they did every night. She didn't stop, didn't even hesitate. As the smell and taste of blood grew stronger, her pace quickened, until finally she was running, away from the crowds and toward something she didn't want to find.

At some point she drew her weapon from her shoulder bag; she was hardly conscious of doing it. She was only aware of running, faster and faster, her lungs burning and her side aching when, finally, she found it.

Him. What was left of him.

She was standing at a construction site, partially cleared for a new building but holding nothing yet except huge earth-moving machines, looming still and silent all around her. Stoic inhuman witnesses to the atrocities committed here.

There was a streetlight just close enough for her to see what he had left this time. The remains of a man's body, naked and bloody. But only part of it.

There was nothing from the navel down except the grisly pulp of hacked-up internal organs.

Too late. Riley was too late. Again. And the taste of blood was still in her mouth.

Missed again, didn't you? But don't worry, little girl. You'll get another chance. I'll see you in Mobile.

She could have sworn she heard the echo of mocking laughter, but it wasn't on the faint breeze blowing around her.

It was inside her own mind.

And this time she knew it wasn't her imagination.

Present Day

"We don't know it's him. Not for certain," Bishop said.

Riley sat in her car at the sheriff's department, the cell phone to her ear, and struggled to keep her voice even and calm. "He's leaving coins, right? Mint-condition coins **inside** the victims."

"That shouldn't have leaked to the press."

"It didn't leak before, we both know that. Which means this killer isn't a copycat."

Bishop's voice held all the calm Riley's lacked, and then some. "What we both know is that hundreds of people worked on the previous investigations over time, so we **can't** be sure information wasn't leaked—even if it didn't make the newspapers."

"He's dead, Bishop. I killed him."

"I believe you did."

Riley realized that with her free hand she was gently rubbing the burns on her neck and made herself stop. "One of us needs to take a look at what they've got. Be sure. I can—"

He didn't let her finish. "We haven't been invited, Riley. And since our previous investigation was officially closed and our killer officially taken off the books, what's happening in Charleston right now is being viewed as an entirely new case, most likely a copycat."

"A full-blown serial killer just popping up out

of nowhere? If his ritual is established, then he's killed before."

"Yes. Which is why I've reached out to a cop friend of mine in Charleston. He's getting duplicate reports to me for an unofficial profile. I'll know soon enough if this is someone we've seen before."

"You mean we'll know soon enough if I missed." There was a bitter taste in her mouth, not unlike the blood in New Orleans.

"You didn't miss. You never miss. You fired your weapon and hit John Henry Price at least three times full in the chest, and he went down."

"They never found the body."

"That river never gave up its dead."

She drew a breath and let it out slowly. "Very convenient thing, wasn't it? That he just happened to fall into the river after I shot him. That he ran out onto that dock but past the tied-up boats, all the way to the end. What if he planned the whole thing, Bishop? He could have. We both know he was smart enough. What if he just wanted to stop for a while, get us off his back and off his trail, and he knew the only way was if we **believed** he was dead?"

"Riley—"

"You didn't get there until later; none of the telepaths or mediums were there to tell us **for sure** if he was gone. Just me. And all I could feel, all I could sense then, was terror, because he'd gotten so damn close. Because I knew he'd been the one to crawl into my head instead of the other way around."

"It happens sometimes when the predator we're tracking has some active or even latent ability."

"And you warned me. I know."

"It's been nearly two and a half years," Bishop said quietly. "If he was alive, he would have been killing."

"He could have been more careful. Picked victims who wouldn't be missed. Hidden or destroyed the bodies when he was done with them. You said yourself at the time that going public the way he did, when he did, leaving the bodies to be found, was because he wanted a challenge, because it had gotten too easy for him. He wanted the world to watch him, to see how clever he was. Maybe the challenge now is to convince everybody else he's not the same killer we tracked for so long. Maybe that's why he's hunting tourists rather than locals."

"Maybe," Bishop said at last. "But we have some time; this killer is apparently on a monthly schedule, and his most recent victim was discovered only a few days ago."

"He's killed one victim a month?"

"For the past six months. The police caught on early because of the coin signature but managed to keep that bit out of the press until the most recent victim last week. Political decision."

"Didn't want to hurt tourism."

"Exactly. But word's out now, and they're getting plenty of heat for not warning their visitors. Not the best example of Southern hospitality on record."

"Hardly." Riley frowned. "If they're taking heat—"

"—then chances are good they'll call for help sooner rather than later. Yes. I'm counting on it. As to whether this killer really is someone we've seen before, I won't know anything until I see those reports. In the meantime, you have trouble enough where you are now."

He was right and she knew it. Riley tried to focus, to put that other killer out of her mind, but it was almost impossible. She had never felt more vulnerable in her life, and even the faintest possibility that John Henry Price was still alive and on the hunt less than fifty miles away had turned the queasiness in the pit of her stomach to churning fear.

Even on the other end of a cell-phone connection, Bishop didn't miss that.

"Riley, what else is going on? Has the situation there worsened?"

She didn't want to but knew she had no choice, so Riley made her report matter-of-factly. She told him about the murder and about the evidence that she herself had been attacked with possibly lethal intent.

And before he could say a word, she finished with, "Don't recall me, Bishop."

"Why the hell not?" His tone was grim. "Riley, I have absolutely no idea what a direct jolt of electricity could do to a psychic's brain, not under those conditions. But I can pretty much promise you there's not much chance of a reversal of whatever damage was inflicted."

"You mean I might never recover my memories. Never get my senses back to normal—any of them."

"That's exactly what I mean. It's more than a chance, Riley. It's a probability. Electrical energy affects us. It can strengthen our abilities, change them—or destroy them."

She drew a breath, then said, "That's all the more reason I should stay here. Look, I know it sounds irrational. But every instinct I have is telling me that if I leave, what's happened to me **will** be permanent. That I'll never get back the lost time—or the lost senses."

"Riley—"

"Bishop, please. It's more than just a case now. Somebody attacked me, maybe tried to kill me. And the same person most probably killed a man on the same night. Tortured and decapitated him. It might be his blood that was all over me, and I don't even know his name, not yet. I have to stay here. I have to work this investigation. Whatever answers I can find will be here, not studying inkblots for some doctor at Quantico."

He was silent for a moment, then said, "Tell me you aren't asking to stay just to be close to Charleston. In case."

"I can't," she admitted. "That's part of it. Because if it **is** Price, I'm the only one who got close once before. I'm the one you'd have to send if—when—they ask for our help."

"The last time nearly destroyed you, Riley. **With** all your senses and memories intact."

"I know. And I'm not looking for a repeat performance, believe me. I don't need a profiler to tell me he would be **really** pissed at anyone who'd taken him out of the game even temporarily. Pissed as in out for revenge and in a major way. That was his nature, right? Vengeful?"

"Among other things."

Riley didn't want to think about those other things. "So we both hope there's a copycat in Charleston. But whether I have to face a worse possibility or not, I'll be no good to myself or to the SCU if I can't fix whatever that bastard with the stun gun broke."

"Which is all the more reason to return to Quantico."

Riley hadn't wanted to but ended the argument with a simple fact neither of them could dispute, because both were cops.

"Memories or not, I did **something** on Sunday night that left me covered with blood. Maybe the blood of a murdered man. Until we know for sure, I can't leave."

9

Leah Wells had wanted to be a cop since she was eight years old. Maybe even longer, but she remembered back to eight. She had turned her dollhouse into a jail, imprisoning three dolls, two teddy bears, and a ninja action figure borrowed from her brother when he hadn't been looking.

The ninja had committed the most heinous act; he had kidnapped Malibu Barbie and held her for ransom. The battle to capture him and free the hostage had been intense.

Leah's mother was somewhat bemused by all this, rightly fearing the childhood games heralded a less traditional life than the one that she, at least, hoped for. But Leah, instead of spending her college years joining a sorority and pursuing a degree in child psychology or some such, had studied criminal psychology and criminal investigation, interning with the state bureau of investigation.

But if her mother had been disappointed in her daughter's choice of careers, Leah herself was somewhat disillusioned by four years spent on the police force in Columbia; she discovered she did not like being a big-city cop. Too much violence. Too many depressing situations with unhappy, tragic outcomes.

Gordon said she'd picked the wrong career for a woman who believed happily-ever-after was the way stories were supposed to end, but the truth was that Leah enjoyed the work—mostly. She enjoyed helping people. So, when Columbia turned out to be too depressing for her, she decided a beach community would undoubtedly be more cheerful, less violent, and provide great fringe benefits.

Especially since she was that rare redhead who tanned instead of freckled.

She had landed in the Hazard County Sheriff's Department by virtue of a pin. With a list before her of law-enforcement agencies along the southeastern coast looking for experienced officers, she had closed her eyes and stabbed the paper with an open safety pin.

Hazard County it was.

Maybe a dumb way to plan a career, let alone a life, but it had worked out well for Leah. Because she liked her work now and loved the beach-community lifestyle. And she had a man she was fairly crazy about as well. Icing on the cake.

"And now," she said to Riley, bringing her story to the present and sounding aggrieved, "some murderous fiend has to come along and ruin paradise."

"Yeah, murderous fiends can really screw up your day," Riley said gravely. She was sitting on a corner of the conference table, idly swinging one foot, waiting for Sheriff Ballard to meet them there with the postmortem report. In the meantime, she had gotten Leah talking with a simple question or two about herself.

Leah sighed. "Oh, you know what I mean. It's not like I'm taking this murder lightly. Every time I close my eyes, I see that poor guy hanging out there in the woods. I feel queasy. And scared. Because if the maniac who killed him isn't a summer visitor, then chances are he's somebody I know."

Riley took another bite of the PowerBar she'd

been eating, then said, "For what it's worth, I'd be surprised if this killer was a summer visitor."

"Shit. Why?"

"Because if he—or they—practice actual satanic rites, it's not something you usually just take on the road when you go on vacation. Not the extreme rituals, at any rate. Plus, secrecy is a really big factor, and that site was awfully public."

"So it could have been—what? A fake ritual?"

"Maybe a smoke screen. To hide the real motive behind the murder. And if that's the case, if somebody is using the trappings of the occult to throw us off the scent, then the reason is, most likely, to deflect attention away from someone who would otherwise be a logical suspect in the straightforward murder of this man."

Leah thought about that. "But we can't know if he had any enemies locally until we know who he is. Was."

"Yeah. So identifying him has to be a priority."

"It is. But so far, nada. The doc serving as our medical examiner gave us a preliminary report last night; he didn't find any identifying marks on the body. No old scars, no tattoos, no birthmarks. We ran his prints a second time just to be sure, but still no luck."

"I wouldn't expect his prints to be on file," Riley said.

"Any particular reason why?"

Neatly folding her empty PowerBar wrapper into a narrower and narrower strip, Riley said, "Because the head was removed."

Leah couldn't help grimacing, but said, "And so?"

"And so I've never heard of an occult ritual where the head of a victim was removed and taken away. And I can't see why that would be done other than to delay identification. That being the case, if the killer had any reason to suppose the guy's prints were on file, and obviously not being the squeamish kind, he would have destroyed the fingertips. Hacked them off, or maybe used a blowtorch."

Leah cleared her throat. "It's not a nice world where you live, is it?"

Riley looked slightly surprised, then smiled a bit ruefully. "I guess not. I don't think about it that way, most of the time."

"It's just a job?"

"Well . . . more or less. I meet some great people through my work. Have some interesting experiences, not all of them negative. I travel a lot. I do work I feel is important."

"Oh, no question about that." Leah lowered

her voice slightly, even though they were alone in the conference room. "And you have a way to use the psychic stuff where it really means something, instead of working in a carnival sideshow or on one of those call-the-psychic hotlines."

"One of the most amazing psychics I know spent years in a carnival, telling fortunes."

"I didn't mean—"

Riley waved that away. "Oh, I know. But you're right—for some psychics, maybe most psychics, there aren't many ways to carve out a decent living using those abilities. That's assuming you even **can** use the abilities, and lots can't."

"Can't control them, you mean?"

"Most of us can't control them, or at least not reliably. My boss says that if ever a psychic is born who **can** control his or her abilities, the whole world will change. He's probably right about that."

"But that psychic won't be you, huh?"

"No. I've been using my abilities as long as I can remember, and it's still hit-or-miss. Even if my concentration is perfect and my energy level optimal, I may not get a damn thing. Other times I'm not even trying and get blindsided by a dump of information or emotions."

"You get emotions? Other people's emotions?"

Leah hadn't intended to sound wary but heard it in her voice.

Riley frowned at the empty wrapper that was now a thin, folded strip; she tied it neatly into a knot. "Sometimes. Not the way an empath would, feeling what somebody else feels. It's just knowing somebody is angry or sad—or whatever. Even if it's all locked inside and they aren't showing any of it."

Leah studied the other woman, wondering what that must be like, to have that window into other people. Not that she wanted to know firsthand; she had trouble enough sorting through her own thoughts and emotions without adding in someone else's.

It wasn't something that appeared to disturb Riley. She was a curiously serene woman, Leah thought. Even out in the woods yesterday, in the midst of that horrific scene, her manner had been calm and matter-of-fact. And today the gun on her hip was worn casually with jeans and a light summer top.

She did **not** look like an FBI agent. Then again, Leah could imagine her in an army uniform only because Gordon had a couple of pictures of them together.

"Don't let those big eyes and that sweet voice fool you," he had warned Leah with a grin. "Riley hasn't got an innocent bone in her body. She's seen battle and she's seen the world, and she can take care of herself on any patch of it fate might see fit to send her to. Hell, I wouldn't want to tangle with her, armed or unarmed."

Something to bear in mind, Leah thought.

"Does being psychic really help?" she asked. "I mean, in an investigation."

Riley tied the plastic wrapper into a second knot, frowned at it as if wondering why she'd done that, and dropped it into an ashtray on the table behind her. "Sometimes." She hesitated, then met the other woman's gaze and said, "But maybe not this time. Just so you know, I'm more than a little off my game right now."

"Ash?" Leah guessed.

Riley was clearly surprised. "Why would you think that?"

"Just relating, I suppose." Leah laughed. "When I was falling for Gordon, I once came to work wearing two different shoes. I thought the guys would never let me live it down."

Riley smiled, but her eyes remained intent, questioning.

Interesting how clearly that came across, Leah thought. That silent question. Without actually intending to, she found herself offering an answer.

"Ash is a very intense guy, everybody knows that. I just figured he was probably even more intense behind closed doors—so to speak."

"He's a little . . . overwhelming," Riley said rather cautiously.

"I bet. Rumor has it he left the Atlanta DA's office because he couldn't control his temper."

"Really?"

Leah shrugged. "Oh, you know rumors. I've never seen any sign of that sort of thing, personally. But it's hard to miss the guy's . . . intensity. I keep coming back to that word, but it does seem to fit, doesn't it?"

"Yeah. Yeah, it does."

Shaking her head, Leah said, "Rotten timing, all this. It looked like things were going really well for you two, that we'd find out all the supposed occult stuff was just nonsense and Gordon was fretting for nothing. Now, with this murder, everybody's tense and jumpy, and none of us can think much about anything else. Occult or not, something's sure as hell going on."

"Yeah."

"It was pretty obvious yesterday that Ash wasn't happy about you working the case. You two get that straightened out?"

"Yes. I told him I'd be working the case."

Leah laughed. "Atta girl. It's probably good

for the man to find out you won't be at his beck and call."

"I think he already knew that."

The sheriff came into the room just then, which effectively put an end to any further confidences. At least for the moment.

"Well, we've got paperwork," he said. "And the crime-scene photos are printing out now. Riley, turns out we **do** have some sort of pattern-recognition software—and a technician who knows how to use it."

"Melissa?" Leah guessed.

"Yeah. Figures, right?" He handed the manila folder he was carrying to Riley, adding, "She's our resident computer geek, and thank God we have her. One of those people with an inborn knack. Anyway, she's going to be concentrating on those blood spatters on the rocks, see if we maybe have something more deliberate there."

"Good enough." Riley opened the folder and began going over the postmortem report.

Jake moved restlessly around the room for a minute or so, then took a seat at the table near Riley. "Still no luck identifying the guy," he offered.

Leah wanted to tell him to give Riley a chance to absorb the report she was reading but kept her mouth shut.

Without looking up, and apparently still reading, Riley said, "With no head, and fingerprints not in the system, I'm not surprised. Still no missing-persons report that matches, I gather?"

"No. No missing-persons reports at all."

"Is that unusual for this area?"

"To have no reports? Nah, it's normal. We don't get too many missing, barring the occasional teenager staying out too late or drunken fishermen falling out of their boats."

Deciding to speak up, Leah pointed out, "If he went missing on Sunday afternoon or early evening, it's less than forty-eight hours. Unless he had somebody waiting for him at home— wherever that was—it's at least even money that nobody's noticed him missing. Especially if he was here on vacation."

Riley nodded. "The needs of vacationers vary; not everybody walks on the beach or visits the restaurants or shops. Some people come with a bag of books or briefcase full of work, park themselves in front of the view, order takeout delivered, and never leave their own little rented piece of sand until it's time for the drive home. If this guy came here alone, his absence may have stirred no more notice than his presence did."

"How are you doing that?" Jake demanded.

She looked at him over the top of the open folder. "Doing what?"

"Reading and talking. Or are you just pretending to read?"

Leah kept her mouth shut again and just listened.

"No," Riley said. "I'm reading. It's a knack I have. Another agent in the unit taught me."

He grunted. "Must come in handy."

"Sometimes."

"That's considered a masculine trait, isn't it? Being able to compartmentalize mentally? Or emotionally."

"I've heard it said."

"You don't agree?"

"Never really thought about it." Riley's voice remained mild, and her slight smile was merely polite, but Leah was certain the other woman was perfectly well aware of what was going on.

Jake was showing off one of his least attractive traits, one Leah had seen often enough to recognize. Quite simply, he was accustomed to women paying attention to him no matter what else happened to be going on. Virtually all women. And that part of him disliked taking second place, to another man or to a murder.

Coming in third where Riley was concerned was obviously bugging the hell out of him.

Leah made a silent bet with herself as to the direction Jake would steer the conversation.

"You're probably good with numbers too," he said.

"I am," Riley confirmed, still mild. "I can also change a tire or the oil, use power tools skillfully, read any sort of map accurately, hit what I'm aiming at on the firing range or in the field, and I play a mean game of pool. Not bragging or anything. Just saying."

"Poker?"

"That too."

"A paragon," Jake said. "Can you cook?"

"Afraid not."

"I guess it's a good thing Ash can then, huh?"

Leah won her bet.

"Guess so." Riley shrugged.

"Doesn't really matter to you?"

"Well, I usually live on takeout, so it's something new. I could get used to it."

Jake was so transparently not pleased by that statement that Leah nearly laughed. But not quite. He was, after all, her boss.

Riley closed the folder and tapped the edge against her free hand. "Getting back to the murder, with no good way to I.D. the body, I say our best bet is to look for a man who isn't where he's supposed to be. Starting from the easier end. Summer visitors."

"That will be the quickest," the sheriff agreed. "We can check with all the motels and realtors for a single guy renting a room, a condo, or a house; in this area, we tend to get more families and groups than singles, so it ought to narrow the field. I'll get my people on it."

"It's a start, anyway." Riley offered the folder to Leah. "Want to take a look?"

"Pass. Wouldn't know what I was reading anyway."

Riley smiled and returned the folder to Jake. "Not much we didn't already know. White male approximately forty to forty-five years old, tortured and then decapitated. No tox-screen results yet. Estimated time of death was between two and six A.M. Sunday night. Or Monday morning, rather."

"Does that help?" Leah wondered.

"Not really. Not without more to go on. Jake, may I see all the paperwork you've got on any of the other possibly related crimes this summer? The arson, vandalism, whatever else you have."

"Of course." He was all business now, the

foray into her personal life seemingly forgotten. "Looking for a common thread?"

Matter-of-factly, she said, "If there was one, your people probably would have seen it. Unless it's occult-related. Those can be very subtle, and I wouldn't expect most cops to pick up on them."

"But you would?"

"Maybe, maybe not." She shook her head. "Sorry to sound vague, but I haven't had a chance to do any research yet; until I work up a list of possibly related occurrences and try to figure out what they have in common, research is tough and fairly useless. The occult is a broad topic."

With a sigh, Jake said, "Yeah, I did an Internet keyword search using **human sacrifice.** You wouldn't believe some of the shit that came up."

"Oh, I'd believe just about anything." Riley's voice was dry. "But I'd rather start at the beginning, not with the end result."

"What do you mean?"

"I mean that the preparations for an occult ceremony are every bit as important as the eventual outcome, possibly more so."

Leah got it first. "So if you find something out of place in the prep work, you'll be more inclined to believe the occult . . . elements . . . were used as a smoke screen."

"Exactly."

Jake was frowning. "That's what you think? Seriously?"

"I think it's possible."

"You've been listening to Ash."

"Actually, I think he's convinced this murder has nothing to do with the occult. I'm not quite ready to rule it out just yet."

"I'm glad to hear that," Jake said. "Thought I'd have to waste a lot of time arguing the possibility."

"I'm always open to possibilities," Riley said. "There are usually plenty of them, and this case is no exception. Maybe it's a garden-variety murder dressed up to look like something else. Or maybe it really is something else."

It was Leah's turn to frown. "Wait a minute. You said there wasn't **much** in the autopsy report we didn't already know."

"That's what I said."

"So there was something. Something you didn't expect?"

"One small thing," Riley agreed. "The stomach contents."

Jake looked at the closed folder he'd placed on the table, then back at Riley, his brows lifting.

"What about them? We don't have the tox screen yet, so—"

"So we don't know if he was drugged or poisoned. Yeah. But what we do know is that his stomach was full of blood. And it wasn't his."

10

Riley bent to pick up a charred bit of wood and straightened, turning it in her hands. "The house was under construction when it burned?"

"Not much more than a shell," Jake confirmed. "The roof was on, and it was mostly closed in, but that was it."

"And it was being built by a construction company, not an individual."

"Yeah, a big company bought up a shitload of land on the island a few years ago, when one of the original owners finally sold out. They've been building on lots ever since. Usually have two or three houses going at the same time. Big crew."

"Insurance?"

"What you'd expect. Nothing excessive." Jake shrugged. "And nothing crooked that I could find. They build a house and then sell it, to either an individual, a co-op, or one of the properties groups that own rentals. Business as usual around here."

Riley dropped the charred wood and absently brushed her hands together. "And your fire marshal is sure it was arson?" She was behaving as though this was her first visit here, although she had to assume that she'd been here to this site at least once before, and unbeknownst to the sheriff. This fire had, after all, been one of the unusual occurrences to rouse Gordon's suspicions this summer.

So it only made sense that she had come here at some point. She might even have found something here to deepen—or erase—her own suspicions, for all she knew.

She didn't remember.

"An accelerant was used," Jake replied. "And not something common, like gasoline or lighter fluid. I don't have lab results on just what kind, but we're sure of that much."

"Anything else we're sure of?" The question was straightforward and not at all sarcastic.

"Not a whole hell of a lot. Happened in the middle of the night, closer to dawn, really. Report called in by a neighbor who was up early to take his dog out. The fire was well under way, and nobody was seen here or running—or driving—away from here."

Riley frowned at the blackened pilings intended to support the house well above the sandy ground as required by code and the only parts of it still upright and recognizable. Around the base of the massive timbers were mounds of charred wood, some of them waist high, where the building had caved in on itself while burning.

"What're you thinking?" Jake asked.

She wished she knew. There was something very familiar about this, but she didn't know what it was. Or even **why** it was. Maybe it just looked familiar because she'd stood here before, studied the debris of this fire before.

Or maybe it was something else.

"Riley?"

Why do I get the feeling it's something else?

"I guess the fire marshal sifted through all this stuff," she said, more to be saying something than because she had any real doubts.

"Twice. And then I had a closer look myself—

early yesterday, as a matter of fact. Except for signs of that accelerant I mentioned, neither of us saw anything that didn't belong here."

Riley looked at him with a frown. "Then why do you have this fire lumped in with the other unusual occurrences? Fires happen. Arson happens." Thinking of the earlier conversation with Leah, she added, "Even in paradise. And burning a building doesn't play a part in any ritual I know of. So why do you believe this might have had something to do with occult practices?"

He sighed. "Well, there **was** one unusual thing here. The fire marshal didn't notice, or at least didn't put it in his report. And I only found it yesterday. Haven't even had the chance to tell Ash, if you want the truth."

"Found what, Jake?"

He led the way through the mounds of rubble toward the beach side of the property, saying over his shoulder, "The company wants to clear all this and start rebuilding, but their insurer's investigator apparently wants to take a look and won't cut them a check until he does. Supposed to be here by the end of the week. Otherwise, all this'd be cleared out by now."

An awful lot of things appeared to be happening—or were supposed to happen—by the end of the week, Riley thought, conscious of a new prickle of unease. As if a clock were ticking off the moments until . . . something. She didn't know what. Or whose clock it was.

Or even if it mattered, dammit.

But all she said, calmly, was, "I'm not surprised the insurer wants to take a look, if an accelerant was used. I gather it was one of those rare policies that actually covers arson, but only if no evidence points to the company?"

"Yeah. Buildings under construction are tempting targets for arsonists, and having a special rider on the policy is usually less expensive than hiring security to watch the place twenty-four–seven all during construction. But the insurers take a harder look when something like this happens, of course. Personally, I don't see how the builder would profit from a fire, not at this stage. The policy is one designed just for a building in progress, so at any given time it only covers what the company can prove it's cost them up to that point."

"Sensible."

"Yeah, and pretty much stops some unscrupulous builder from throwing up shoddy workmanship and then burning it and claiming the loss as market value. Apparently, you've gotta have the paperwork to back up your claims of cost—actual cost of materials and manpower, not appraised value when finished. That sort of policy keeps the cost down for the builder but still makes it so they don't lose their shirts if something happens during construction."

"I bet it's saved the insurance company some major bucks too. Jake, where are we going?"

"Here." He stopped near the edge of the dunes, which presently hid their view of the ocean and over which a wooden walkway had already been partially constructed, with more thick pilings sunk deeply into the sand.

Ignoring the STAY OFF THE DUNES! signs posted liberally up and down the beach and near every walkway, Jake stepped behind a piling and crouched down.

"Almost missed it," he said.

Riley joined him, going down on one knee in the soft sand, and stared at the rough surface of the massive post. "I don't suppose it could be natural," she said.

"No. Found the same thing at the abandoned building that burned in Castle last week. I'd say this was a brand—or at the very least made with something hot enough to burn the wood."

After a moment, Riley reached out and traced the very clear shape that did indeed look as though it had been deliberately charred into the surface of the post.

An inverted cross.

It was nearly lunchtime when Riley and the sheriff finished what little they could do at the second arson site, an abandoned building on the outskirts of downtown Castle. What little they could do having consisted of looking at a burned-out hulk of a building that had once been a small store and studying the inverted cross that had been burned into an otherwise untouched plank jammed upright into the ground and left conspicuously behind the building.

"Not very subtle," Riley murmured as they headed back toward the street.

"Was it supposed to be?" Jake asked. "I mean, isn't a sign supposed to be . . . well, a sign?"

"A sign of what? Here there be devil worshippers? Most practitioners keep pretty quiet about it, Jake."

"That group down the beach from you has been vocal."

Which led Riley to believe they were likely to be harmless, more apt to be on the candles-and-chanting "conventional" end of Satanism rather than out on the extreme fringes, where blood rituals and attempts to harness the elements or some supernatural force were practiced.

But all she said was, "Leaving signs of occult activity for outsiders to find isn't smart. Unless you have a very good reason."

He frowned. "Okay. Then, maybe . . . a warning of some kind?"

"I guess it's possible." She couldn't seem to think clearly, and Riley was aware of another chill of unease. How many PowerBars had she eaten since breakfast? Two? Three? That should have been enough. More than enough. For Christ's sake, it wasn't as though she'd been running an obstacle course—

"Are you okay?" Jake demanded. "You've been acting sort of weird all morning."

"Have I?"

"Yes, you have. And that wasn't an answer. What the hell's going on with you?"

She wouldn't have pegged the handsome sheriff as being particularly sensitive to undercurrents, which told her that it was only too screamingly obvious something unusual **was** going on with her.

Great. That was just great. She really **couldn't** fake it anymore, apparently.

Falling back on the tried and true, she said, "I'm different when I'm working, that's all."

"No offense, Riley, but if this is you working, I don't know how much help you're going to be to this investigation."

Despite the beginning of that sentence, his tone was aggressive and his entire attitude impatient, and it didn't take any extra senses to tell Riley he was in the mood to pick a fight. Probably, she thought, because needling her at the station hadn't achieved whatever results he'd been after.

She wondered now if she had stopped dating Jake less because she'd met and been attracted to Ash and more because she really didn't have much time for men who believed they were God's gift.

Under different circumstances, she probably would have given him the argument he so clearly wanted to start, but today she simply didn't have the energy for it.

In any case, he was distracted before Riley had to come up with some kind of response. And she didn't know whether to be relieved or irritated when the distraction proved to be Ash. His Hummer was parked beside Jake's Jeep out on the street.

"How'd he even know where we were?" Jake muttered.

"He didn't have to know," Riley pointed out mildly. "All he had to do was drive the few blocks between here and the courthouse and look for your Jeep."

Jake grimaced. "Yeah. Sometimes I forget how small this place really is."

"I wouldn't think you could hide much here," she agreed.

"You ever lived in a small town?"

Riley nodded.

"Then you know that there are secrets everybody in the entire town knows—and then there are secrets that stay that way, sometimes for generations."

"True enough." Something was nagging at her mind, had been for at least the last hour, but Riley couldn't make it come clear. Something about one of the arson sites? Something Jake had said? A memory trying to surface?

She didn't know. Whatever it was, it remained maddeningly elusive.

It's like an echo of something I only half-heard in the first place. How the hell am I supposed to figure out what it was?

Especially with her Swiss-cheese memory and still-dulled senses.

Ash had gotten out when he saw them approaching and, when they joined him on the sidewalk, asked Riley, "Any ideas about our mysterious arsonist?"

"Nothing helpful, I'm afraid," she replied, pushing the useless worries out of her mind for the moment.

"Still thinking it could be part of some kind of occult activity?"

"I still can't rule it out." Riley shrugged. "I've got to do some research, see if any of this fits any known pattern."

"Would you expect it to?"

"Well, yeah, at least to some extent. There are basic tenets to every religion, every belief system. The bells and whistles may change over the years, and some strong leaders may invent their own rituals or their own methods of conducting them, but the broad outlines tend to stay the same."

It was Jake who said, "And in occult practices, the broad outlines would be?"

"All black-occult rituals center around the theme of summoning supernatural power to effect a change."

"Supernatural power? Like magic?"

His scornful questions didn't surprise Riley. Neither the paranormal nor any supernatural force or forces were a part of most people's lives, so ignorance abounded. She had, in fact, grown accustomed to explaining to perfectly intelligent people that **paranormal** had nothing to do with vampires or werewolves and that **magic** could mean something other than illusion or the twitch of a TV witch's nose.

So, patiently, she said, "In this context, supernatural power would be the energy forces of nature, of the elements. Wind, water, earth . . . fire. In occult rituals—magic—that elemental energy is created or summoned and then channeled, directed, toward a specific end."

Ash said, "So somebody burned down two buildings to—what?—harness the energy of the fire for their own purposes?"

"It's possible, Ash."

"You don't sound too sure of that."

Riley was perfectly aware of Jake frowning at her and wondered if he was once again thinking that she was being little help to his investigation. But she kept her gaze on Ash.

"A fire used in occult practices is common. Even a bonfire. But a burning building? I'd call that excessive. And I haven't a clue why someone would need that much energy or would believe they could harness it if they had it. There's always a purpose in any ritual, and so far I see no purpose for all this. So, no, I'm not sure how or even **if** these fires are connected to any occult practices that may or may not be taking place in Hazard County."

He grunted. "You sound like you're on the witness stand."

"I've been there a few times."

"Yeah, I figured."

Riley looked at the sheriff. "I'll have to do some research before I can even speculate much more, maybe get in touch with a couple of experts back at the office."

"There are experts on the occult in the FBI?"

"A few, yeah." She was one of those but was still reasonably sure she hadn't shared that knowledge with the sheriff.

She was less sure about Ash, but since he didn't say anything, she didn't worry about it, at least for the moment.

"My tax dollars at work," Jake muttered.

"You may be glad of their expertise before this is over," Riley told him. "Because if somebody **is** killing people and burning down buildings as part of occult rituals, you have a serious, serious problem on your hands."

With a sigh, Jake said, "I have that even if none of this is occult-related."

Trust me—if it's occult-related, it's worse.

But Riley didn't say it out loud. And wasn't sure why.

Ash said to her, "I gather you copied a friend at Quantico on the postmortem results?"

She nodded. "With Jake's permission, of course. Couple of hours ago."

"Your friend works fast. I stopped by the station after I left the courthouse, and Leah gave me a message to pass on; apparently, your cell phone is off or dead."

"Damn." She didn't bother to check her bag, knowing she had turned the phone on before leaving the house. It was dead—and losing its charge even faster than what was normal for her. Yet another sign of things out of whack in her world.

To Jake, Ash added, "Your phone seems to be off as well."

"I left it in the Jeep."

"Good thing there was no emergency requiring the sheriff."

"We're a block and a half from the station, Ash; somebody could have stuck their head out one of the doors and yelled for me."

Riley wasn't in the mood for a pissing contest, so she stopped this one before it could really get going by saying to Ash, "The message?"

He looked at her. "Short and fairly enigmatic.

Quote: **First test, human. Second test, same type as donor.** End quote. Hope it means more to you than it does to me."

Riley laced her fingers together around the strap of her shoulder bag, hoping neither man would notice them shaking. Or would simply believe she was just in need of calories if they did notice. But that wasn't why.

The message was all too clear to her. The blood on the clothing she'd awakened wearing the previous afternoon was human. And the blood type was the same as that found in their victim's stomach.

Which meant it was pretty damn likely there was another murder victim out there somewhere.

Someone whose blood Riley had been covered in.

"**Is** it something Jake should know about?" Ash asked as he drove Riley to the café where they'd planned to have lunch. They had left behind a frustrated sheriff who wasn't at all happy that she wasn't willing to completely decipher the message from Quantico.

"He already knows what's important; his own M.E. told him. That the blood in the victim's stomach is human but doesn't belong to the victim. Which means there's probably another victim we haven't found yet."

"So why did your pal at Quantico have to verify that?"

I can't think. Why can't I think?

She needed fuel, of course, yet again, which was one reason she hadn't protested Ash's arrival at the arson scene. She needed fuel, and once she had that, once her energy level was optimal, then she could begin to make sense of the bits and pieces of information scattered in her mind.

Occult activity: possibly. Arson: definitely. Murder: definitely—probably two of them, dammit. Connection? God knows.

Replying finally to Ash's question, she said, "Just . . . making sure, that's all."

"Riley, what aren't you telling **me**?"

She took a chance. "A lot."

Ash didn't seem surprised by that. Or else he had a great poker face. "I see. Professional reasons, or personal ones?"

Taking another chance, she answered honestly. Sort of.

"Six of one, half a dozen of the other. I'm sorry, Ash. It's just . . . I'm used to working alone. And I'm not used to being personally involved with someone while I'm working, I told you that." **And I can't read you at all, can't tell what you're thinking or feeling, but I look at you and feel . . . uneasy. Uneasy and I don't know why.**

"And I'm the DA of Hazard County."

"That too. I can't—I can't just tell you everything I know, or think I know or suspect, not without evidence to back it up. Without evidence, it's just speculation, useless speculation. And most of it's probably dead ends anyway, because most investigations are full of them. That's one reason I haven't told Jake much of what I'm thinking either."

"Because he'd grab what might look like a lead and run with it. Focus all his suspicions on one person or one area to the exclusion of all else. Rush to judgment."

Riley was glad Ash seemed to understand that. She nodded. "He's the type, or at least I think he is. Wants to do something ASAP, frustrated because he can't. He's more than ready for concrete answers. And that would be fine—if I was right. But I'm not sure of anything yet. Until I am sure, or at least reasonably sure, I'd rather keep most of the speculation to myself."

After a moment, Ash said in a deliberate tone, "The danger in that is your isolation, Riley. Keep everything to yourself, and if the murderer even suspects you might know something, he could also believe that taking you out would eliminate or at least lessen the threat."

"I know," she said.

"You're willing to risk that?"

"I usually do." Usually—but not always. Because Bishop tended to know, even if she hadn't told him, what was going on in her investigations. In her life. Hell, in her mind. Other team members often knew as well because, hey, hard to keep most things secret among a group of psychics.

But not this time. With Bishop and the other members of the unit obviously preoccupied with their own demanding cases and scattered across the country to boot, the sense of unity she had felt since joining the SCU was missing.

Or maybe that was just her, just the disconnect of her own dulled or missing senses. Either way, this time the inherently risky nature of her job felt more dangerous than ever.

This time she felt alone.

Really alone.

"I don't know that I'm willing to risk it," Ash said in a thoughtful tone. Then, almost immediately, added, "As a matter of fact, I'm sure. I'm not willing to risk you, Riley."

"Ash—"

"Yes, I know your job is dangerous no matter what the circumstances. Situation normal, for you. I also know you're highly trained by the army **and** by the FBI, which means you can more than take care of yourself in just about any situation I could name. Including, undoubtedly, this one. And I know you've done just fine without me for thirty-odd years."

He pulled the Hummer into a parking space outside a busy café, turned off the engine, and looked at her steadily. "But I am asking you, in this investigation, in this place and time, just this once, to break a few of your rules and talk to me about what's going on."

"It's never just once," she murmured. "Break a rule, and before you know it life is chaos. You're running with scissors, coloring outside the lines, putting your elbows on the table. Anarchy."

"Quit stalling. Look, I can separate personal confidences from my professional responsibilities."

"I'm not sure I can," she admitted.

"I'm sure. Trust me, Riley."

Hating the gambit, Riley nevertheless fell back on a handy excuse and tried to keep it light. "It's not fair to ask anything of me when I'm starving and can't think straight. You don't want to win that way, do you?"

"I," Ash said, "am willing to win any way I can. Haven't you figured that out yet?"

He didn't press her for a response just then, which was good since Riley didn't really have one. Instead, he got out of the vehicle, and as she followed suit Riley was aware of the unsettling realization that she was going to have to decide whether to trust Ash completely—and decide without the aid of the extra senses she had counted on her entire life.

Blind trust.

Something she wasn't at all sure she was capable of.

11

Riley decided to approach the Pearson house casually, from the beach. Having made that decision, she returned to her own house after the lunch with Ash, exchanged her shoulder bag for a fanny pack just large enough to hold her weapon, I.D., a couple of PowerBars, and house keys, found a pair of sunglasses behind which she could at least partially hide a multitude of uncertainties, and went out for a seemingly casual stroll.

"Casual" out on the beach meant carrying her gun out of sight. Or at least that was what she told herself.

**Judgment call. Sometimes I wear the
weapon on my hip and sometimes I hide it
away. That makes sense. Right?**

Her wavering was both uncharacteristic and
unprofessional—and scary. Riley pushed it
away, telling herself one more time that things
would become clearer.

Eventually.

Other people were hitting the beach as well,
since it was after two and therefore considered
a safer time of day for the sun worshippers.
A number of people nodded and smiled as Riley passed, but nobody called out to her—
which was a relief, since the faces were those of
strangers.

She was, in any case, more intent on scanning
the oceanfront houses as she passed; no one had
been specific as to the actual location of the
Pearson house, other than to say it was "up the
beach from your place."

Jake had been so pissed at her when she'd left
the arson scene with Ash that she hadn't wanted
to ask him. As for Ash, she'd been preoccupied
wondering when he was going to repeat his request that she confide in him about everything
and had forgotten to ask him.

Oh, yeah, some cop I am.

Rather than repeat that request, he had instead talked casually of casual things, and Riley had reached the uncomfortable conclusion that he was simply going to wait until she brought up the subject.

Either he knew her well enough to know that she despised both ultimatums and feeling cornered, or else he was utterly confident that she would, sooner or later, confide in him.

She found either possibility disconcerting.

"Hey, Riley!"

She stopped but remained where she was on the beach, just above the high-water mark. A man, waving an arm to get her attention, was walking rapidly toward her across the wooden walkway that provided beach access from one of the houses.

The Pearson house? Riley didn't know. Had she visited the house at all? She didn't remember. The house at which she was looking was no more familiar to her than any other one in the neat row of attractively individualized yet basically similar houses along the beach: lots of deck space, lots of windows, colorful beach towels fluttering in the breeze as they hung over deck railings to dry. Nothing made this particular house memorable.

But the man . . .

I know you. Your face is in my mind.

One of the faces in her mind, at least. Not a bad face, on the thin side with the bones a bit too prominent. It matched his thin body, which was currently dressed in an old T-shirt featuring the logo of a seventies rock band and a pair of slightly baggy, too-long shorts.

At least he's not wearing a Speedo. . . .

Riley did her best to shake off the irrelevant thought and concentrate on the man trudging awkwardly toward her through the deep sand piled up at the bottom of the walkway stairs.

Early to mid-forties, at a guess. Fairly tall, thatch of dark hair in no particular style, and very pale skin already showing the first pink signs of sunburn.

Already? Do I know he's only been here a short while or just assume it from what Ash said?

"Sunblock," she said casually as he reached her. "You can get burned before you know it on the beach. It's that nice breeze coming off the water." She was still groping in her mind but so far had found no name for this vaguely familiar face.

He grimaced. "Yeah, that's what Jenny keeps

telling me. She also says the punch lines are too easy when you're a sunburned satanist."

"That is a point," Riley said. **Satanist? Oh, shit. But if he's this open about it . . .**

"Anyway, I'm wearing sunblock today. Plenty of punch lines for that, now that I think about it. But never mind. Riley, what's this we're hearing about the body found yesterday? He was a sacrifice?"

"You must know I'm not free to discuss any of the details with civilians. It's an ongoing investigation"—**Your name, dammit. What's your name? It's**— "Steve." **So ordinary? Damn, bet I've got it wrong.**

But apparently not.

"Riley, if he **was** killed and hung above the altar inside a circle of salt, we both know that's ritual."

She pulled her sunglasses down her nose and peered at him over the tops.

"Not **my** ritual," he added hastily. "Or ours, rather. Come on, Riley, you know we don't do that kind of shit. I don't know anybody who **does.** And a human victim is sure as hell not what we expected when we were invited out here."

Invited?

"Yeah, about that," she said, testing the waters cautiously. "About that invitation."

"What about it?" Steve frowned. "I told you when we talked about it Saturday afternoon."

"A lot's happened since then." She kept it vague.

Steve didn't appear to find that strange. "No kidding. I guess the sheriff has you on the murder officially, huh?"

Riley pushed her sunglasses back up her nose so she could hide behind them. "Like I said, Steve, it's an ongoing investigation."

"Right, right. Well, just so you know, I'd a lot rather talk to you than the sheriff. He thinks we're a bunch of nuts—probably dangerous nuts, at that. You know better."

Do I?

Mildly, she said, "Well, you can't really blame the sheriff. You've been talking to people. About your beliefs."

"We have nothing to hide," Steve insisted.

"Mmm. Having nothing to hide is one thing. Going around telling people you practice Satanism when weird things have been happening in the area is asking for trouble."

"Yeah, so you said when we talked on Saturday."

Riley waited, hoping that silence on her part

would keep him talking. It was a technique that had worked for her often in the past, and it worked now.

"I know you warned me, Riley, but, Jesus, I didn't know some poor bastard was going to get killed. If I'd had any idea **that** was in the wind, I never would have brought my people here. We concentrate on compassion rituals, I told you that. We don't do **any** destruction rituals; the energy required and expended is just too negative. We don't want that coming back to us."

"Even if you had an enemy you'd prefer to get . . . out of your way?"

"Even if. And we don't make those kinds of enemies. I told you. We're harmless."

"Okay. So who invited you out here?"

Steve frowned at her. "I told you that too. He said his name was Wesley Tate."

Desperately trying to read his expression and pick up on verbal clues, Riley said, "I'm still having a hard time believing you'd bring your people here on the word of a stranger, Steve. I would have thought you'd know better than that. You've been practicing—what? Twenty years?"

"Nearly that." He sighed. "Yeah, I know it could have been a setup of some kind. At best somebody trying to take our money, and at worst a hate group out to make an example of us. But he just sounded so damn charming and welcoming, Riley. We've been taking heat back home, getting pressure to go elsewhere, so the invitation to visit Opal Island came at a perfect time."

A suspiciously perfect time.

Riley mentally crossed her fingers and guessed. "But to accept the invitation of a man you hadn't even set eyes on . . ."

"I know, I know. Not something I'd normally have considered, except that he knew all the right things to say. I mean, we're not some secret brotherhood with code words and bullshit like that, but you know as well as I do that there are . . ."

"Code words?" she supplied dryly.

"Well . . . yeah. The right words, anyway. The right names. He knew people. He checked out. And it wasn't like he was inviting us to his own place or asking for anything. Just suggesting we might want to check out Opal Island and Castle because people were laid-back here and because there were some even like-minded."

"And have you found them?"

"No. But it's just been a few days, after all. We've sort of put out the word." He grimaced. "As you said, rotten timing, obviously. And I've gotta tell you—if those **like-minded** people are into human sacrifice, we're not gonna have much in common with them."

"If anything at all," a new voice added pleasantly.

Riley looked past Steve, unsettled yet again that she hadn't noticed the approach of the tall, dark woman now joining them on the beach. Especially since the woman was strikingly beautiful and had a strong, definite presence. Probably in her mid-thirties, she was both exotic and sensual, her centerfold body ripe to bursting and her dark eyes practically smoldering.

"Hey, Riley," she said as she joined them. Her voice was as sultry as the rest of her, low and rather throaty. And her night-black hair fell straight and gleaming down her back all the way to her hips.

Put her photo in the dictionary beside the name of the alternative religion of your choice and she'd look the part.

Even wearing a very brief swimsuit. Maybe especially wearing a very brief swimsuit.

Riley dredged in her mind and produced a name. "Hey, Jenny."

"Guess the shit's really hit the fan with this murder," Jenny said, shaking her head. "Is that what you came to tell Steve? That we should pack up and get out?"

Though the other woman's voice was casual, the question was, in some peculiar way Riley couldn't define, some sort of challenge. She was sure of that, even if she didn't understand what lay behind it.

At least . . . I think I'm sure.

"I was just stretching my legs after lunch," she said mildly. "Steve was the one who wanted to talk to me."

"**Should** we pack up and leave?" Jenny asked.

"Not my place to say. But there's been a murder, and plenty of evidence left behind to point toward the occult. So if I were you, I'd be careful. Maybe stick close to the house. Maybe keep my beliefs to myself for the duration."

"If you were us."

Riley nodded. "Something like this happens, and people get jumpy as hell. Things snowball. So I'd lay low for a while. If I were you."

"Understood." Jenny smiled. She linked her arm with Steve's and with her free hand reached out to pat Riley on the shoulder. "You don't worry about us. We'll be fine."

. . . the candlelight cast dancing shadows around the room and shimmered off the velvet hangings and silken robes. On the wall

above the altar hung an inverted cross fashioned of some metallic material that also caught the light. Below the inverted cross was the usual platform, and upon it the altar.

She was naked. Her head raised on a pillow, she lay in the center of the rectangular platform so that one of its long edges came to the backs of her widely parted knees. Her arms were stretched out to either side, and each hand grasped a silver candlestick containing a black candle.

The candles were lit.

Her body was pale, her long black hair arranged to frame her bold nakedness with no attempt to coyly conceal. Her lush breasts were tipped with artificially blood-red nipples, and as Riley watched, the robed celebrant—the "priest" conducting the ceremony—stepped between the altar's spread legs and dipped his thumb into the silver cup he held, then drew with the viscous liquid an inverted cross onto the pale flesh of her lower stomach.

Red. Blood.

The room smelled of incense and blood, and Riley had to breathe through her mouth to avoid coughing.

Couldn't cough.

Couldn't give herself away.

She peered through the narrow opening in the draperies, trying to look for anything familiar in the robed individuals. Height, build, a gesture—anything to help her identify at least one of them. But it was an exercise in futility. They were eerily featureless, their faces concealed by the hoods.

They were chanting in low voices, in Latin, and she could only catch a few words of what they were saying.

" . . . Magni Dei Nostri Satanas . . ."

Riley sat up with a smothered gasp, her heart pounding.

A Black Mass. That was what she'd seen, part of a version of the satanic ceremony known as a Black Mass.

Seen? Seen when? Seen where?

She was in bed, Riley realized. In her own bed, in her own bedroom of the beach house with moonlight streaming through the blinds on the windows. When she turned her head cautiously, it was to see Ash sleeping beside her. Beyond him she saw the clock on the nightstand.

5:30 A.M.

Wednesday?

No, that wasn't right. That couldn't be right. She'd been on the beach, talking to Steve and Jenny, and it had been no later than three or so on Tuesday afternoon. And then . . .

Here. Now. Waking in bed with Ash.

More than twelve hours later.

Resisting panic, she slipped from the bed without waking him. She found one of her sleep-shirts on the floor and put it on, then crept from the bedroom.

As usual, several lights had been left on dimly in the main living area of the house, and the blinds in there were firmly closed against the night. The latter fact told her only that she must have, as usual, closed all the blinds at dusk; Riley disliked the exposed sensation of uncovered windows at night, especially when people were likely to walk along the beach on the other side of those windows.

A holdover from her army days, when being too visible and presenting too much of a target had never been a good idea.

Riley paused for a moment and held out her hands, studying them. Not too shaky, but hardly steady. Rather the way she felt inside.

She went to the kitchen to collect an energy bar and a glass of orange juice. The TV remote

was on the breakfast bar, so she used it to turn
the set on, hitting the MUTE button as she did
so. Automatically turning it to CNN, hopeful
of verifying the date, she swore softly to see a
commercial for some diet product.

Figured.

She got her juice and the PowerBar, then carried both to the small table in one corner of the
living area, where it looked like she'd been
working on her laptop.

**Looks like? Jesus. Why don't I remem-
ber this?**

It would have been easy to panic.

Very easy.

She sat down and tapped a key to take the
computer out of sleep mode. When the dark
screen brightened, the first thing she did was
check the time and date, just to confirm that
this was indeed very early on Wednesday. And
it was.

She'd lost more than twelve hours.

But there was lost . . . and then there was **lost**.

From the looks of things, she'd been functional, even working. In one window was an
FBI report on recent occult activities in the
U.S., while another window contained the beginning of a report apparently written by her.

"Huh," she murmured. "Since when do I write—Oh."

The first line explained the otherwise inexplicable: **Since I have no idea what the long-term effects of my current situation might be, I've decided to keep this written journal/report for the remainder of the investigation.**

Current situation? That was worded so ambiguously she must have feared someone else might read it. Maybe Ash, for instance, since he apparently spent most nights here.

In any case, the rest of the entry was pretty bare-bones, detailing only the previous morning's visit to the sheriff's department, the autopsy results on their murder victim, and her visits with the sheriff to the arson sites. Not a word about her stroll up the beach and meeting/conversation with Steve and Jenny.

Then again, maybe she'd imagined all that. Or dreamed it.

Like the Black Mass, where Jenny had served as the altar. Maybe Riley had dreamed that? It had certainly seemed unreal, at least in a sense. Blood. Blood played no part in a Black Mass, despite popular belief; it was supposed to be a ceremony all about mocking traditional Christian beliefs and ceremonies, twisting and corrupting them. Blasphemous, certainly, from any conventional point of view, but neither dangerous nor inherently evil, and it didn't involve blood or actual sacrifice.

At least, it wasn't supposed to.

Riley looked around the quiet, peaceful space, listened to the surf pounding out on the beach, and wondered what was real. What she could trust. What she could believe in.

Had she actually witnessed that ceremony?

Had she dreamed it?

A touch on the nape of her neck found the burns left by a Taser. That was real. The man sleeping in her bed was certainly real.

Though the presence of both in her life was baffling.

She didn't sleep with men she barely knew, most **especially** during an ongoing investigation. And her training and experience made it highly unlikely that anyone could sneak up and blindside her with a Taser attack. Particularly in a situation where all her instincts and senses would have been on alert.

Unless . . . unless whoever had attacked her had been with her all along. That was possible, she supposed. Maybe more than possible. Someone she had trusted could have been close enough to surprise her, to catch her off her guard.

Nice little theory, that. The problem was proving it, identifying who that someone might be, and accomplishing both objectives without giving away her own ignorance on the subject.

No one so far had volunteered any information about where she had been or who she might have been with on Sunday night. At least not that she remembered, dammit.

All I really know is that I was Tasered. That I was covered in some of the same blood found in our victim's stomach—

Damn. Was he identified in the last twelve hours? That was the priority, to I.D. him. Though surely I would have made a note in this damn report of mine. And what about that other probable victim? Has he—or she—even been discovered yet?

She didn't know. Couldn't remember.

All she knew was that another twelve hours of her life were gone, and she didn't have the faintest idea what she had been doing all that time.

She put her head in her hands and slowly rubbed her face.

"Riley?"

She looked up to see Ash approaching her and hoped her face didn't show the growing panic she was all too aware of feeling.

"It's not even dawn," she told him, outwardly calm. "I didn't wake you, did I?"

"I'm getting used to these predawn urges of yours to work." He bent down to kiss her briefly, adding, "They seem to come most often after a restless night. You tossed and turned a bit."

"Sorry."

"Didn't disturb me. Much, anyway." He smiled. "I gather you're up for the day? I'll grab a shower and shave, then fix breakfast."

Somewhat involuntarily, she said, "You're almost too good to be true, know that, pal?"

"I keep trying to tell you. If you're not careful, somebody else is going to steal me away from you." He kissed her again, then headed off for his shower.

Riley sat there at the table, her computer humming quietly, and gazed after him. Right now, in this moment, she felt safe with Ash—but what did that mean? That she trusted him? That she felt no threat from him? Or simply that she was thinking and feeling with a part of her anatomy quite a bit south of her brain?

Could she even trust her feelings—any of

them—when her senses and memory were, to say the least, unreliable? When she could lose more than twelve hours without warning and apparently without some external cause?

There's a reason, a trigger. There has to be. I just have to figure it out.

Easily said. Not so easily done.

12

Riley finished the PowerBar and juice, hoping the calories would help clear the fog in her brain but not very surprised when it didn't happen. She couldn't seem to think except to ask herself questions for which there were no answers.

Yet, at least.

I've been functioning. Normally—or surely Ash would have commented. But I don't remember what I've said or done. And lost hours and a restless night culminating in a dream—or memory—of some kind of Black Mass can't possibly mean anything good.

The panic was crawling inside her now, cold

and sharp and no longer something she could deny to herself. This was out of control, **she** was out of control, and she had no business whatsoever being part of a murder investigation. The right thing to do, the safe and **sane** thing to do, would be to return to Quantico.

Today. Now.

Something on the TV broke through the panic to catch her attention just then, and she lunged for the remote to turn on the sound.

Bishop. He hardly ever made the news, went out of his way to avoid being photographed or videoed, and **always** kept a low profile during investigations. So what the hell was he involved in that was making the national news?

"... the agent in charge refuses to comment on the ongoing investigation, but sources within the Boston police confirmed only minutes ago that the latest victim of the serial killer terrorizing the city these last weeks was indeed twenty-one-year-old Annie LeMott, daughter of Senator Abe LeMott. The senator and his wife are in seclusion with family, as police and FBI agents continue to work around the clock to catch their daughter's killer."

The CNN anchor went on to the next subject, her voice turning perky as she reported on something less tragic.

Riley hit the MUTE button on the remote and returned to her laptop. It didn't require either memory of recent events or senses to tell her what to do next; within two minutes, she was reading a more detailed FBI report of the Boston serial killer. And the report explained a lot.

Bishop was hip-deep in his own investigation, all right. In fact, he was tracking a particularly vicious killer with, so far, at least a dozen notches on his belt. Twelve known victims in just under twenty-one days, all young women, all murdered with bloody abandon.

No wonder Boston was going nuts. No wonder this particular series of murders was making national news.

And no wonder Bishop had accepted Riley's assurances that she could handle the situation here, even when she had failed to report in. She doubted he'd had much time to sleep or eat in the past few weeks, let alone worry too much about any of his primaries—people he had handpicked as team leaders **because** they were highly intelligent, capable agents with all the skills and initiative required to operate independently of both him and the FBI if necessary and for as long as necessary.

It just . . . usually wasn't necessary.

With that thought in mind, Riley remained

online and connected to a special database at Quantico reserved for the SCU, wended her way through the layers of security, and checked on the whereabouts of the rest of the unit.

Jesus.

Chicago, Kansas City, Denver, Phoenix, L.A., and Seattle, plus two small towns she'd never heard of in the Gulf Coast region. The unit was literally scattered across the map, manpower and resources spread thinner than she'd ever known them to be. And every team was involved in high-risk operations ranging from murder to possible terrorist threats—the latter being investigations the unit had only recently begun to be called into as consultants.

As far as Riley could tell, she was the only agent operating without a team, partner, or any kind of backup. But then, she was also the only one who had set off on a very unofficial investigation of a few oddities—not murder or any other major crime.

Then. Now the situation was definitely high-risk. And being on her own here now was both a very bad idea, and seemingly unavoidable.

Unless she bailed. Returned to Quantico. Nobody would blame her for that, not under the circumstances. Hell, when—if—she told Bishop

about this latest wrinkle, he'd undoubtedly recall her without even allowing her time to pack.

Riley realized she was fingering the burn at
the base of her skull. She forced herself to stop,
swore under her breath, and disconnected from
the SCU's database.

She couldn't bail. Couldn't leave.

She had to **know.** Had to figure out what was
going on.

"Let's pretend," she whispered. She could do
that. It's what she did best, after all. Pretend.

Pretend everything was normal. Pretend there
was nothing wrong with her.

Pretend she wasn't terrified.

The sheriff said to Ash, "You realize, of course,
that you have no business being involved in this
investigation. This part of it, at least. Your part
begins when we catch the son of a bitch."

Ash leaned back in his chair at the conference
table and shrugged. "I've gotten involved in the
past long before the trial stage, we both know
that."

"Not in a murder, Ash."

"We haven't had a murder until now, not
since I've been DA. And not since you've been

sheriff. I'm betting if we'd had one, we'd have worked together. I may not be a cop, but I have experience in investigations—murder investigations included. And you're too good a cop to ignore that."

Leah glanced at Riley, interested to know how the other woman was reacting to all this, and wasn't very surprised to see that Riley was apparently engrossed in reading reports concerning what little information had come in since the previous afternoon.

There wasn't much. Teams had been canvassing Opal Island as well as Castle, literally going door-to-door in search of an identity for their murder victim. So far, the search had turned up three temporarily misplaced teenagers and one temporarily misplaced husband (the former all found sleeping off a late party and the latter discovered on a nearby golf course), but no man missing since sometime Sunday night.

Leah had read and reread the reports Riley was now studying, and wondered what the federal cop found so interesting. Then again, she decided, maybe it wasn't interest so much as a refusal to get involved in the "discussion" going on between the two men.

"I'll take any resource I can get," the sheriff was saying. "But don't you have to be in court?"

Ash shook his head. "Not at all this week, and hardly next week. Unless something unexpected happens, at least. Even my paperwork is all caught up."

"Just bored and have time on your hands, huh?"

"Jake, it's your investigation. Want me to keep my nose out of it, just say the word."

It wasn't really a challenge, Leah thought. And yet it was. If Jake refused Ash's offer of help, it wouldn't be a smart move; Ash had worked as an assistant DA in Atlanta for several years, and whatever rumor had to say about why he left, nobody doubted he had gained considerable experience with murder investigations while he was there. More than Jake had, when it came right down to it.

Refusing the offer of that sort of experienced help might well be something the voters would remember come the next election, particularly if the situation worsened. Plus, it made Jake appear either insecure or jealous of his authority.

Or just plain jealous, period.

So Leah wasn't very surprised to see her boss accept the offered help, albeit with little grace or gratitude.

"As long as we're clear about who's in charge, I got no problem with you helping out, Ash."

"We're clear."

"Okay, then." Jake looked at Riley. "See anything there the rest of us missed?"

"I doubt you missed it," she said calmly. "The blood in the vic's stomach contained glycerol."

"An anticoagulant, yeah. I got that. And an ingredient in all kinds of things, from antifreeze to cosmetics, so not exactly difficult for someone to get their hands on. Which means virtually impossible to trace."

Leah asked, "So what does that mean? That there was glycerol in the blood?" She hated to admit to ignorance, especially when the sheriff had—rather surprisingly, to her—chosen her to assist him on this case, but she didn't feel less of a cop for not having specialized knowledge, and she needed to understand.

It was Jake who said, "Somebody didn't want the blood to clot too quickly."

"I'm still in the dark," Leah complained.

Riley said, "What it probably means is that the blood the victim drank—whether willingly or because he was forced to—wasn't fresh. Someone had kept it for that purpose. Maybe for quite a while."

Leah grimaced. "Bucket of blood. Oh, yuck."

"Was it so much?" Ash asked.

"At least a quart," Riley answered. "That's way more than is used in any ritual I know of."

Ash said, "And more than anybody could have swallowed without vomiting some of it back up, I would have thought."

Riley looked at the M.E.'s report again. "Some minor abrasions inside the esophagus. I'm betting they used a tube. Probably while he was unconscious. Poured the stuff straight into his stomach. And I doubt he lived long enough after that to get rid of it."

"Then what was the point?" Jake demanded. "Fill his stomach with blood and then decapitate him—why?"

"I don't know," Riley said. "But there had to be a reason. Blood in a ritual represents life, power. Human blood much more so than animal blood."

Leah's thoughts were running along a different track. "You mean the stuff I've heard about that is true? Human blood really is used in occult rituals?"

"Some very rare black-occult or satanic rituals, yeah. But the donor—or donors—offer up only a small amount of their blood, willingly, as part of the ceremony. By pricking a finger, usually, or a cut across the palm. It's pretty much a symbolic thing. Nobody gets bled to death."

"But somebody did this time? I mean, other than the guy we found in the woods?"

Riley frowned slightly as she gazed at the now-closed folder on the table before her. "Like I said—there was at least a quart in his stomach. All of it the same blood type, so likely from the same donor, though we can't be sure without DNA testing. But if it all did come from one person, that's a lot of blood to lose at one time."

"Too much?" Leah asked.

"Could someone have lost that much blood and lived? Sure. Five or six quarts in the human body, depending on size and weight. Losing a quart would be serious but not necessarily fatal, especially if it was a ritual blooding and not some traumatic injury."

"Thing is, at least some more got splashed all over the scene." Jake nodded when Ash looked at him. "We've got two blood types in all that, most from the vic but some apparently from the same . . . donor . . . who provided what was in his stomach. No real way to measure how much, especially since the ground soaked up a lot. I'm betting it was more than a couple of quarts, all told."

"Then there's likely to be another murder victim we have yet to find."

"Maybe." Riley was still frowning. "Or maybe not. Maybe the anticoagulant was necessary because it took a while to get enough blood without killing the donor. Or donors. You could probably take a little bit every day for several days without too much danger, if you were careful, knew what you were doing."

Ash said, "So, we're looking for somebody with anemia?"

"Failing a second victim. Or a first victim, rather." She looked at the sheriff. "Any luck finding some kind of pattern in the blood spatter at the scene?"

"So far nada. Melissa says the software hasn't run its course yet, but her gut feeling is that there's nothing to find."

"It was a long shot." Riley shrugged.

"What would you have expected, if there had been a pattern?" Ash asked.

"Well, whoever this is seems to be big on signs. So I would have expected another sign or symbol."

"Here there be devil worshippers?" Jake suggested dryly.

"Something like that. Subtle they aren't."

"They?" Leah asked. Then she shook her head. "Of course—it would be a group, wouldn't it?"

"Probably. There are solitary practitioners in most religions, but for any major ritual there would have to be more than one. Anything up to a dozen or so participants is most likely."

"Conspiracy in murder," Ash noted neutrally, "is very rare."

"They wouldn't have viewed it as murder," Riley said.

"Still, for a group of people to keep this sort of secret . . . How likely is that?"

"If they practice Satanism, very likely. Or at least very possible. Ash, these groups can only survive if they keep their . . . less conventional activities to themselves. And they learn that early. They're just too far out of the mainstream for community tolerance, much less acceptance."

Leah was faintly surprised. "Do they need community acceptance?"

"If they live in the community, sure. Their religion is only a part of their lives; they shop, go out to eat, go to the movies and the theater, usually send their kids to school. It's not all that uncommon for some of them to hold public office, especially at the local level. So, generally speaking, they keep quiet about occult practices."

Ash was frowning. "But you said whoever we're looking for in this case isn't being very subtle. Deliberately?"

"Maybe. Or desperate. That was a very public place for a ritual," Riley said. "Especially a major ritual involving sacrifice. Add that to the obvious arson sites, all the signs and symbols . . . It's either deliberately blatant or very careless. Either way, somebody is moving fast. Maybe too fast to avoid mistakes."

"Any idea what that **major** ritual would have been?" Jake asked her. "You said these things had a purpose, right? So what purpose was there in torturing a man and then beheading him?"

Riley shook her head to the repeated question, and repeated her earlier answer. "I don't know. Yet."

He nodded as though expecting it. "Well, while you're working on that, I've got some people checking out that group in the Pearson house. Because as far as I can tell, they're the only ones in the area who worship Satan."

"Openly, at least," Riley murmured.

He ignored that. "Soon as the background

checks are done, probably in the next couple of hours, I mean to have a talk with that bunch. You game?"

"I wouldn't miss it."

"Okay," Ash said as soon as they were left alone in the conference room, "I did what you asked. Got myself included in the investigation. Want to tell me now why that matters?"

Riley felt a little shock, and her mind raced. She didn't remember asking him to do any such thing and, since awakening to the missing twelve hours or so, had been too preoccupied to ask or even wonder why he had accompanied her to the sheriff's department.

She didn't doubt he was telling the truth, but she also had no idea why she would have asked this of him. Unless . . .

"Riley? Look, I'm not running away with some fatuous idea that you need me to hold your hand, but—"

"Actually," she said slowly, "I think maybe I do. In a manner of speaking."

He waited, brows lifting in a silent question.

Riley hesitated only a moment. "Jake said the background checks he's waiting for would take a couple of hours. There's something I want to check out myself in the meantime. And I don't think I should do it alone."

"Let's go," he said.

It wasn't until they were in his Hummer in the parking lot that he asked the obvious question.

"Where to?"

Riley drew a breath. "The clearing where the body was found."

He frowned. "I know Jake's kept the area roped off and guarded, but you've already seen whatever there was to see. Haven't you?"

"With my eyes, yeah."

He didn't need that explained. "But you said you weren't able to pick up anything clairvoyantly."

"I wasn't. But there were a lot of people around. It might be different now."

"Might?"

"I need to try, Ash." **Because I lost more time, and maybe that changed things. Maybe.**

He looked at her steadily for a moment, then started the engine. "Mine not to reason why."

"Long as you don't do and die," she murmured. "Or even ride into the mouth of hell."

Ash smiled. "Have I mentioned how much I appreciate having a well-read lover? I would have had to explain that reference to just about anyone else I know."

"Books and imagination see you through a lot as an army brat." Riley dug into her shoulder bag for a PowerBar. "I have a mind filled with facts, poetry, and way too much useless trivia."

"It's only useless until you need it."

She paused in unwrapping the bar to eye him. "You get that out of a fortune cookie?"

"Probably." He glanced at her. "I do have one question. Why me rather than your pal Gordon? He knows all about the clairvoyance, right?"

"Yeah."

"So why not pick a former army buddy as backup if you're expecting trouble of some kind? Not that I'm complaining, you understand. Just wondering."

Riley was wondering about that herself. She had no way of knowing for certain that she had asked Ash to join the investigation for this reason; it was merely logical to assume. Because she'd known from the beginning that she couldn't just accept the status quo, accept her MIA psychic abilities, that she'd have to push herself at some point, have to try with all her strength to tap into what that Taser's electrical surge had damaged.

She had no idea what would happen then. But logic also told her she shouldn't be alone when she tried. As for why she'd picked Ash over Gordon, logic provided a possible answer for that as well.

"Gordon's a civilian now," she said finally. "He can't be officially involved in a murder investigation. You can."

"Ah. Makes sense."

Yes, it made sense. It was logical.

She wasn't sure she believed it, however.

The problem, of course, was that Riley had no memory of what had prompted her request that Ash involve himself in the case officially. Maybe it was because of this, because she'd intended to try her damnedest to tap into her seemingly absent abilities and wanted someone she trusted standing by in case it knocked her on her ass.

Maybe.

Or maybe it was something else. Something that had occurred to Riley as her mind raced when Ash told her about a decision made, apparently, in those missing hours.

What if it happened again? What if she decided things, did things, made choices today that she wouldn't remember tomorrow? It had happened a second time now; had she somehow

guessed or known that her spotty memory and
damaged senses had only been the beginning of
her problems? What if her mind, her brain, had
sustained even more damage from the attack
on Sunday night than she had any way of esti-
mating?

What then?

Again, logic demanded that if she intended to
remain on the case under these circumstances—
and she did—then she needed someone trustworthy who not only knew the truth but was
also in a position to stick close and observe her
virtually around the clock. At any other time,
another SCU member would have been the
automatic choice. But that simply wasn't possible now.

Her lover, the DA of Hazard County, was the
best choice she was left with.

But to say that Riley felt either confident in
or comfortable with that decision would have
been to overstate the matter. For one thing, it
was a very unofficial way to conduct herself during an investigation, and not at all in character
for her. For another and far more vital thing . . .

**Can I trust him? I feel I can. Sometimes.
Most of the time. But not always.**

Doubts she couldn't even put into words
nagged at her. It was like catching a glimpse of

some movement from the corner of her eye, only to see nothing when she looked directly at it. She felt that way about Ash, that there was more going on than she could see, could know, and it made her wary.

But can I trust my feelings? Any of them?

And even if I can trust him, will he understand?

Can he?

13

She hadn't yet made up her mind how to explain the situation to Ash. How much to tell him.

Do I tell him how out of control I feel? Do I tell him I'm scared? Do I tell him I don't remember us?

She didn't know.

"Riley?"

She realized she had tied the empty PowerBar wrapper into a knot, twice, and forced herself to stop. "Yeah?"

"You haven't told me a whole lot about the work you do, at least in specifics. But what you have said, and what I know of you, tells me that you've used your abilities most of your life. Yes?"

"Since I was a kid, yeah."

"And we've already discussed the fact that both your army and FBI training and experience have prepared you to face just about any eventuality."

Riley didn't reply since it wasn't a question, and as he pulled the Hummer into a space near the dog park she turned slightly in her seat to look at him.

Ash turned the engine off, then met her gaze and nodded slightly. "All that being the case, I have to ask what makes this situation different for you."

"I told you I'd never gotten involved with anyone during an investigation."

"Yeah, but I'm not talking about us. I'm talking about you."

"Ash—"

"You're scared. And I want to know why."

After a moment, she said, "Does it show so plainly?"

He shook his head. "As a matter of fact, if I didn't know you so well I never would have seen any sign of it. There was nothing you said or did that gave you away, not really. You've just been . . . a bit off the last few days. Quieter. Slower to react, to answer a question. And you've been tossing and turning a lot every night. So not quite yourself."

"And you read that as fear?"

"Not at first. I'd venture to guess very little scares you, and I'm pretty sure you've seen things that would make my hair stand on end. So fear wasn't the first possibility I thought of when I realized something was wrong."

Riley waited.

"But then it dawned on me that despite what you were telling me, the way you've been burning energy so quickly during the last few days **was** unusual. Even for a case. And that either you didn't know why it was happening, or you were shaken because it wasn't something you could control. Control is a big issue for you, we both know that. It's a trait we share."

"Which is why you realized I was probably afraid."

"If there's something you can't control in your life, fear is possible; it's a natural response no matter what kind of training you've had. If there's something you can't control in **yourself,** fear is fairly inescapable, at least for people like us."

"Makes sense," she said, echoing his earlier comment. "And it's a good read."

"Accurate?"

Riley nodded reluctantly. "Accurate enough. This is—I haven't encountered a situation like this one before."

"In what way?"

She hesitated again, her mind still racing, still torn with uncertainty and wariness, then finally took that leap of faith. She had to trust him. She had no choice. "The burns on the back of my neck?"

His eyes narrowed. "Yeah?"

"Not from a curling iron. Apparently, I was . . . immobilized by a stun gun sometime Sunday night."

"You were attacked?"

"Apparently."

Ash drew a breath and let it out slowly. "That's twice you've used that word. Apparently. You don't know?"

"I don't remember."

He got it quickly. "The electrical charge. It affected your mind?"

Riley nodded. "My memory. My senses. All my senses, even the extra ones. I've been scrambling ever since. To catch up, to remember. To figure things out."

"Christ, Riley. Do you remember what you were doing, who you were with?"

"Not so much. And it's been a bit difficult to piece things together without admitting I don't have a clue what happened."

"And I'm hearing this only now?"

She kept her tone even. "Imagine waking up with your memory full of holes. Imagine that when you woke up, you had dried blood on you. And then imagine that before you could get your feet under you and try to figure out what had happened, you were called to the scene of a grisly murder." Riley managed a shrug. "It took me a while just to get all the characters straight, never mind the plot. I'm still working on that."

"Dried blood on you?"

"That was the part of the report from Quantico that I didn't want to explain to Jake. **First test: human.** The blood on my clothes was human; my boss ordered it tested."

Slowly, Ash said, "And the second test said the blood was the same type as the donor. So the blood on you matched what was in the victim's stomach?"

Riley nodded. "I don't have a clue how it got all over me, but the obvious possibility is that I was there. At some point before, during, or after that murder, I was there. Involved somehow."

"You didn't kill anybody," he said immediately.

"I certainly hope not. But I can't explain that blood. And until I can, admitting all this to Jake doesn't seem like a good idea. Especially since he's not all that happy with me right now."

Ash frowned. "Wait a minute. On Sunday night, you told me—unexpectedly—that you needed some time alone and sent me away. Which means you knew something was going to happen."

"Or at least knew I wanted to do some investigating on my own, yeah, we can assume that."

"But you don't remember where you were planning to go or why?"

"Afraid not."

He turned his gaze forward, staring through the windshield as his long fingers drummed on the steering wheel for a moment. Then he looked at her again, this time with a certain amount of anger. "This was never just a vacation for you, was it, Riley?"

So I hadn't confided in him about that. Why not?

Dammit, why not?

"Riley—"

"It's never just a vacation for me. Never."

Mobile, Alabama
2½ Years Previously

By now, Riley could have been blindfolded and taken anywhere in the Southeast or along the Gulf and would have been able to recognize a coastal or river city from the smell alone.

She was also beginning to really dislike it. Musty, muddy, faintly sour, it made her think of damp and decay and blood.

Not so surprising, really, considering how many butchered bodies she'd stood over in otherwise lovely coastal cities.

This time, Riley didn't wait for the killer to strike. She didn't just drift into Mobile and blend in, vanish into anonymity while allowing her senses time to adjust, which had been the game plan up to that point.

After New Orleans, waiting patiently was somewhat beyond Riley. Whether because this particular killer had thrown a gauntlet at her feet professionally or because she felt personally violated, the fact remained that she was certain he had somehow managed to touch her mind more surely than she had touched his.

And that, to Riley, was a hell of a strong motivation to get this case resolved and this killer behind bars ASAP.

So, despite Bishop's warnings, despite her own uneasy misgivings, she used every trick of concentration and focus she had learned in her life to begin trying to connect the moment she hit town.

It wasn't the way her abilities were supposed to work, really. She had connected with other minds before; Bishop said her secondary or ancillary ability was telepathy, and being a telepath himself, he'd know. But generally speaking, telepathy was barely a blip on her personal radar, and her clairvoyance took the form of picking up bits of information from her surroundings or from other people. Touching objects or people tended to make it easier, but not always. Sometimes she got absolutely nothing. And on a few memorable occasions she had been slammed by a "dump" of information that had left her mentally disoriented and physically exhausted—a truly disconcerting experience she was wary of repeating but had no way of controlling or predicting.

Cosmic irony, that. A not-so-gentle reminder

from the universe that the gifts given never came without strings.

In any case, her own "gifts" tended to be far more benign than those many psychics experienced. No pain, no disorientation, no visions yanking her from the here and now. Mostly, she just became aware of something rising in her mind, bobbing about to attract her notice, like flotsam on a wave. A fact, a feeling, a certainty.

Reaching beyond that, opening herself deliberately to contact from a dark and twisted killer, was a move as risky as it was unprecedented, at least where she was concerned.

She wasn't even sure how to do it other than to focus, concentrate, think about this butcher and how badly she wanted to stop him—

Welcome to Mobile, little girl.

Riley stopped in her tracks. She stood on a side street in downtown Mobile, near a well-lighted corner where people passed on foot and in cars on a typical weeknight like this.

They went about their business, oblivious, as Riley put out a hand to the building beside her, steadying herself not so much physically as emotionally.

There weren't words to describe how cold and slimy his thoughts were in her mind. Everything in her recoiled, yet she made herself stand still and silent, ignoring her surroundings until she saw nothing, felt nothing, heard nothing except that voice in her mind.

That presence.

I knew you'd come. Knew you'd follow me.

"Where are you?" she whispered, not even aware that she'd shut her eyes, the better to concentrate.

I'm close, little girl. Closer than I've ever been.

"Where?"

Can't you feel my breath on the back of your neck?

She forced herself not to turn, not to betray the icy shiver chilling her all the way to her bones on the warm, humid night.

"Where are you, you bastard?"

Fast as you were, I got here before you. I've been waiting, little girl.

"God damn you—"

I've left you a present.

Riley's eyes flew open and she jerked as though physically struck. "No," she murmured. "Oh, no . . ."

He had left her another victim to find. Another butchered body. Another family destroyed.

She had failed. Again.

Poor little girl. In such pain. But don't worry. You'll get another chance. We'll meet again, Riley.

Present Day

"Riley?"

Dragging her mind back from the past, fighting to focus on the here and now, Riley had to wonder why, if she was sleeping with this man, she hadn't told him the real reason she'd come to Opal Island.

Had she trusted him before the Taser attack? Or was there, among her lost memories, a reason why she had allowed him to share her bed without sharing her truths?

But she had already taken the leap of faith, so she pushed the doubts aside, drew a breath, and answered him honestly.

"Gordon got in touch just before I came down here. The fires, the signs and symbols pointing to the occult, worried him. He's seen enough of the world, walked through enough jungles, to know when something bad is walking there too. He believed something was going on and that it was going to get worse. He asked me to check it out. Unofficially, of course. When he called, I'd just come off a case, I had vacation time piling up, and the unit wasn't busy. So my boss okayed it. Not a formal investigation, just a favor for a friend."

"Why didn't you tell me, Riley? We talked about the arson, the way people were getting edgy—even about the possibility of occult activities. You told me the occult was one of your specialties in the SCU. You never said it was why you'd come here."

Because I didn't trust you enough? Because I was afraid—or knew—that you were involved? Or only because for the first time my personal life meant more to me than my professional one and I didn't want them to get tangled?

Why couldn't she think straight? Why couldn't she make up her damn mind about him?

"Riley?"

"I don't know. I don't know why. I don't remember, Ash."

Once again, his eyes narrowed. "You don't remember? Do you mean it isn't just whatever happened on Sunday night that you can't recall?"

She nodded reluctantly. "When I woke up on

Monday, most of the last three weeks was pretty much a blank."

"Pretty much?" A lawyer's determination to get things straight.

"Almost entirely," she admitted. "There were flashes. Faces. Threads of memory that vanished like smoke when I tried to catch hold of them. I had to be told, by Gordon and by my boss, what I was doing here."

"Then you didn't remember us."

"No," Riley said. "I didn't remember us."

"You sure as hell fooled me," Ash said.

Riley looked at him for a moment, then unfastened her seat belt and got out of the Hummer. She headed for the entrance to the dog park, not surprised that the area was deserted but for the bored deputy standing guard at the break in the fence near the woods.

Murders made people nervous. Particularly gruesome murders with possible satanic elements made them downright panicky. Riley figured most dog owners were taking their pets to the beach for exercise these days.

"Riley—"

When he grabbed her arm and swung her around to face him, she almost reacted in self-defense. Almost. Those instincts, at least, were very much alive in her, and that training went so deep it was an ingrained part of her character; her father had begun teaching her how to throw a larger opponent over her shoulder—and disable said opponent—before she started kindergarten.

She was more than a little surprised she hadn't taken Ash's head off. Interesting, that. Important? She didn't know.

She looked at the hand gripping her arm, not moving or speaking until he swore under his breath and released her. Then she merely folded her arms and waited.

"Look, if anybody has a right to be pissed about this, I think it's me," he said, keeping his voice low so that the deputy some yards away wouldn't hear.

"Oh, really?" She stared up at him, matching his quiet steel with her own. "Somebody **attacked** me. He or she put a stun gun to the back of my head and emptied electrical current into my **brain.** And not just the electrical current standard in a Taser, meant to temporarily incapacitate. This was an amped-up weapon, Ash, a weapon quite probably intended to kill. It didn't kill me, but it put me down and it damn sure screwed up more than my memory. So forgive me if I chose to pretend nothing had happened for a few days while I tried to figure out who the hell I could trust."

"So far," Leah said to the sheriff, "nothing unusual's shown up in any of the background checks."

He scowled. "What, not even a parking ticket?"

"I didn't say that." She handed a printout across the desk. "Three of them have bad credit ratings."

Jake eyed her. "Are you being funny?"

"Obviously not." She perched on the arm of one of his visitor's chairs, smiling faintly. "I'm just saying that not a single one of them has a criminal record of any kind. A few court appearances on civil matters—divorce, child custody, a property dispute—but absolutely nothing criminal. As far as we've been able to determine, the group in the Pearson house is clean."

He grunted. "Unless somebody gave us a false name."

"They had I.D.," she pointed out.

"And how hard is that to fake in this day and age? Hell, you can buy a new identity on the Internet."

Patient, she said, "The paper trail looks genuine."

"Yeah, yeah." He frowned down at the report she'd given him. "Keep digging."

"And when we hit bottom?"

"Dig a little deeper."

"Right." She stood up, but paused before turning toward the door to say, "You know, if we don't find anything, and they don't want to talk to us, we won't have a legal leg to stand on in questioning them about the murder. Not one thing we've found so far ties any of them to the scene, and until we find out who the victim was . . ."

"That's another thing I don't get," Jake said. "We should have an I.D. by now. With the size of this county, we've had time to talk to nearly every soul; we've certainly had time to knock on every door."

"Almost," she said. "Tim thinks by the end of the day our teams will have done that. Every door on the island, at least, and most of those in Castle. The whole county will take a few more days."

"We need more people," he muttered.

She hesitated, then said, "Well, in general we don't need them."

"Don't remind me that I could call in the state police."

"I don't have to remind you." Leah shrugged. "Anyway, they'd have to waste time getting up to speed before they'd be any real help. I'm betting Riley's going to make the difference here."

"I'm not so sure about that." Before she could respond, he added, "She and Ash still in the conference room?"

"No, they left a little while ago."

"To go where?"

"Didn't say."

His frown became a scowl. "Find out, dammit."

Leah didn't question or argue, she merely nodded and left his office to obey the order. She'd been one of Jake Ballard's deputies long enough to recognize the signs of a frayed temper, and though he seldom lost his entirely, when he did it wasn't pretty.

She returned to her own desk, nearly alone in the bullpen with virtually every available deputy out doing the house-to-house. She tried Riley's cell first, not really surprised when she got only the voice mail.

"I don't know why she even bothers to carry a cell," she muttered to herself as she hung up without leaving a message. "It never seems to be working."

A downside of being psychic, Riley had explained. Something about electromagnetic energy; as Leah understood it, it was sort of like Riley carried around with her a permanent static charge. Even her credit cards had to be carried in a special case, and the SCU-designed cell cases were only partially and sporadically protective because the phones had to be able to send and receive signals to be useful.

Difficult, Leah supposed, to design a way in which to shield a device from electromagnetic energy when said device required energy to function.

She was rummaging on her messy desk looking for the business card Ash had given her earlier with his cell number on it when the deputy manning the front desk approached her.

"Hey, Leah—we might have something."

She looked up at Tim Deviney, her brows lifting. "Yeah? With the door-to-door?"

He nodded. "We got a renter not answering his door, and neighbors haven't seen him at least since the weekend. Team's been back twice, and still no answer, no sign of him."

Leah frowned. "A single renter? Was he on our first list?"

"No, the realtor thought he was coming down with his family, and it's one of the big houses, so they had no idea he was alone."

"We have a name?" she asked.

"Yeah. Tate. Wesley Tate."

14

After a long moment, Ash let out a short sigh. "Okay. Point taken. You have more right to be pissed."

"Thank you."

They stared at each other, and then he finally smiled. "So I'm the one you decided to trust, huh?"

Becoming more aware of the deputy watching them, Riley lowered her voice again. "Well, I was sleeping with you, after all. I don't know if you're aware of this, but I just don't make a habit of sleeping with men I barely know."

"So you said."

She narrowed her eyes at him. "Want to tell me why I made an exception for you?"

His smile widened. "You know, I think I'll wait awhile and see if that part of your memory comes back."

"Bastard."

"I said you had more right to be pissed; I didn't say I wasn't still pissed too. You're a hell of an actress, Riley. It might have dawned on me slowly that something was wrong, but I never guessed I was a stranger to you."

She cleared her throat. "Not a total stranger. My memory might have been AWOL, but other parts of me were . . . Let's just say some things came back to me quicker than others."

"Yeah, we were great in bed right from the start," he said. "I would have been seriously offended if you had forgotten that."

"I'll bet."

"It's a guy thing."

"Uh-huh. Well, while you beat on your chest, I'm going to go see if I can pick up anything from the murder scene."

Turning serious, he said, "Riley, I don't have to know much about psychic abilities to guess this isn't a good idea."

"Probably not, but it's the only one I have right now." She shook her head. "Look, Gordon couldn't tell me much because I hadn't told **him** much. I've never kept notes or an ongoing report during an investigation—something I've just started doing here in case my mind is more screwed-up than I think it is—so it's not like I left a trail of bread crumbs for myself to follow. I don't know what's going on. I don't know what I may or may not have learned in the last few weeks. All I **know** is that somebody attacked me and a man's dead."

"And your boss left you here without backup?"

Riley briefly explained just how occupied the remainder of the team was with their own cases, then added, "Bishop wanted to recall me to Quantico, but I talked him out of it. I have to report to him every day, though, and when I report in today I damn sure want a few answers to offer him. Otherwise, when he hears what happened yesterday—"

"What happened yesterday?"

Shit.

Reluctantly, she admitted, "I lost a few more hours."

"What?"

"You heard me. About twelve hours, this time. From yesterday afternoon until this morning."

"Riley, you seemed perfectly fine last night."

"So I gather. It's fairly obvious that I was . . .

functional. Working at my laptop, starting that damn report. I just don't remember doing it."

"Jesus Christ. You want to explain to me why you aren't in a hospital?"

"They wouldn't know what to do with me. Ash, about the only thing medical science knows about the human brain is that they **don't** know what most of it's used for. And as far as the SCU can determine, that's probably the part psychics **do** use."

He was frowning. "You're telling me medical tests wouldn't show any organic cause for the blackouts?"

"I'm telling you they wouldn't provide any information I don't already have. And that it isn't something a doctor can slap a Band-Aid on and send me home with a prescription for."

"Riley—"

"Look, you're going to have to trust me on this. Whatever damage that Taser did, medical science can't fix. Maybe if I can tap into the clairvoyance, use my brain and senses the way I always have, then I can straighten myself out. Maybe."

"No guarantees."

"No."

"It could make things worse."

"That's as likely as any other outcome," she admitted.

"Is that why you finally decided to tell me the truth? Because you're afraid you could get worse, lose more time? Is that the sort of trouble you're expecting?"

"I'm hoping there won't be any trouble, of course. But if there is, if I do lose more time, I'll need someone to keep me on track." Riley drew a breath and let it out slowly. "I really don't know what could happen if I manage to tap into the clairvoyance. Maybe nothing. Maybe that sense is entirely gone; I certainly haven't been able to tap into it so far."

Ash reached out and pulled her into his arms.

Riley was a little surprised, but she found her arms going around his waist and was aware of a rather shaky sense of relief.

Maybe she wasn't as alone as she'd thought.

"We'll get through this," he told her. "And no matter what you believe, you're a hell of a lot more than just a psychic."

"Preparing me in case it really is gone for good?" she murmured.

"It's only a part of you, Riley. Not all of you."

"If you say so."

He kept an arm around her as they continued

through the dog park to the break in the fence. "It's your turn to trust me on this. Besides, I'm a lot more worried about these blackouts."

"You and me both, pal."

The deputy stationed at the fence obviously knew both of them and only nodded and touched his hat with a polite murmur when they passed, but the faint smile he wore said plainly enough that he had observed the embrace with interest and without surprise.

"So I gather everybody knows about us," she said dryly.

"We weren't secretive. Why should we be? We're both unattached and past the age of consent."

"I just . . . tend to keep my private life private, that's all."

"Another question in your mind?"

"Let's just say it's another sign that something was different. That something changed after I got here. And it's very frustrating to not remember what that was."

His arm tightened around her, but all Ash said was, "I'm betting on you, if that's worth anything. I doubt very much you've ever lost a fight in your life. Not one that mattered, at any rate."

Riley started to tell him he'd lose that bet, but by then they had reached the clearing still roped off with yellow crime-scene tape, and she did her best to push everything else out of her mind.

"What now?" Ash asked.

"Now," Riley replied, "I try to do my job. Wait here, if you don't mind."

He didn't protest, just watched as she ducked under the tape and headed for the boulders at the center of the clearing. "Anything I can do to help?"

"Well, if my head starts to spin around and I spew pea soup all over the place, please drag my ass out of here."

"Please tell me you're kidding."

She looked back over her shoulder to smile at him. "Yeah. Just keep an eye out, okay? If anything looks weird or wrong to you, break the connection."

"What connection?"

"This one." Riley turned her gaze back to the boulders, drawing a deep breath and concentrating on opening every sense she possessed. Then she reached out and placed both hands firmly on the stone that might have helped make up an altar.

She had unconsciously closed her eyes the moment her hands touched the rough stone.

Though the bloodstains had faded to rusty marks that might have been mistaken for natural color variations in the rock, she was all too aware of what they really were, and it took all her willpower to deliberately open herself to them.

She hadn't really expected anything to happen, not given the generally absent state of her senses.

Almost immediately, however, Riley knew that something had. As if a switch had been thrown or a lid closed, she found herself abruptly surrounded by utter silence.

No birds. No distant sounds of traffic and people.

All she heard was her own suddenly shallow breathing.

Riley forced herself to open her eyes and recoiled violently from the altar, stumbling back.

The acrid smoke from the fire stung her nostrils, sulfur making the stench worse. Beyond the firelit clearing, the dark woods might have been miles deep, and ancient, impenetrable guardians for the ceremony taking place here.

The robed figures dancing around the fire some feet away were familiar to Riley, but only in that she recognized the movements and gestures, the low chanting in a language most of the modern world had forgotten. She couldn't see any of their faces. None of them seemed to be aware of her presence.

In any case, it wasn't the robed celebrants that held her fascinated gaze but the open coffin placed upon the rock altar.

Riley's first thought was that it must have been a bitch to carry the obviously specially designed coffin all the way out here. And even more of a problem to hide from observers while it was being transported, large as it was. But then she realized that, ornate and gilded though it first appeared, the coffin was actually made of some kind of sturdy cardboard. It fit fairly well on the flat rock they had speculated might be used as an altar.

And it was occupied.

The woman wore a black hood, so it was impossible for Riley to see her face. She was otherwise naked, her arms folded across her breasts in the traditional death pose. But her knees were raised, her legs parted, in a clear if obscene invitation to a lover.

Standing at the foot of the coffin, on one of the smaller boulders, was another robed celebrant, this one wearing a death's-head mask rather than a hood. His arms were raised as he chanted a bit louder than the others, clearly leading them. His robe was open, and he was naked beneath.

He was also very aroused.

Riley took another step back, and then another, thoughts and questions clashing in her mind. This was wrong, and not just in the sense that most people would undoubtedly be horrified by the scene. It was wrong because the **ceremony** was wrong. There were familiar bits, things she recognized, the chanting, the candles and incense; even the coffin had a place in a satanic ceremony—but not like this.

It was supposed to be, above all, a celebration of life, of the strength and power of the human animal. And sexuality was a very large part of that, but . . . this was wrong.

Before she could make it all come clear in her mind, she raised her gaze for the first time and was stunned to see a naked man hanging over the coffin.

He appeared to be unconscious.

Riley tried to get a good look at his face, but when three of the celebrants moved out of the circle around the fire and went to the altar, she couldn't help but watch what they were doing.

In a weirdly graceful acrobatic movement, two helped the third one to climb to the top of the tallest boulder, so that he stood parallel to the hanging man.

There was a short sword in his hand, a kind of weapon Riley had never seen before, its sharp blade gleaming in the firelight.

The other two celebrants went to the hanging man, and each reached up to grasp one of his ankles. Then they moved slowly back toward the far side of the altar, pulling his feet back and holding them high until his upper body hung over the coffin and the woman waiting inside it.

Riley almost started forward instinctively when she realized what was going to happen, but that involuntary movement was halted when she reminded herself that this had already happened. Or it was a vision. Or even a figment of her Taser-disordered mind and imagination.

Bottom line, what she was seeing wasn't actually taking place before her.

There was nothing she could do except watch in horror.

The chanting became louder, the group around the fire danced more frenziedly—and then someone Riley couldn't see struck a bell sharply three times.

And everything stopped.

Only the snapping, popping fire offered any

movement or life for what seemed an eternal moment. And then the man at the foot of the coffin spoke a phrase in Latin, sharply.

Blood is the power? That's what he said?

The man on the topmost boulder leaned forward, grasped the hanging man's head by the hair, and drew it back far enough so that he was able to place the sharp blade against that unprotected throat.

The man at the foot of the coffin spoke, again in Latin, a short phrase Riley tried to brand in her mind.

Blood is the life.

Then, her voice muffled and unidentifiable behind the hood covering her face, the woman in the coffin spoke. Her words were also in Latin, and her tone was eerily seductive.

I offer . . . this sacrifice . . . and draw from blood spilled . . . life spilled . . . the power of darkness . . . the power of evil . . . to do my bidding.

The bell was struck three more times, and on the third strike the hanging man's throat was cut.

Blood gushed out and down, splashing the coffin and the woman in it. She unfolded her arms, holding them out as though welcoming the blood or beckoning a lover. Her hips lifted

and undulated. Scarlet coated her breasts and
stomach and streamed down the insides of her
thighs.

The robed celebrants grouped around the fire
began their dancing and chanting again, this
time more frantically, their voices rising as the
hanging man's lifeblood was drained from his
limp body.

The priest at the foot of the coffin chanted as
well, his voice growing louder, more frenzied,
until finally the woman convulsed and cried
out in an orgasmic tone, and he cast off his robe
and climbed into the coffin, mounting her
writhing body.

Riley's stomach heaved. She wanted to close
her eyes or look away, but she was helpless to
do either. She could only stand there and watch
the obscene copulation taking place, while the
chanting of the other celebrants became shouts,
and the dying man's blood continued to spatter
the two in the coffin, and the smell of incense
and blood stung her eyes and her nostrils.

This was wrong. Wrong in so many ways—

"Riley!"

She opened her eyes with a gasp, momentarily dizzy as she stared at the daylit clearing. No

coffin. No robed celebrants. No victim hanging above the altar.

She could still smell the blood.

"Riley, what in God's name—"

Realizing only then that Ash's arms were around her, that he had undoubtedly pulled her away from the altar, she fought for the strength to get her feet under her and turn to face him. She was grateful when his hands continued to grip her arms.

She thought she would have collapsed onto the ground otherwise.

"What did I do?" she asked, the thick, rusty sound of her own voice unfamiliar to her.

"You went white as a sheet," he said grimly, frowning down at her. "And cried out something I couldn't quite catch. By the time I got over here, you were shaking and—"

He lifted one hand and touched her cheek, showing her the wetness on the tips of his fingers. "—crying."

"Oh." She stared at the evidence of her tears. "I wonder why I did that. I was horrified, but—"

"Horrified by what? Riley, what the hell happened?"

She looked up at him, wishing she didn't feel so weak and drained, so utterly bewildered. "I—

saw what happened here. At least, I think I did."

"The murder?"

"Yeah. Except . . ." She fought to think clearly. "Except it wasn't right. He hadn't been tortured beforehand. And blood couldn't have splashed the flat altar stone because there was something lying across it, covering it almost completely. And there was too much noise, someone would have heard. And it was . . . wrong. What they said, what they did. Wrong in too many ways."

"Riley, are you telling me you had some kind of vision?"

"I think so. I've never had one before, not like that, but some of the others on the team have talked about them and—and I think that's what it was. But it was wrong, Ash. The details were wrong. The whole ceremony was . . . was like something you'd see in a horror movie."

He seemed to understand what she meant. "Over the top? Exaggerated?"

"In a way. As if someone who didn't really know what Satanism was imagined how it must be. Or knew and wanted to—to twist it into something truly evil."

"Maybe one of those fringe groups you mentioned earlier?"

She shook her head. "I don't know. Maybe. It's nothing I've ever heard of, I know that much. An actual human sacrifice is about as evil as you can get; add that to a weird ceremony that includes getting drenched in a dying man's blood while you screw in a coffin, and—"

"Screw in a—Jesus, Riley."

"Believe me, it looked as horrifying as it sounds. And from what I heard, I gather the purpose of the ritual was to draw power from the sacrifice and the sex."

"Power to do what?"

"I have no idea. But there has to be some reason behind it, some need for supernatural power."

"Same as with the arson? Attempts to harness elemental energy?"

"Yeah, and a hell of a lot of it. I can't imagine why someone would need so much power, but—" She felt herself slump a little, and thought her energy reserves must be **really** low.

"Riley—"

"I'm fine, Ash. I'll be—"

Riley sat up in bed with a gasp, her heart racing. She almost immediately recognized her bedroom, quiet and lit only by moonlight filtering through the blinds on the windows. A quick look showed her Ash sleeping peacefully beside her.

The clock on the nightstand said it was 5:30 in the morning.

Oh, Christ.

She slipped from the bed, finding her sleepshirt on the floor and putting it on with an icy sense of déjà vu.

It couldn't be happening again.

Not again.

She went into the living room and found the remote to turn on the TV, her hands shaking so much that just pressing the right small buttons on the device was a challenge.

CNN confirmed her fears. It was Thursday.

She'd lost more than eighteen hours this time.

15

Riley tried to think and realized that her energy reserves were so drained she was literally swaying on her feet. She went into the kitchen and drank orange juice straight out of the carton, then ate two PowerBars, one right after the other, barely chewing them and not tasting them at all.

She had a terrifying sense of being completely out of control.

I'm not just losing time. I'm losing me.

She ate a third PowerBar and finished the juice while she waited for the coffeemaker to do its job, and by the time there was caffeine to join the calories, she felt steadier.

Physically, at least.

What's happening to me?

The last thing she remembered was the experience in the clearing and talking to Ash, briefly, afterward. She thought he had said something to her, asked her something, and then . . .

Here. Now.

There was no trigger she could recall, no definitive word or action she could point to as the cause of these . . . blackouts. One moment she had been having a perfectly ordinary conversation with someone—at least as ordinary as conversations could be in her line of work—and the next moment hours had passed.

Too many hours.

Riley carried her coffee to the table where her laptop was set up. Once again, it was obvious that she had been here, working, during at least some of the most recent missing time. But there was one difference from the previous day.

She had to enter a password to access her report.

She didn't remember setting that up but had no difficulty in deciding what the password had to be. Because it was always the same, a nonsense word from her childhood, the secret name of a mythical kingdom she had created as a little girl's escape from the rough-and-tumble world of older brothers and military bases and living all over the globe.

She typed in the word, unsurprised when it proved to be the correct one.

There were, it seemed, at least a few truths in her life she could hold on to.

What she couldn't figure out was why she had decided to password-protect her report. She hadn't when she first began the report.

Or maybe I did. Maybe I just don't remember that either.

She hoped the report itself would answer at least a few of her questions, but she found herself reading only details she actually remembered. Going to the sheriff's department, meeting with Jake, Leah, and Ash. Noting that she herself had asked Ash to join the investigation, **primarily** because she was afraid she might lose more time and needed someone she trusted to keep an eye on her.

Well, I called that one. Dammit.

Riley winced when she reached the end of that very brief "report." Because it ended quite abruptly with:

Returned to the murder scene with Ash. Experienced a highly unusual variation of clairvoyance I can only describe as some kind of vision. Extreme black rites, possibly gen-

uine but darker and more twisted than any I've ever heard about. I was unable to positively identify any of the individuals participating in it, though the purpose of the ritual was, clearly, to gain power.

But for what? I don't know. I hate to admit that my mind is still affected by the Taser attack, but it must be, because thinking clearly is still difficult, sometimes impossible. One moment I'm certain of something, someone, and in the next I find myself doubting, questioning, worrying.

I don't understand. Something is happening to me, has happened, something more than the Taser attack. The only possibility I can think of, incredible as it sounds, is—

"Shit," Riley muttered.

The entry broke off, presumably because she'd been interrupted. And for whatever reason, she had never finished that sentence, never noted whatever possibility it was that had occurred to her.

Now she couldn't remember what it had been.

If it had been.

"Oh, Christ, I'm losing my mind." She put her hands up and rubbed her face slowly. Trying to think. Trying to understand.

"I was going to ask if you were feeling better, but I guess not."

Riley put her hands down, automatically touching the laptop's keyboard in a macro command that would instantly bring up an innocuous screen saver. The motion was so smooth and practiced that she doubted Ash had even noticed.

I'm doubting him now? Why?

"'Morning," she said, vaguely surprised that her voice sounded so normal. Even a chameleon had her limits, and Riley suspected she had reached hers days ago. At least.

"I guess I shouldn't be surprised that you're up early," Ash said as he joined her at the table. He bent down and kissed her lightly. "But last night I had the impression you were going to sleep for a week. Or three."

"I . . . just needed a little rest."

"You needed a lot of rest. And still do." He frowned slightly as he studied her.

"I know I look like hell," she managed, suddenly realizing she hadn't even bothered to run her fingers through her hair in her bolt from the bedroom.

"You never look like hell. But you do look worried."

"I **am** worried." She drew a breath. "Ash, I've had another blackout."

"What?"

She nodded. "I don't remember anything after having that vision yesterday morning in the clearing. That's more than eighteen hours this time."

Ash pulled out the chair beside hers and sat down. He was still frowning. "Riley—"

"I thought I might have written more down in the report, but it's just what I remember anyway. Meeting with Jake and Leah in the conference room at the sheriff's department, talking. Then the two of us going to the crime scene so I could try to pick up something. And having that weird vision. Ash, I don't have visions, not like that one, and I don't understand it. I don't understand what's happening to me. Jesus, I don't even know if I've checked in with Bishop—"

"**Riley.**" He reached over and covered one of her restless hands with his. "What are you talking about?"

"I'm trying to tell you—" She broke off abruptly, really looking at his expression, and felt a chilly wave sweep over her. "Yesterday," she managed. "Yesterday morning. I told you about the attack on Sunday night."

He nodded. "Yeah, you told me about that."

"And—the blackouts? The missing time?"

Ash's fingers tightened around hers. "Honey, you never said anything about blackouts or missing time. This is the first I've heard of any of that."

It was still early, just before eight, and Riley sat curled in one of the comfortable big wicker chairs on the deck of her rental, hoping the bright sunshine of the warming day would do something about the coldness inside her.

A hot shower hadn't helped, nor had one of Ash's excellent breakfasts. Not that she had noticed what she was eating; it was merely fuel to provide the energy she so desperately needed.

And she wasn't even sure that was still working.

She stared at the ocean, her gaze occasionally roaming as she absently watched more than a dozen of the island's dog owners taking their pets for a last run before the "dog curfew" that kept them off the beach during most of the day.

Such a nice, pleasant summer morning, filled with nice, pleasant activities. Normal activities. Normal people. She doubted any of **them** was watching the world as they knew it spinning out of control.

"Here." Ash sat down in the chair beside hers, handing her a large mug of coffee. "Even in the sun, you're still shivering."

"Thanks." Riley sipped the coffee for a few minutes, aware that he was watching her, waiting. Finally, she sighed and turned a bit in the chair to face him. "So. Where had we gotten to?"

"We had gone over the meeting at the sheriff's department yesterday morning. You seem to remember all that clearly."

She nodded.

"Okay. And I gather you remember most of the conversation between us afterward, about why you'd asked me to get involved officially in the investigation. That was when you finally told me about the attack on Sunday night. That it had affected your memory a little and your senses a lot. You said you wanted someone you could trust to keep an eye on you in case the attack had caused more damage than you already knew about."

Riley sorted through what "memories" she had, wondering again which knowledge or seeming knowledge she could trust. "I didn't tell you I had forgotten most of the last three weeks?"

Ash frowned. "No, that's not what you said. You didn't remember the attack or the hours before it happened. You didn't remember why you had gone out or where you had gone that night. That's what you told me. That's all you told me."

"Oh."

"Riley, are you saying now that you didn't remember **anything** about the last few weeks?"

"Bits and pieces, but—" She sighed. "Dammit, in my head we've had this conversation before. I didn't remember us, but once you touched me I knew we were lovers, I felt what was between us, and that was the one thing in this whole damn screwy situation I was sure of. So don't get pissed that I was faking my way through our relationship, because I **wasn't,** not in any way that counted. Fumbling a little, I'll grant you. But not faking."

"You were . . . very convincing," he said finally.

"Now, see, you're getting pissed again. Please don't make me repeat the speech about how I was affected by what happened to me on Sunday night and how it left me scrambling to catch up on **everything,** not just us."

Dryly, he said, "Sorry, but I wasn't there the first time."

"Yes, you were." Riley shook her head. "At least that's the way I remember it. Damn, it was—is—so real in my mind. I don't understand this. Any of it."

Ash eyed her thoughtfully. "Well, you're still shaking a bit, but you also seem to be taking this very calmly."

She didn't bother to explain that in the SCU, one learned to handle unexpected things thrown at one without warning.

Or else one washed out of the SCU. Rather quickly.

Instead, all she said was, "I'm not calm, I'm numb. Big difference."

"Riley, maybe you should go back to Quantico."

"No." The response came instantly, without thought, and as soon as she heard herself say it Riley felt the rightness of it, the certainty. She wasn't sure of much, but she was absolutely certain she had to stay the course here. It went against logic and reason, to say nothing of all her training, but it was what she felt.

And how can I trust what I feel any more than what I think? Is this genuine instinct fighting its way through all the bewilderment of lost memories and unreliable senses, or just bloody-minded determination not to quit before the job is done?

It could have been either. Or neither.

Ash reclaimed her attention, saying, "Look, we both know—or at least I hope you know—

that I do **not** want you to leave. I've been gathering all the arguments I can think of for you to transfer down here, maybe work out of the Charleston FBI field office. But you'd said you were considering taking a full six weeks off, so I thought I had a bit more time to make my case."

Momentarily distracted—not surprisingly, considering the current state of her mind—Riley said, "Six weeks? I said I was thinking of staying—what is it now?—another two weeks?"

He nodded. "Saturday, you'll have been here four weeks."

"That doesn't make sense either," she murmured. By the previous Sunday night, she had to have known that Bishop and the rest of the team were all but overwhelmed with cases; she might not have checked in with him, but it was her habit to keep tabs on the unit wherever she was, and she couldn't imagine a situation in which she would have been contemplating an extension of her "vacation" knowing how thinly stretched the SCU resources were.

"Thanks a lot," Ash said.

Riley shook her head. "It has nothing to do with us. Bishop's current investigation is a serial killer on the rampage in Boston, making the national news on a daily basis, and I would have known the other teams were just as busy; the SCU is strained to its absolute limits right now. It wouldn't have been in character for me to decide to stay here on what was supposed to be a minor **and** unofficial investigation."

"Minor?"

"In the general scheme of things, sure. At least until what happened on Sunday. To that point, all we really had in the way of violence were a couple of instances of arson, property damage; nobody got hurt, and that wasn't something Jake and his people needed my help to investigate. Why would I have stayed here knowing I was badly needed elsewhere? Unless . . ."

Ash was watching her intently. "Unless?"

"Unless I knew that, however unthreatening the situation looked on the surface, Gordon's instincts were right and there was something very dangerous going on here. You're sure everything I was telling you pointed to—"

" 'No big deal,' I think were your exact words." He frowned. "Although if your . . . performance . . . since Sunday is anything to go by, you could have been telling me that while believing the opposite, and I'd never have known. Apparently."

She sighed. "I knew we were going to have to have this conversation again."

"Riley—"

"Ash, I can't apologize for not confiding in you during those first weeks because I'm not sure there was anything **to** confide. Or if there was, why I decided to keep it to myself. And since waking up on Monday I've spent most of my time just trying to figure out if my mind and senses will ever get back to something I fondly call normal. I'm sorry if you're pissed. I'm sorry if you're hurt. But put yourself in my place for just a minute and think about it. If you had no idea why you had done something uncharacteristic—why you had done a **lot** of things that were uncharacteristic—how quick would you be to push aside all your doubts and confide everything to the woman unexpectedly sharing your bed?"

After a long moment, he sighed and nodded. "Okay, point taken."

"Thank you." Half to herself, she muttered, "I just wish I could be sure we won't be repeating all this tomorrow. The term 'déjà vu' has taken on a whole new meaning for me."

"You think there'll be more blackouts?"

"I don't know what to think. Except that

whatever I'm experiencing, it's like nothing I've ever heard of before. Blackouts and lost time aren't unknown among psychics. In fact, if anything they're fairly common. But they tend to present as either total unconsciousness or radically different behavior."

"What do you mean?"

"I mean that if you and everybody else around here noticed nothing odd about how I was acting during the time I've lost, it can only mean I didn't actually **lose** those hours. I was functional. I was here, doing normal things. I was me. But then, for whatever reason, those memories and experiences . . . ceased to exist for me. I've lost the perception of their reality."

"Why does that sound a lot more scary to me?"

"Probably for the same reason it feels a lot more scary. Because how we perceive the world **is** our reality. And if I've lost that, even pieces of it, then . . . I can't trust anything I think, or feel . . . or believe. Especially now. It's not just holes now; my mind has apparently begun filling in the holes, the blank spots, supplying **memories** that aren't real at all."

"Assuming you can believe me," he noted.

"I have to believe you," she said flatly. "I have to have something solid to hold on to, to anchor me. And that's you. Because you're in my bed. Because before all this started, I trusted you that much. It's never casual for me, in case I didn't mention that. Sex. So you being my lover has to mean I trusted you absolutely within days of meeting you. I may not remember why, but I have to believe that. I have to hold on to it. You're my lifeline, Ash."

"I wish you sounded a little happier about that."

Riley made a determined effort to lighten her tone. "Well, what can I say? It's those control issues, remember? No matter how happy I am, I'll always want to steer my own boat."

"I am the captain of my soul," he murmured.

"Yeah. We're none of us master of our fates, but that doesn't stop us trying to be."

"You and I have debated that before."

"Have we?" Riley shook her head. "Then I imagine we will again. In the meantime, if you want to bail, better now than later."

"I don't bail, Riley."

"Didn't really think you would. Just thought I'd offer."

"Noted. And refused."

She found herself smiling. "I've got a hunch I picked a pretty good lifeline. And it doesn't take anything but common sense to know I'm going to need one. Things may get worse, Ash. A lot worse."

After a moment, he asked, "Is all this due to the Taser attack?"

"I don't know what else it could be."

"You said something once about—Riley, could it be the influence of another psychic?"

"Theoretically? Yeah. Energy to energy. Electromagnetic fields can be manipulated, electronic impulses cut off or redirected. Even created. It's how the brain works, and it can be affected by plenty of external factors. But as far as I know, we've never encountered a psychic with the ability to influence another psychic's mind even in small ways. Not without a very strong blood connection."

"Which isn't possible in this case."

Riley shook her head. "My brothers are scattered around the world and my parents are in Australia. And none of them is psychic anyway."

"There's no way a psychic unrelated to you could be doing this?"

"No way I know of. To alter my memories? To create new ones? Even in theory, the sheer amount of energy anything like that would require is . . . almost unimaginable."

Burning buildings. A blood sacrifice.

No . . . not just a blood sacrifice . . . a human sacrifice. How much dark energy would that create?

For a moment, Riley thought there was something on the edge of her mind, but then it slipped off.

"Would you know if your mind was being influenced?"

"Maybe. Probably." Surely she would. Surely. It made her skin crawl to think otherwise, to consider the possibility that her actions weren't her own, her memories and even her very thoughts shaped for her by someone else.

It was far less scary to believe a simple electrical discharge had scrambled all the circuits in her brain.

Still . . .

Could that be why I'm using up energy so quickly? Because my mind is working to fight off a kind of attack I'm not even consciously aware of? Is that even possible?

"Is that why you're so sure it was the Taser attack?"

"I think that's more likely." **I hope it is, anyway.** She reached up to rub her forehead. "Not that my thinking is all that clear. But I do know that memory is a tricky thing at the best of times; add in an electrical blast of unknown strength and duration, and the brain is very likely to go haywire. Especially a psychic's brain, which tends to have a higher-than-normal amount of electrical activity going on at any given time anyway."

Ash shook his head. "This is beyond me."

"It's beyond me too," Riley admitted. She hesitated, then added, "I have to report in. Because it's the right thing to do and because if there's anyone who might understand what's going on in my head, it'll be Bishop."

"You sound doubtful."

"Not of that. I'm just wondering how much even he can juggle before one of the plates crashes to the floor."

16

And you have absolutely no memory of anything you said or did during the two blackouts?" From Bishop's calm tone, no one would have guessed either that he found anything unusual in the situation or that he was in the middle of an incredibly intense investigation of his own. For the moment, at least, he appeared to be perfectly capable of juggling multiple tasks.

"No," Riley answered. "It's like I passed out and then woke up hours later."

"Which," he pointed out, "is different from the first memory loss, immediately after the Taser attack."

It took a moment, but then Riley realized. "When I woke up Monday afternoon, there **were** bits and pieces of memory. Uncertain, even wispy, but they were there."

"Yes. A reasonable physical result of a temporary disruption of the brain's own electrical activity. Like an explosion of energy that caused a scattering, a . . . fragmentation of memories. You lacked the ability to stitch them together, but all the pieces, all the experiences, were still there."

"Just memories?"

"You tell me."

Riley stood there with the beach house's phone to her ear and gazed absently through the ocean-side windows. Ash was out there on the deck, waiting patiently, his own brooding gaze fixed on the water. She wondered what he was thinking, feeling.

She didn't have a clue.

Drawing a breath, she answered Bishop. "No, not just memories. More. Senses. Emotions. Even the normal ability to read other people, to have some idea of what they're thinking and feeling. It's all scattered, distant."

"But not knowledge. Not training. That you can still access."

"I think so," she said cautiously.

"Then I'm betting it's all still there, Riley."

"In pieces."

"You can reconnect the pieces."

"Yeah? How?" She was afraid her voice sounded as shaky as she felt.

"You made a start. You were able to use your clairvoyance at the murder scene."

"Not like I've ever used it before."

"There's at least a chance the electrical jolt may have changed that for good."

She realized her short nails were biting into her palm and forced herself to unclench her right fist. Staring down at the reddened crescents as they faded, she said slowly, "There's a precedent?"

"Of sorts. Electrical fields affect us, Riley. Virtually all of us. But how depends on the individual. It can have unpredictable side effects ranging from very mild disorientation to a radical change in our abilities. But a direct jolt to the brain . . . The only similar case I know of involved a second-degree medium who was accidentally electrocuted. His heart stopped, but they brought him back."

"And? He still sees dead people?"

"He couldn't see them before, just barely hear them. Now he sees them in Technicolor and hears them as clearly as you're hearing me. All the time, if he drops the shield it took us more than a year to teach him how to build."

"Like living in the middle of a noisy crowd only you can see and hear."

"Yes. Not pleasant."

"He's not with the team."

"No. Maybe someday, but not yet. Right now it's all he can do to have some semblance of a normal life."

Riley would have preferred to go on talking about someone else's troubles but reluctantly focused on her own. "So . . . the shock of that Taser might have strengthened or altered my clairvoyance to the point that I can actually experience visions."

"It's possible."

"You didn't mention that possibility before. Did you? Jesus, I don't even remember if I reported in yesterday."

"You did, briefly. And I noticed absolutely nothing unusual in the conversation, so you obviously were functional during those missing hours. As for whether we discussed the possibility that your abilities may have been altered, no, not specifically."

"Did you think this might happen?"

"Honestly?" For the first time a hint of weariness crept into his voice. "There's been so much going on here that I haven't had a great deal of time to consider possibilities elsewhere."

"Yeah, I saw you on the news. Looks like a tough one."

"It is. But all the teams are currently involved in tough cases. Including you. Riley—"

"I know. I should return to Quantico. But the answers are here, Bishop. Besides, at least one man has died and there's a strong possibility of another victim. And I'm involved. Somehow, I'm involved. I can't just walk away from that."

"An unknown assailant managed to blindside a trained agent and put you down hard on Sunday night."

"Don't rub it in," she murmured.

Bishop ignored that. "You don't know if it was meant to be a lethal attack, though all signs point that way. Your memories and instincts are, to say the very least, unreliable, and you've been burning energy at a rate far greater than normal for you. You've had two blackouts in the last forty-eight hours, losing well over half that time. You're experiencing dreams and visions of what appear to be extreme black-occult rites, which we both know are as rare as hen's teeth. And you have no backup."

"What's your point?" she asked, deliberately flip and not at all sure he'd let her get away with it. He usually didn't.

"Riley."

"Okay, it's insane. I'm insane. Probably. I'm also scared, in case you're not picking up on that."

"I'm picking up on it," he said. "Even without telepathy. The worse a situation gets, the more flippant you get."

Riley frowned. "I'm that predictable?"

"It's a defense mechanism. In your case, a survival tool."

"As in 'Don't bother to kill the poor little lunatic blonde, she's obviously out of her mind and, so, harmless'?"

"That's part of it. And a different sort of . . . protective coloration. If you're laughing about a situation or taking it lightly, then it can't be all that serious, now, can it? Puts other people at ease and tends to stop them crowding you."

Riley returned her gaze to the man waiting outside on the deck, and said, "I don't think it's going to work this time."

"Not with everyone, at any rate. If Ash Prescott is your lifeline, you need to be totally honest with him."

It didn't surprise Riley that Bishop had picked

up on her specific uncertainties; she wasn't at all sure he wasn't actually reading her thoughts, long distance. "I told him he was my lifeline. But . . . do you really think it'll come to that?"

"I think it might. You've experienced two blackouts in two days, Riley, the second one longer than the first. That alone suggests your condition is deteriorating rather than improving."

"Yeah, I was afraid of that. But the brain's designed to repair itself, right? To build new pathways when old ones are destroyed?"

"Yes, more or less. Which is why I would expect your condition to stabilize. The fact that it hasn't indicates some kind of continuing damage."

Riley considered that for a moment, trying to think clearly. There was an idea on the edge of her mind, something she couldn't quite reach, and it was maddening because she thought it represented at least part of the answer.

There was something . . . something I realized? Something that made sense?

Bishop said, "It's also distinctly unsettling that you were functional during the blackouts."

"You're telling me. Ash has been filling in most of the missing time for me, and as far as I can tell, I was behaving normally."

"So the most likely scenario we're left with is that you experienced the time, lived through it with perfect normality, and afterward, for some unknown reason, lost the memory of it. Or at least can't access it."

"That's what it sounds like."

"And we don't know what triggered either of the blackouts."

"If something did."

"Blackouts are always triggered by something, at least in our experience. You were using your abilities the second time, but not the first; do you recall any commonalities in the moments just before the blackouts?"

She was about to say no, but then Riley paused and thought about it more carefully. "Just before the first blackout, I was talking to two people from that group of satanists I told you about here on the island, Steve and Jenny; when I woke up after that blackout, it was from a dream in which I was watching the celebration of some version of a Black Mass—with Jenny serving as the altar."

"And the second blackout?"

"Happened just minutes after I experienced that vision at the crime scene. In the vision, the celebrants were masked, but the woman could

have been Jenny again. The priest might have
been Steve. I can't say for sure, but . . ."

"A possible connection."

"The only one I can think of." Riley was conscious of a chill as she realized it was becoming
more difficult to concentrate, to focus. She
was losing energy again. Already, she was losing
energy.

Damn, damn, damn . . .

She forced herself to go on. "Ash . . . sug-
gested the possibility of another psychic. So did
Gordon. Someone able to influence my mind.
My memories." **And maybe sap my energy?**

"It is possible. Your deteriorating condition
argues there's something more at work than the
single Taser blast. And if there is a combination
of black-occult practices and genuine psychic
ability manipulating the situation down there,
clearly with some success, you can't handle it
alone."

"Bishop—"

"Nobody handles that sort of thing alone. A
psychic with the drive to create dark energy and
the ability to tap into it? With the ability to use
it? We know evil exists, Riley, that it's a real, tangible force."

"Yeah, but—"

"A force you're vulnerable to, especially now. Your natural defenses have been weakened, all but destroyed; how could you protect yourself from an attack on that level?"

Riley didn't have an answer.

Bishop didn't wait for a response. "If nothing else, black-occult practices would provide the perfect opportunity to channel negative energy. Whether in an attack meant to disable or destroy, or to achieve some other specific purpose. You're the expert on the occult; you know better than most that such rituals are incredibly dangerous in the wrong hands. Whether intentional or not, controlled or not, they create an enormous amount of negative energy— which could well be one of the things affecting you now."

She hadn't thought of that; it had never happened to her before. Then again, she could count the genuine black-occult rituals she had been witness to on the fingers of one hand. With fingers left over.

"Damn."

"Assume the worst, Riley. Assume you have a very powerful enemy out there. The Taser attack may only have been the beginning."

"I don't know who I could have threatened in such a short time, at least not to that extent."

"Which is the answer you need to look for. Whatever's happened to your abilities, your memories, the one thing you know for certain is that you were attacked."

It was, perhaps oddly, something Riley needed to hear, to be reminded of, and by someone who could view the situation with cool logic.

She felt a bit steadier, a bit more centered. She could do this. She was a pro, after all, experienced in investigation. Trained in self-defense and more than able to take care of herself. Knowledgeable about the occult.

She could do this.

She was almost positive she could.

"So you'll let me stay on the case?"

"There are conditions, Riley."

"Okay, but—"

"Listen to me. You chose Ash Prescott as your lifeline, and we both have to trust that you knew what you were doing. Keep him close. Follow what leads you can, look for what connections you can—and report back tomorrow. By the end of the day on Friday. Just as we originally agreed. If there's been no progress in the investigation, or you black out again, even for ten minutes, then you'll be recalled to Quantico. Period."

This time, Riley knew better than to argue.

"Understood." She was still fighting to hold on to her concentration and hoped he wasn't picking up on it. "Bishop, one last thing. The serial killer in Charleston. You were going to look at the files?"

"Yes, I have. You don't have to worry about John Henry Price, Riley."

She leaned against the counter, too relieved to even attempt to hide it. "You're sure?"

"I'm sure."

"Bad enough it's a copycat, but—"

"Investigate your case, Riley. Report in tomorrow, sooner if anything changes. And **be careful**."

"I will." She cradled the receiver and continued to lean against the counter for a moment, then pushed herself away and went to grab another PowerBar before heading back out to the deck to talk to Ash, trying to convince herself that she couldn't actually feel the energy draining out of her as though someone had pulled the plug.

Bishop closed his cell phone and stared down at the folder open on the table before him.

"You lied to her," Tony noted, his tone neutral.

"I withheld part of the truth."

"A lie by omission is still a lie, boss."

"That," Bishop said, "depends on whether the end justifies the means. In this case, it does."

"And is the end going to be a happy one?"

Without directly replying to that, Bishop said, "Riley needs to feel certain of her trust in her lifeline."

"And one truth too many cuts that line?"

"In this situation, probably. With her abilities, instincts, and memories unreliable, the smallest doubt could cause her to pull away from him. Isolate herself even more. Put her in greater danger."

"This wouldn't exactly be a small doubt."

"No. Not from her point of view."

"It's a little shaky from mine," Tony admitted. "I love a good coincidence, but if working with you has taught me anything it's that we're usually not that lucky. A connection between two seemingly unrelated things—or people—usually means something nasty. For somebody. And for there to be any connection at all between John Henry Price and Ash Prescott at this stage is more than a little creepy. To say the least."

"Price is dead," Bishop said, and reached out to close the file in front of him.

"Mmmm. Except that, in our business, dead

doesn't necessarily mean gone. And it sure as hell doesn't mean harmless. Somebody is, after all, killing those people in Charleston."

Bishop got to his feet. "We aren't in Charleston, we're in Boston. Where people are also being killed."

"You'd think there was something in the water," Tony offered.

"You'd think. I'll be in the interview room, going another round with that so-called witness."

"Pity you haven't been able to read him."

"That won't stop me from trying again."

Tony waited until he reached the door of the conference room before saying, "Boss? You don't like hanging one of us out on our own, do you?"

"Is that what you think I've done to Riley?"

"It's what you think you've done. What you feel you've done."

"Tony," Bishop said, "sometimes working with an empath—"

"—is a real pain in the ass. Yeah, I know. But I'm not really an empath. The emotions have to be pretty strong for me to pick up on them."

"You're not helping."

Tony grinned faintly. "Sure I am. It's my job to point out that Riley's a big girl—so to speak.

She can take care of herself. I was there that day in the gym, remember? She took on you **and** Miranda. At the same time. And damn near beat you both. I'd call that tough enough."

"Physically, no argument."

"But this isn't about physical toughness, is it? It's about knowledge. Whoever put her down with that Taser knew they couldn't do it any other way."

"It's a dangerous enemy who knows you that well."

"An enemy you should keep close?"

Bishop didn't answer.

"You didn't warn her."

"I warned her."

"Not specifically."

"She knows she has an enemy there. Nothing I could say would make her more guarded or wary, just . . ."

"Paranoid?"

"No. Dangerously uncertain of the one person who can help her survive the next few days."

"Let's hope she figures out who that is," Tony said. "Because he looks suspicious as hell even from where I'm standing, boss. All of them do. Who does she really trust when the crucial moment arrives? A new lover with a bloody connection to the serial killer who almost killed her? An old army buddy who's been less than honest with her? Or the small-town sheriff with his own agenda? Who does she pick to hang her survival on? How does she make that choice?"

"She listens to her instincts."

"And?"

"And pays attention to what they've been telling her all along."

Riley had finished one PowerBar and was eating another when she rejoined Ash on the deck and reclaimed her sun-warmed chair.

"What did Bishop say?" he asked.

Condensing the conversation, Riley replied, "He thinks it's unlikely—but possible—that another psychic is having an effect on me. Far more likely it's the Taser attack. He mentioned a case where a jolt of electricity changed a psychic's abilities. If that **is** what's happening to me, there's no way to really know what was damaged or changed in my brain until we see the effects of it."

She decided not to go into the possibility that negative energy created by black-satanic rites could also be having an effect on her, though she wasn't quite sure why.

Who am I doubting? Myself? Or Ash?

"It's a miracle it didn't kill you," he said.

Riley began tying the empty PowerBar wrapper into knots. "I'm still trying to figure out how somebody could sneak up and blindside me. That's not supposed to happen, you know, not to us ex-army types with FBI training to boot."

Slowly, Ash said, "Maybe they didn't have to sneak. Maybe whoever it was . . ."

"Was already with me? Yeah, the thought had occurred."

"Which, I suppose, explains your reluctance to trust anyone."

"Wouldn't you be reluctant?"

"I'm not arguing. Just saying."

She eyed him, hesitated, then said, "You might as well know. I told Gordon about the attack on Sunday and the amnesia. At least, I'm pretty sure I did, unless that's another memory I can't trust."

Ash didn't appear to be upset by that. "You two served together and have known each other for years; it makes sense that you'd trust him before anyone else. Does he know about the blackouts?"

"No, I haven't talked to him since those started. At least . . ." She frowned. "I don't remember talking to him. Unless I did on Tuesday afternoon during that missing time. After we had lunch, I walked along the beach to the Pearson house and talked to Steve and Jenny—and the next thing I remember, it was yesterday morning."

He was also frowning. "I picked you up around six-thirty Tuesday; we had drinks and dinner, then came back here. You wanted to do some research online, and I had paperwork to deal with."

"Um . . . is that usual for us? Both working here?"

"I wouldn't call it usual, but we've done so a few times. Here or at my place."

"I've been to your place?"

A little laugh escaped him. "Of course you have, Riley. But we're usually here at night because my condo is on the small side. I'm keeping an eye out for a bigger place, by the way."

She decided to ignore that last comment. "So . . . between the time I was talking to Steve and Jenny and when you picked me up here, there are three or four hours unaccounted for. I may or may not have been alone. May or may not have gone to talk to Gordon or someone else."

"Easy enough to check with Gordon, at least."

"Yeah, I'll call him." Riley looked at her half-empty coffee cup and tried once again to gather her thoughts; she seemed able to do so for brief periods, but then they scattered again and she could almost literally feel herself beginning to drift, even despite the calories she had consumed since talking to Bishop.

Minutes ago. Just minutes this time.

"Riley?"

"Yesterday," she said finally, struggling to keep her focus. "After that . . . vision or whatever it was in the clearing. What did we do?"

"Immediately after? Came back here."

"We did? But wasn't Jake planning to talk to the group at the Pearson house?"

"Yeah. But the background checks turned up nothing, which meant he had no cause to question any of them, no legal leg to stand on. When he called anyway and asked if he could pay them a visit, he was politely referred to their lawyer." Ash shrugged. "Not so surprising a reaction, from a group probably accustomed to . . . nosy cops."

"And they would be."

"I imagine so. Anyway, Jake was frustrated but hamstrung. There was nothing we could do at the station, and you wanted to do more research in some occult database you knew of, so we spent the afternoon and evening here. We went out for a walk just before sunset, and I tried to teach you the finer points of making spaghetti sauce a bit earlier, but other than those breaks, up until nearly midnight I was channel surfing and you were on the Net. You didn't say, but I got the impression you were looking for something specific."

"I guess you don't know whether I found it?"

"You didn't say."

"Sounds like a boring evening for you," Riley said, bothered by that and not entirely sure why.

"It had its compensations."

Riley was tempted to follow the intriguing tangent but forced herself to focus. "There was **nothing** new in the investigation in all those hours?"

"Riley, we talked about—" Ash shook his head. "You're right, this is a very confusing minefield. Our memories don't match."

Half to herself, Riley said, "There's probably something profound in that, but never mind. What don't I remember?"

"By late afternoon, Jake called with a positive I.D. on the victim. The house-to-house finally turned up an empty rental where someone was supposed to be, and they were able to match prints found there to those of our former John

Doe. Not that it's been much help so far to know who the poor bastard was, since we haven't been able to connect him to anyone on the island or in Castle. As of last night, Jake's people hadn't even been able to contact his family. You don't remember any of this?"

This time, Riley didn't even pause to think about what she didn't remember; she was too busy trying to concentrate. "No. Who was he? What's his name?"

"Tate. Wesley Tate. A businessman from Charleston."

A jumble of thoughts crowded into her mind, and Riley did her best to sort through them. What was real? What memories could she actually claim as her own? "He lived in Charleston?"

"Yeah. Jake's people were still working on the background check when we talked last night, so that's all I know for sure."

"He lived in Charleston, but chose to vacation here?"

"Struck me too. If you live in a beautiful coastal city, why rent a house on an island fifty miles away?"

"Maybe he didn't have an ocean view at home."

"He didn't have much of one here. The rental isn't oceanfront, it's three rows back."

"So he didn't come for the view."

"It's a good bet. Neighbors saw him arrive on Saturday, but nobody seems to have seen him after that. Another weird thing is that it's a big house, not really the sort for a single man to rent. Especially with plenty of smaller houses and condos available on the island. The realtor was under the impression that his family or a group of friends was set to join him later."

"And nobody's shown up."

"Not so far."

Riley drained her cold coffee, then got to her feet, relieved to find her legs relatively steady under her. "I want to take a look at Tate's rental. After that, I think Jake and Leah should meet us at the Pearson house."

Ash was also on his feet. "There's a connection between that group and Tate?"

"If I can trust this part of my memory—yes. A big one."

"You didn't seem to recall a connection last night. What if your memory about this is faulty?"

"I'll jump off that bridge when I come to it," Riley said.

17

She called Gordon from Ash's Hummer, using his cell and plugging it into the car charger even before she began to place the call.

"Saves time," she explained to Ash. "It's why I didn't even bother to bring mine; I seem to be pulling energy out of them."

"I gather that's new," he said, not really a question.

"They never last long as a rule but, yeah, the speed they're dying on me is new. At this rate, I'll count myself lucky if the Hummer doesn't die on us."

Ash eyed the vehicle's power outlet and shrugged. "I'll keep the engine running."

Riley placed her call, and as soon as Gordon answered, asked without preliminaries, "Did I talk to you yesterday?"

Gordon, unflappable under even extreme conditions, replied simply, "No. Haven't seen or heard from you since Tuesday morning."

"Damn."

"Why? What's changed?"

"I'll fill you in later."

"Yes," Gordon said. "You will."

"It's okay, I'm with Ash. Will you be home this afternoon?"

"Yeah."

"All right. I'll be in touch."

Riley closed the phone and placed it, still plugged into the vehicle's power socket, on the console between the two front seats. Then she automatically leaned back away from it.

Ash said, "Have another PowerBar."

Riley dug into her shoulder bag for one of the half dozen she'd brought with her, saying only, "It's getting obvious, isn't it?"

"Your hands are shaking," Ash replied. "There are a few bottles of orange juice in the cooler behind your seat. After what happened yesterday at the crime scene, I figured I'd better stock up."

She managed to get a bottle without having to climb back there, and washed down the PowerBar with the juice. "This," she said, "is getting ridiculous."

"It's getting scary," Ash said, his tone remaining calm, almost offhand. "I know you said things could get worse, but . . ."

"This isn't what you bargained for. Sorry."

Ash sent her a glance. "I can handle whatever I have to, Riley. You're the one I'm worried about."

She drew a deep breath and released it slowly, trying to focus, to steady herself. "I have to figure out what's going on. If there really are black-occult rites being practiced here, and why. Why Wesley Tate died and whether I was somehow involved in his murder. Why I was attacked. Even why I'm getting worse instead of better when the attack against me was days ago. It all fits somehow. It's all part of the puzzle. I just have to find all the pieces."

"And then put them together so they make sense."

"Yeah." Riley reached for another Power-Bar. "And I've got around thirty hours in which to do it. Otherwise, by the end of the day tomorrow, Bishop will recall me. And I'll spend the next month being tested from my DNA

outward and looking at inkblots for SCU doc-
tors."

"For a number of reasons," Ash said conversationally, "I'd rather that not happen."

"Me either."

"So how can I help?"

"Just try to keep me focused."

"Do my best." He turned the Hummer into
the short driveway of Wesley Tate's rental and
parked.

It wasn't a crime scene, so the big third-row
house hadn't been taped off or left under guard.
But Riley had nevertheless called Jake before
they left her rental to ask his permission to go
through the place, and also requested that he
and Leah meet them at the Pearson rental in an
hour or so.

He had agreed to both requests and cleared
their visit to Wesley Tate's rental with the realtor, so someone from that office met them at
the house with the key.

She was a gorgeous brunette dressed to kill—
or seduce—and Riley knew the instant she set
eyes on Colleen Bradshaw that here was one of
those "available" women in Ash's life.

It wasn't just the outfit, far more dressy than
was the norm on the island; realtors showed
houses to prospective renters and buyers, and

Riley had seen enough of them to know that most dressed well during office hours for just that reason. It wasn't even the warm smile or the way Colleen touched Ash's arm three times during the brief introduction to Riley.

It was the way that smile never reached her chilly gray eyes.

This woman hates me.

Riley was mildly surprised but not disturbed; she had too many things on her mind to worry about Ash's former lovers.

Much.

"Jake said I was to give you the key," Colleen said to Ash, handing it over as if it were a precious jewel that needed to be placed reverently into his palm. And caressed for a beat or two.

Riley shifted her stance slightly, just to make the gun she wore on her hip more obvious. "Thanks, Ms. Bradshaw," she said in the indifferently polite tone reserved for bank tellers and waitresses. "We'll see that it gets safely back to your office when we're done here."

"Of course. It was nice to meet you, Agent Crane."

"Likewise. Oh—Ms. Bradshaw? Did you meet Wesley Tate? Speak to him?"

"Sorry, no. Another agent handles this account."

"I see. Thank you."

"My pleasure. Ash, I'm sure we'll be talking."

"See you later, Colleen."

They both watched the tall brunette fold herself—with quite unnecessary ceremony, Riley thought—into her little sports car and drive away, and it wasn't until then that Riley said, "How long did that last? You two?"

Ash didn't seem surprised. "A few months over last winter."

"Obviously she wasn't the one who broke it off."

"No." Ash held up the key she'd given him. "Shall we?"

"Ah. You don't kiss and tell. Good to know."

"There isn't anything to tell." He led the way to the front steps of Wesley Tate's rental. "An attraction, but not a lot in common."

"A spark but no fire."

"Exactly."

"So how come she hates me?"

Ash was smiling faintly. "Does she hate you?"

"Innocent isn't a good face for you, Ash. There's something completely unnatural about it."

"Why would you think she hates you?"

"Let's just say I'm glad I was the one with the gun."

He paused at the top of the steps to look at

her, still smiling. "Jealousy. This is a new side of you. I think I like it."

"I am not a jealous person. And I have nothing to be jealous about. Do I?"

"Of course not."

"Well, then." **So what if that Amazon is six feet tall and dresses like she should be standing on a street corner somewhere? So what? Why is this bugging me so much?**

Why am I even thinking about this?

"Okay, you're not a jealous person." Ash unlocked the door and opened it. "Shall we?"

"I'm really not a jealous person. And, anyway, you're supposed to be helping me stay focused."

"Right. Sorry."

I am a cop, and this is where a murder victim lived the last days of his life. At least—

"How long was Tate here before he was killed?" she asked, putting leggy brunettes out of her mind as they went into the house.

"Not long. He got here on Saturday." Ash was all business now.

"Jesus. Did he even have time to unpack?"

"According to Jake, there's clothing from an overnight bag in the master bedroom and a shaving kit in the master bath. Either he wasn't planning to stay long or expected to buy whatever else he needed."

They walked from the foyer into the great room, a living and dining area that lived up to its name; it was not only a huge, open space but had been decorated with high-end products and furnishings and the very latest thing in amenities, including a large-screen plasma TV and a fireplace.

Momentarily distracted yet again, Riley indicated the fireplace. "Does anybody around here even use those?"

"We have a few chilly nights in winter. Not many, as a rule, but a few. Rentals with fireplaces do better in winter, obviously."

"Oh. Makes sense, I guess." **Focus, dammit. Focus.** Riley looked around at what was a very large house, clearly designed to hold a dozen or more people. "How many bedrooms?"

"Six. And seven baths. There's a level below this floor and one above."

Frowning, Riley went over to one of two refrigerators and opened it. "Curiouser and curiouser," she said. "It's stocked." She checked the other one. "Both of them are stocked. Bet the pantry is too."

"Yeah, Jake said the local grocery store made a big delivery on Saturday, before Tate arrived. Prearranged. People go online and make out

their shopping lists ahead of time; the store de-
livers as soon as the cleaning crew is out behind
the previous tenants. The delivery people put
away perishables and leave the rest on the
counter for the renter."

"I had no idea you could do that," Riley said,
closing the fridge door. "I just stopped on the
way in and bought what I needed."

"Frozen pizza and PowerBars mostly. Yeah, I
remember."

"If you don't cook, that's what you buy." She
frowned again. "Question is, why did Tate have
so much food delivered? What's in there would
feed a dozen people or more for a couple of
weeks."

"I would say he was expecting company. And
for more than just a meal or two." Ash studied
her. "Are you getting anything clairvoyantly?"

"I haven't tried. Yet." As difficult as it was for
her to concentrate, Riley was more than a little
bit wary of dropping her guard.

Assuming she still **had** a guard, which was
probably arguable.

"So what's the plan?" Ash was still watching
her. "I don't know much about this kind of
thing, but I'm guessing the guy didn't leave a lot
of his own . . . energy . . . here anyway, not con-

sidering how little time he spent here. A cleaning crew was here the day he checked in, and
Jake's forensics team is neater than most and
clean up after themselves, so this place has pretty
much been spit-shined."

Riley wondered if he was offering her an out
because he was afraid she'd fail—or afraid she'd
succeed.

She wasn't sure which one **she** was afraid of.

"Where's the master?" she asked.

"Usually has some of the best views, so I'm
guessing upstairs," Ash replied. He led the way,
adding over his shoulder, "It's not that I mean
to hover, but I'd rather stick close just in case."

"I appreciate that," Riley said. Because she did.

The master bedroom was spacious for a
rental, and boasted both a large adjoining bathroom and a private deck with a—distant—view
of the ocean.

Riley ate a PowerBar and prowled the space,
looking, touching, cautiously trying to open
senses she wasn't sure were doing anything except
barely functioning. She was getting nothing. No
scents, no sounds, no appreciable texture; even
the brightly decorated room looked oddly
washed-out to her.

The strange veil was back, a layer of something indefinable separating her from the world. And it was getting thicker.

Riley was cold. So cold. But she tried not to shiver, tried to keep doing her job.

"He was neat," she said, peering into a closet where a suit jacket and two shirts hung evenly spaced.

"He didn't have time to get messy," Ash pointed out.

Riley opened a dresser drawer and pointed to several pairs of socks and Jockeys, folded precisely. "He was neat."

"Okay, he was neat." Ash paused, then said, "You know, if there's a possible connection between Tate and the people in the Pearson house, why not just follow that lead to get information? Why put yourself through this if you don't have to?"

She looked at him, frowning. "Put myself through this. Does it seem to you this is an effort for me?"

Ash returned her stare for a long moment, then came to her and turned her to face the mirror above the dresser.

"Look," he said.

For just an instant, no more than a split second, Riley thought she saw another woman standing there with Ash behind her, a weird sort of double image, the way slight movement shows as a blur in a photograph.

And then it was gone, and Riley saw herself. With Ash standing behind her, his hands on her shoulders.

At first, she couldn't see whatever it was that caused him concern; the weird veil that had faded colors and muted her other senses lay between her and the mirror, just as it lay between her and the world.

But then, slowly, the veil grew thinner, more wispy. And Riley felt curiously stronger, steadier on her feet. In the reflection she watched, fascinated, as the room behind them became brighter, the colors more vivid. Her pale blue short-sleeved blouse and jeans, Ash's khaki slacks and dark shirt, even his vivid green eyes, all became clearer, sharper.

No longer distant.

No longer out of her reach.

She looked at his hands on her shoulders, and her scattered thoughts began to focus.

Damn, Bishop was right. Again.

"Look at your face," Ash began. "It—"

Riley held up a hand to stop him. "Wait. Just a minute." Taking the chance of further depleting her energy reserves, she concentrated on listening, on reaching out to hear the ocean, too far away from this house to be easily discernible through insulated walls and triple-pane glass.

Almost immediately, as though a door had opened just yards from the beach, she heard the waves, the rhythmic crash of water against earth. She could almost feel the foamy surf lapping around her ankles, smell the slightly fishy salt air.

Her spider sense was back.

She reached farther, tried harder—

—he was already dead by the time she reached the otherwise-deserted clearing.

Smoke from the final glowing embers of the fire curled upward, and the smell of sulfur and blood was almost overpowering. She didn't approach the headless corpse, still dripping blood, but circled the clearing warily, gun in hand and senses flaring.

All her senses.

She wasn't getting much, just faint impressions of dark figures that had moved here, danced here, damned their souls here. The lingering echoes of chanting, and bells, and invocations in Latin.

But no sense of identity, and no real sense

of life. It was . . . weird. As though the ghosts in her mind were only that, unreal figures conjured like a nightmare of images super-imposed on this place.

Yet the corpse was real. He had been tor-tured and killed in this place, without doubt. She knew that if she touched it the body would still be warm.

The blood-spattered rocks were real. The dying fire. The circle of salt she found on the ground.

To sanctify the circle, or protect whoever had stood within it?

She didn't know. And the harder she tried to open her senses, the more Riley had the uneasy realization of . . . a barrier. There was a muffled quality to the normal night sounds she heard. The acrid stench of sulfur was fading more rapidly than she expected, more rapidly than it should have, and the blood—

She couldn't smell the blood anymore.

Riley looked quickly at the corpse, half-convinced she would find that it had been conjured by her own imagination. But the lifeless body hung there still.

She took a step toward it and then froze,

abruptly aware that she had stepped inside the circle for the first time.

The unbroken circle.

Utter silence closed around her, and her vision began to dim. She tried to move but couldn't, couldn't even lift her gun or make a sound, and the darkness became a tangible thing, wrapping her in a cold embrace she couldn't escape.

There was barely time for the first faint hints of comprehension to fight their way through the dark fog of her mind.

Barely time for her to begin to understand what was happening to her.

And then the force of a train slammed into her, hot agony blazing along her nerves, bright fire in her mind. For an eternal instant she felt herself literally connected to the ground beneath her feet, a spear of burning energy impaling the earth.

Discharging all her strength into it, like a lightning rod—

"Riley."

She realized she had closed her eyes only when his voice pulled her back to the room in which they were standing, and she opened them to see the reflection of his worried frown. And feel his hands still on her shoulders but tighter now, almost holding her upright.

With an effort, she steadied herself. "Sorry. But, Ash—"

"Look at your face, Riley."

She realized she had been looking at his, and turned her gaze instead to her own.

The earlier chill came back with a vengeance.

Her face looked . . . gaunt. Not so much as if she had aged, but as though she were starving.

Riley lifted probing fingers, shaping the sharp cheekbones and the hollows beneath them. Hollows that hadn't been anywhere near this pronounced only hours before.

"This isn't normal," Ash said, his voice roughening for the first time.

"No . . . it isn't **natural,**" she corrected slowly.

"What's the difference? Christ, Riley, you're burning calories so fast there's no way you can keep up with the demands of your body. You've got to stop pushing yourself, stop trying to use abilities that Taser must have destroyed."

Still looking at that haggard face in the mirror, at eyes staring back at her with a feverish intensity that belied the chill shivering through her body, Riley said, "I don't think that's it. The start of it, maybe. Probably. The first step. Only it wasn't intended to take me out of the game. It wasn't intended to kill me. It was intended to weaken me. To make me vulnerable."

"What are you talking about?"

"The biggest piece of the puzzle, Ash. It's me."

He turned her around to face him, keeping his hands on her shoulders. "How could that be? Honey, all this occult shit started weeks before you got here. Weeks before you had any intention of coming here."

"But it was a dandy lure, wasn't it?" She was working it out even as she spoke, slowly putting together what had seemed to be disparate facts and events. Ragged memories and uncertain visions. "Possible occult activity in a sleepy little seaside community, nothing violent or vicious, no need for a whole team to come investigate. Just one. Just me. Just the unit's expert in the occult."

His hands tightened on her shoulders. "Gordon Skinner is the one who called you down here. Someone you trust. Right?"

"Yes. And that had to be part of the plan. Going into a situation knowing a trusted friend had my back if necessary, I wouldn't have felt any hesitation in coming alone."

"Are you saying he's involved?"

"No." Riley shook her head, hesitated, then lifted her hands to grasp Ash's wrists. Almost instantly, she began to feel a little stronger. Her head was clearer, thoughts and conclusions falling rapidly into place in her mind.

She was right about this.

It's about connections. And this is a connection I need to work this case. Hell, maybe I need it just to survive.

"No, I don't believe Gordon's part of it. Willingly, at least. Knowingly. But he could be a pawn. Maneuvered just like so many other people and events have been maneuvered."

"Riley—"

"Ash, this isn't **natural,** what's happening to me. It shouldn't be happening. What damage the Taser did my brain should be repairing, even now. Which means there's something else here, something else affecting me. Something that was here from the beginning. Stealing my strength, my abilities, playing with my memories, my sense of time, of what's real and what isn't."

"What could be doing all that?"

"Negative energy. Dark energy. Created, controlled, channeled, directed by someone."

"Another psychic? You said that wasn't likely."

"I don't think it is another psychic. Or at least

not like any psychic I've ever heard of. I think this is someone who went looking in very dark places for enough power to achieve whatever it is they're after."

"Which is?"

Slowly, she said, "Whatever it is, I think it has everything to do with me. I had a flash of memory just now. At least, I'm pretty sure it was a memory. Of Sunday night. Of reaching the clearing, finding the body hanging there, already dead. I was alone. But I felt uneasy, my senses didn't seem to be working well. And then I stepped inside the circle."

"The circle made up of salt?"

"Yeah. It had been left unbroken. When I stepped over it, stepped into the circle . . . I was trapped. Caught. I couldn't move. Couldn't hear. Everything was going dark. That was when I was Tasered. I was held in place like a fly in resin, then deliberately electrocuted."

"Held? How? Are you talking about elemental forces? Or something supernatural?"

"Both. I'm talking about someone with the ability to harness negative energy. Torturing and killing a human being? That's about as negative as it gets. Suffering generates power. Dying violently creates an incredible amount of power; destruction always creates something to replace what's destroyed, even if it's only sheer energy. Couple that with a black-occult ceremony intended to generate even more dark energy, and you'd have enough psychic poison to cripple even a strong enemy."

"You?"

"I'm the one who walked into the trap. I'm the one who woke up crippled."

"I'd argue with that assessment, but never mind. You're saying it was all designed for that end? To disable and then harm you? Using energy?"

His doubt was clear, and Riley hardly blamed him for it. What she was suggesting **was** incredible.

I bet that's the conclusion I'd come to just before the blackouts, what I began to explain in the report, that—incredible as it seemed— someone was manipulating energy deliberately, dark energy, and that it had all been a setup to get me here. And then destroy me.

But there was something Riley's enemy hadn't counted on, she was almost sure of it. Something she herself was only beginning to understand.

The wild card was Ash.

R iley—"

"Ash, there's nothing magical about it. Nothing unnatural, except in how it was used. It's . . . the corruption of a perfectly human ability to manipulate electrical and magnetic fields. We all do it every day in small ways; our bodies are filled with electrical impulses firing off all the time. Automatic. Unthinking. But in this case, someone has found a way to absorb dark energy, negative energy, and use it, even direct it back outward for a specific purpose."

"Riley, is that even possible? To absorb energy from something else? From someone else?"

She drew a breath and let it out slowly. "I really hope this doesn't creep you out. Take a closer look at my face."

He did, and his frown deepened. "You look . . . your face doesn't seem so thin. So exhausted as it did a few minutes ago. What—"

Ash was nothing if not quick. His gaze dropped to her hands gripping his wrists—and he got it.

"Wait a minute. You're pulling energy from me? From us?"

Glad he had added that last bit, she nodded. "I'm pretty sure, yeah. Feeling stronger by the moment. It's not something I've ever been able to do before. And we've tried, believe me."

"We?"

"The SCU. One of the ways Bishop matches some partners is by complementing abilities. Matching a strength with a weakness. My weakness has always been that I use so much energy during a case I end up exhausted, sometimes at very critical moments. So he tried matching me with team members who have . . . energy to spare. But that never worked, because I could never tap another source, even someone I trusted, someone entirely willing to share. Bishop said—"

"What did he say?"

Riley hesitated. But however uncertain her memory, her body knew, had clearly known for some time, at least one truth.

"He said there's a rare kind of trust he's only seen between some siblings and lovers. A trust so deep and so absolute that all the barriers that separate people from each other disappear. He's like that with his wife; they share their thoughts, their abilities, everything they are. Like two halves of a single soul."

She drew another breath and finished, "He said I'd probably find that when I fell in love. And if I did, I'd also find an amazing source of strength I'd be able to tap into. He and Miranda are precognitive, so when he says **probably,** you can pretty much take it to the bank."

When Ash didn't immediately respond, she added hastily, "It's not like I'm an energy vampire or anything like that, it's just—"

Ash kissed her. Long, slow, and impossibly deep.

When she could, Riley murmured, "Wow."

He smiled, but his voice was husky when he said, "Honey, the first time we made love, we generated enough heat to ignite a small star. So believe me when I say that I understand how human beings can create and channel energy.

Especially the right human beings in the right combination."

She cleared her throat. "Man, I wish I remembered that."

"I'll remind you tonight. If not sooner." He kissed her again, briefly this time, and added, "Whatever energy you're drawing from me at the moment, I'm more than willing to give, especially if it's helping you. Besides, far as I can tell, it's nothing I can't spare."

"No, you're one of those people who have . . . excess. More than you need or would ever use." Something she had sensed in him from that first moment at the crime scene, memories or no memories, that palpable force of intensity radiating from him. "You have to buy a new watch every month or so, because they always stop running, and I'll bet you have problems with ATMs and other computers."

"I do, as a matter of fact. On both counts."

"Some people produce a lot of energy and can't really productively channel the excess. Others burn it off quickly. Even too quickly."

"So we match perfectly. What I don't understand is why you're just now realizing you can tap into my energy. Correct me if I'm wrong, but up until now, I was under the impression

that I was one of the major **drains** on your energy. Or our relationship was, at any rate."

"You're not wrong." She thought about it.
"My best guess is that because of my uneasiness
about not being in control I wasn't able to try to
tap into your energy, consciously or even sub-
consciously, until I was desperate. Until my reserves had gotten so low it was a matter of sheer
survival. You showed me my reflection, and on
a very primitive level I realized I had to reach
out—or die."

With a half smile, he said, "Have you talked
to somebody about these control issues of yours?"

She couldn't help but laugh, albeit briefly.
"Yeah. Besides, you're just the same. It's hard
taking a leap of faith."

"And putting your fate in someone else's
hands. Yes, I know. You were fairly pissed off
about it."

Riley had to laugh again. "I'll just bet I was.
But it does explain some of this uncharacteristic
behavior of mine, huh? I've never been in love
before."

"So you said. Scowling at me."

"I didn't."

"Yes, you did. Scowled. Not that I cared. I've
never been in love before either, and I was a bit

cranky about it in the beginning myself. You asked about how open our relationship was around here; I don't think either of us was able to hide much, and we were . . . fierce . . . about each other from the moment we met."

"The moment?"

"Yes. Unfortunately, you were on a date with Jake when we met. He introduced us."

Riley winced. "Ouch."

"Yeah."

"Well, no wonder he's been . . . difficult."

"I've tried to make allowances," Ash admitted.

She pondered for a moment, but then shook her head. "I can't think about that right now. We'll mend fences or build bridges or do whatever we need to do with Jake later."

With a lawyer's ability to stay on subject when necessary, Ash said, "Okay, so back to your belief that losing energy the way you have is due to someone else's influence."

"Yes. If I'm right about that—and I think I am—then the purpose of all this ritualistic occult activity, including the murder or murders, isn't so much a smoke screen as it is a device."

"To tap into dark energy and use it."

Riley nodded.

"But isn't that always the purpose of black-oc-cult activities?"

"You could get arguments either way. In my experience, most practitioners are more inter-ested in flouting everything even remotely tradi-tional in the way of religion, giving God the finger like gleefully misbehaving children, and convincing themselves it's liberating to be able to act like animals."

"Dressing up in robes and screwing in a coffin?"

"Yeah, basically. Only without the human sacrifice."

"So, usually, nobody dies."

"Virtually always, nobody dies. It's rare that anybody bleeds. The only exceptions I know of have been cases when someone genuinely evil is leading or otherwise controlling a group. As in sadistic killer types. A few have tried the Char-lie Manson bit, convincing followers to kill for them, but most like to do the killing them-selves. It just amuses them to dress up in robes and pretend they're summoning or channeling Satan and it's all for the noble cause of enlight-ening the ignorant."

Ash was frowning. "Okay. So if human sacri-fice was only a . . . by-product of the ritual to create energy, and if you don't believe Wesley Tate was killed the way he was as a smoke screen to hide a murderer with a motive, then—"

"Who he was may not be so important as I first believed." It was Riley's turn to frown. "But he's part of the puzzle nevertheless. He fits in somewhere, and not just because he provided his lifeblood for some ritual. Victims are chosen. No matter how insane the killer, their logic makes sense in their reality."

"So the next step is talking to the group at the Pearson house."

"They are the only avowed satanists we know of so far. And even if they missed the preliminaries—which is troubling and not helping me put the pieces together—they were certainly here in time to participate in whatever happened Sunday night." She frowned.

"What?"

"That memory flash I just had. I don't know how trustworthy it was, since I was just getting my strength back, but **if** it was what really happened to me on Sunday night, then when I got to the clearing I had the weird feeling the whole thing had been staged. Or manipulated somehow. The body was real enough, but everything else, even my sense of an earlier ceremony there, had a feeling of unreality about it."

Ash shook his head slightly, not following.

"You said it yourself. Conspiracy in cases of murder really is rare. Maybe there was no conspiracy. Whatever occult ceremonies may or may not have taken place here might have all concluded without a murder."

"And the murder took place later, committed by a single individual?"

"Why not? The satanists have their fun and harmless ritual, dance and chant around the fire, drink a lot of wine and have a fair amount of sex, then go home to sleep it off. The killer comes back later and does his thing, staging it so that it appears to be part of what took place. Ritual. He uses the place and the murder as a means to help generate more negative energy, both through that act and by scaring the shit out of the populace. And he keeps us distracted. So we waste time looking in the wrong places, asking the wrong questions."

"Like who has a motive to murder Wesley Tate?"

"Maybe."

Slowly, Ash said, "If this killer has the ability to tap into energy, of places or rituals or whatever, and channel it, use it, then **something** has to be driving him. You don't just wake up one day and decide there are better ways of literally destroying people than using guns or knives."

"No. Even if it's a natural gift, the time and effort required to learn to control it . . . Channeling raw energy is really not that much fun. You'd have to be strongly motivated."

"Maybe by hate?"

"That," Riley said, "would probably do it."

"So the real question is—who might hate you enough to do all this in order to destroy you."

"Yeah," Riley said. "That is the question."

"My bet," Jake said to Steve, "is that forensics will place at least some members of your group in that clearing. Preliminary tests indicate both semen and vaginal secretions from a number of different . . . donors . . . on the ground out there. What, Satan doesn't let you bring a blanket to the party?"

"Sheriff," Steve said calmly, "whatever we may have been doing on Sunday evening, everyone in this house was **in** this house well before midnight. We had a big pizza delivery around eleven; I'm sure that can be verified by the restaurant and by the guy who carried in six large pizzas."

"So? Wesley Tate died sometime between two

and six A.M., which means any or all of you had plenty of time to finish your pizza and return to the clearing."

"I never said we were at the clearing."

"We'll soon find out, won't we? Because Riley's statement that you spoke to Wesley Tate before you arrived here, coupled with your own statements to local citizens that you and your group practice Satanism, are enough for the judge to issue a warrant compelling all of you to submit to DNA testing."

When Steve sent a betrayed glance her way, Riley said, "Sorry, Steve, but a man's dead. We have to find out who murdered him and why. We **will** find out. If you and your people had nothing to do with it, now's the time to convince us."

Jenny spoke up then to say, "I still believe we should have our lawyer present."

Riley studied the dark woman thoughtfully. She was the only member of the group other than Steve who had anything at all to say; the other ten people—five men and five women—seated in the great room of their rental house were all silent and fairly expressionless.

They were a rather varied group, ranging from mid-twenties to nearing retirement age, but otherwise looked like any other visitors to

Opal Island in their bright-colored shorts and thin tops, with most sporting at least faint cases of sunburn.

Riley was picking up a general low-level anxiety in the room, which made perfect sense given the situation, but nothing to make her overly suspicious of the group as a whole.

Jenny, though . . . Jenny was different.

Jenny was worried.

. . . not what I wanted. How could it be? But . . . I didn't know. I thought his mind had finally been opened, that he . . . I thought he had changed.

Interesting. And told Riley a lot. But before she could follow that lead, Jake was pressing again, determined to get his questions answered now that they had a tangible connection between these people and the murdered man.

"People who have nothing to hide don't need a lawyer," he said. "No offense, Ash."

"None taken." Ash was sitting slightly behind Riley at the big dining table, their chairs turned so that they faced the group ranged around the living room, and only he and Riley knew that the hand he rested casually on her shoulder was neither casual nor possessive but a necessary conduit between them.

And a vital source of strength for Riley.

Sitting on the other side of the table, Leah had noted the contact with a smile; Jake appeared more irritated every time he looked their way.

He doesn't hide his thoughts very well. Definitely doesn't like me being with Ash. But whether it's because of me or because of Ash, I can't really tell. . . .

Why am I thinking about this shit?

"I think Jenny's right," Steve said, clearly uneasy now. "Why don't you go away and get your warrant, Sheriff, and we'll get our lawyer, and then we'll see."

Riley didn't have to be able to read him to know Jake was on the point of saying something hotheaded and completely unnecessary, so she spoke before he could.

"Steve, I promised your group wouldn't be harassed and I'll make sure that doesn't happen. But we need to know what you know. Wesley Tate was the one who called you, yes?"

"Yeah."

Ignoring Jake's affronted body language as he stood before the entertainment center and in what should have been the focal point of the group, Riley continued to calmly question Steve.

"But you had never met him?"

"No."

"Then why were you even willing to talk to him? You must have gotten plenty of calls from reporters on fishing expeditions, calls from others intent on causing you trouble. What made the call from Tate so different?"

"I told you. He knew people."

"What people?"

"Dammit, Riley, you can't expect me to answer that. Some of them don't practice openly."

"Gee, I wonder why?" Jake muttered.

Instantly, Steve said, "Because of suspicious people like you, Sheriff. We're **supposed** to have religious freedom in this country, you know."

Before Jake could follow what would certainly be a hotly impassioned tangent, Riley surprised most of the people in the room by asking a quiet question.

"How long had you been divorced, Jenny?"

Going pale beneath her tan, Jenny said, "What?"

"You heard me. Wesley Tate was your ex-husband, wasn't he?"

Steve reached for his partner's hand. "She doesn't have to answer that."

"Steve, don't be an idiot." Riley kept her voice matter-of-fact. "A connection like this would certainly show up in a deep background check, so why try to hide or deny it? Besides, they were legally divorced, right? So she wouldn't benefit financially from his death. And if they've been divorced as long as I think they have, any old hurts and resentments are undoubtedly past and forgotten. Jenny has no motive to have murdered Wesley Tate."

At least . . . I don't think she has. Focus, dammit!

Steve frowned but didn't try to stop her when Jenny finally spoke.

"We were divorced more than ten years ago," she said, something of relief in her voice. "Married less than five. He . . . couldn't accept my nontraditional lifestyle choices."

Flashing back to her dream—or memory—of seeing this woman serving as a naked altar in a ceremony about as far from **traditional** as it was possible to get, Riley wasn't sure she blamed him. But all she said was, "And since then? Any contact with him?"

"Not much. He sort of made it a habit to call around Christmas, just to check and see how I was doing."

"Do satanists celebrate Christmas?" Jake wondered aloud, either too intrigued by the question or too pissed at having the interview taken out of his hands to care about going off topic.

"Not the way Christians do," Steve said flatly.

Riley got them back on track. "So why did he contact you out of the blue?" she asked Jenny.

"He **said** he just wanted to help. There'd been . . . a few incidents, as Steve told you, where we were living near Columbia. Made the local news. Wes saw it, he said. He was worried things would get worse, that there was a general climate of intolerance in the area. All the supposed occult stuff during the last year or so here in the Southeast."

Riley nodded. "Yeah, we investigated some of that." **Bishop reminded me about that too. But it was all bogus. Or most of it was bogus. . . .** "So Tate was worried about you. And?"

"And he said he knew of a safe haven. He told us about this house, said it was a nice, peaceful place with gorgeous views and that nobody would bother us. He said he knew—for certain—that there were like-minded people living in the area."

"But he didn't name names."

"No. Afraid not."

"And you still haven't been contacted by any of these like-minded people?"

"No."

"Okay," Riley said. "Did he say he'd meet you here?"

"He said he might spend some time here on the island, that maybe we could get together and talk," Jenny replied. "But it was all very casual, nothing at all set in stone. He said he'd call if he did come. He never called."

"And you didn't suspect he might be the man killed on Sunday night?"

"No. Why would I?"

Jake broke in again to say, "Well, excuse me, but you didn't seem all that surprised **or** broken up when we told you it was him."

"Not all of us show everything we feel, Sheriff," she said, rather pointedly scanning him up and down and then looking away dismissively.

Riley was conscious of a fleeting wish that she and Ash had come out here alone to talk to these people, but reminded herself silently of her unofficial status. And spoke quickly before Jake could explode—as he showed every sign of doing.

"Did you really think he'd changed his mind after all these years?" she asked Jenny.

The dark woman hesitated, then smiled faintly. "No. Not really. I wanted to think so, but it was far more likely he just wanted to find out if I was still serious about my lifestyle. He never remarried. I don't think he ever really gave up on us."

"Which," Jake said to Steve, "gives **you** a motive to murder."

"Hardly," Steve said. "You see, I **know** Jenny is committed to our lifestyle."

"Assuming we accept that," Riley said without looking at Jake, "you still need to account for your presence in the clearing where Wesley Tate's body was found on Monday morning. You **were** there Sunday night, weren't you?"

"**If** we were, it was only to perform a sunset consecration ritual," he said.

Riley knew how much rituals could vary from group to group, but she was picking up enough from Steve to feel fairly confident in saying, "No fire except a candle, black clothing rather than robes. Salt to form the circle and chanting inside it. It wasn't, strictly speaking, a sexual ritual, but at least three couples . . . indulged. You had intended to use the stone altar in future, more elaborate rituals but wanted to make sure the area was consecrated first."

"That was the plan," he admitted. "Until some

lunatic decided to sacrifice a human being. Believe me, any rituals we conduct now will be private and inside the house. With the blinds closed."

"You have a permit for a bonfire tomorrow night," Jake said.

"We're going to roast marshmallows, Sheriff. You're welcome to come, but bring your own stick."

Riley decided that Jake's blood pressure probably couldn't take any more and rose to her feet. "We may want to talk to you again later," she told Steve. "In the meantime, I'll suggest again that it might be wise to stick close to home for the duration."

Steve frowned but nodded, and Jenny merely said quietly, "Thanks, Riley."

19

Jake maintained his silence until they reached their vehicles, and then demanded, "Jesus, Ash, can't you keep your hands off her for five minutes?"

Holding Riley's hand, Ash smiled and said, "I really can't."

Leah coughed to cover the beginning of a laugh, and then said hastily to Riley, "You don't think they're involved, do you?"

"I think we were meant to believe so, but . . . no." Riley shook her head. "I think whoever killed him is the person who advised Wesley Tate to invite his ex-wife and her group here."

Jake said, "Wait a minute. Are you telling me

I've got **another** group of satanists around here?"

"Not a group, no. That would be stretching the odds past breaking, I think. Maybe two people, a team, more probably just one."

"Using this group as a diversion," Ash suggested.

"A diversion from what? Some other reason Tate was killed?"

"Well," Riley pointed out, "it has worked. I mean, first we were running around trying to find out who he was, and now the obvious suspects don't look like such a good fit. We all know the longer it takes to solve a murder the colder the trail gets."

She wasn't about to confide in the sheriff her suspicions that she herself was the linchpin of the entire situation, the target of someone's rage. What evidence she had of such a conclusion was something he was not at all likely to understand, much less accept.

"Stalling tactics?" Jake shook his head. "Then why leave him hanging over that altar? Why not just dump his body in the ocean or bury it somewhere? Since he was never reported missing, we probably wouldn't even have known to start looking for him until new tenants showed up at that house. **And** why torture and decapitate him?"

"It was meant to look like an occult-related death," Riley said. "That doesn't mean it actually was one."

"So far, we haven't looked past the occult as a motive," Ash said neutrally.

With a definite growl in his voice, Jake said, "I've got a motive for you. It might have been dressed up in black robes and salt circles, but I've got a dead man **and** his ex-wife both on this island, and that can't be a coincidence. Look, spouses kill each other all the time. And, yes, even years after they divorce. Maybe he just inherited family money and she's still named in his will. Maybe there's a kid involved somewhere and it's a custody issue. Maybe Smiling Steve in there is a hell of a lot more jealous than he let on."

Riley frowned, then shrugged. "It's your investigation, Jake. I just don't believe anybody in that house killed Wesley Tate."

"Then **who**?" Jake practically roared.

"I don't know. Yet."

He settled his shoulders with the air of a man about to do things. Possibly intensely physical things. "Fine. I'm sure you won't mind if I dig a little deeper with those background checks."

"I think that's an excellent idea. Because there **is** another connection between that group, Wesley Tate, and either Castle or Opal Island."

"What sort of connection?" Leah asked.

"Find that," Riley said, "and we'll have a very big piece of the puzzle."

Jake motioned for Leah to get into their Jeep, then said to the other two, "So what're you going to be doing in the meantime?"

Riley knew Ash was tempted to reply that it involved nakedness and the Kama Sutra, and replied hastily, "Oh, nosing around. Trying to find out if there really are other occult practitioners in the area."

"Good luck with that. Let me know if you find anything."

"Will do." She watched the sheriff's department Jeep pull away, then looked at Ash with lifted brows. "You were a lot of help."

"I've discovered I enjoy pissing Jake off. It's like having a new toy."

She had to laugh, but added, "Well, stop it, okay? At least until we figure out what's going on. It's distracting."

Sobering, he said, "Yeah, you're right. I did

notice that you haven't been in any hurry to tell Jake what you really suspect is going on here."

"It's not like I have any proof. And it all sounds so incredibly Byzantine, for someone to go to all this trouble to lure me here just to mess with my head. The more I think about it, the more unlikely it seems."

Ash glanced back toward the house, then led Riley around to the passenger side of the Hummer. "Maybe we should talk about this on the way," he said.

Riley waited until he joined her in the vehicle and had the engine going before saying, "On the way where?"

"You tell me. How is the head, by the way? You seemed to be picking up on undercurrents back there, if not actual thoughts."

"Actual thoughts," she confirmed. "Jenny's, anyway. Faint and fuzzy, but perceptible. So the head is definitely improving. On every count except memory; the blackouts are still blanks, and my time here before the Taser attack is still weirdly distant and definitely spotty."

Ash guided her hand to rest on his thigh. "So energy isn't a problem now?"

"Not so much. But I am hungry." She thought about it. "I guess food is still the fuel for the physical furnace, but your energy is helping with the psychic end of things."

"As long as it's helping." He glanced at his watch and put the Hummer in gear. "Lunch first, I think. I know you wanted to talk to Gordon this afternoon. What else?"

"I want to look at those arson sites again. Something's been nagging at me." She looked at him and, very conscious of his hard thigh beneath her hand, added dryly, "We'll get to the Kama Sutra later."

Ash smiled. "You really are getting back to normal."

"Because I knew what you were thinking?"

"From the first time we touched," he confirmed. "You said it wasn't complete thoughts, like conversation, just the general impression of what was on my mind at any given moment."

"And you're okay with that?"

"Actually," he said, "it's been a bit of a revelation. And a relief. I never have to explain myself or what I mean when we're talking."

"There's always a downside," she warned.

"Yeah, been there."

Riley lifted a curious brow.

"I had one of those random sexist-pig thoughts all men occasionally have. According to you."

"Must have been a doozy if I called you on it.

I'm mostly used to them. The military life, you know. And growing up with brothers."

"Um. Let's just say it led to a . . . spirited . . . debate. And great sex afterward."

"Well, at least we didn't go to bed mad. My mother insists that's the secret to happy relationships. Never go to bed mad."

Ash smiled, but said, "I know this psychic deal with us is one-sided, but I don't have to be clairvoyant or telepathic to know that all this casual humor is more of that dandy camouflage you pull on the way other people pull on their socks. So what's really bothering you?"

Riley looked at her hand on his thigh, to any outward observer the casually intimate touch of a lover but to her a connection that might well be vital to her very survival, and spoke slowly.

"When I woke up after that Taser attack, it was like there was a kind of veil between me and the world. Everything was . . . muffled. Muted. Faded. Once I was able to tap into your energy, that veil began to disappear."

"But?" he prompted.

"Back there, in the Pearson house, a couple of times I . . . felt myself starting to drift. Even with you touching me, even with plenty of energy, it was difficult to focus."

"Any idea why?"

"That's what worries me. It felt like something outside myself."

"But you were picking up information outside yourself while we were there. How was this different?"

"Because it wasn't just there in my mind, like the clairvoyant bits or Jenny's thoughts. It was . . . pulling at me."

"Sounds like a confirmation of your theory."

"Yeah. Which is all fine and dandy, except that if I felt the attempt, whoever was on the other end felt the failure of it."

"You mean, if there really is somebody out there trying to mess with your mind—"

"Then whoever it is not only is still trying, but may now be aware that the attacks are less successful. That I somehow have the means to fight back. And I'm guessing the next attempt will be the sort with teeth and claws."

"You know," Gordon said after having been brought up-to-date, "I really wish now I hadn't called you down here, babe."

Riley shrugged. "I have an enemy, that's clear. If it hadn't been here, this way, it would have been somewhere else and maybe another way.

I'm glad it was here, Gordon." She nodded toward Ash.

"Well, I'm glad for you, on that account. You been needing somebody to run in harness with as long as I've known you." He looked at Ash, adding, "A lightning rod for trouble. Can't say you haven't been warned."

"Trouble she can mostly handle," Ash pointed out dispassionately.

"Yeah. But, see, the thing is, it never occurs to her that maybe she **shouldn't** handle everything that comes along all by her lonesome. That it's not just about what she **can** do, but also about what she **should** do. And sometimes that means acceptin' a helping hand."

"Stop talking about me as if I weren't here, Gordon. Besides, I have help now—you two."

"And you managed to keep both of us out of the loop for the better part of three weeks," he countered.

"Okay, okay. But you're in the loop now, so some brainstorming would be helpful. I hope."

They were seated around a patio table and under the shade of an umbrella behind Gordon's house and near his dock, a place which provided both privacy and a refuge from the hot afternoon sun.

Gordon pursed his lips. "I guess you've already made your enemies list?"

"More or less." She and Ash had discussed that over lunch. "You know as well as I do that I made a few in the army when I worked intelligence and investigation. And since I joined the SCU I've helped put away some genuinely evil scum. But that's the thing—they **were** put away. Or killed."

"None of them on the loose?"

"Not that I can find out. We went back to my place after lunch long enough for me to get online and check the databases."

"Which she had apparently done before, during one of the blackouts," Ash added.

Gordon frowned. "So you been thinking about enemies for a while now."

Riley nodded. "Looks that way. My computer log shows I not only checked but also double-checked the whereabouts of every perp I helped put away during the last five years. They're all dead or safely locked up still."

"Maybe you need to go back further."

With a slight grimace, Riley said, "That takes me back to active service overseas, when enemies were all over the place. But I doubt any of them would target me specifically, at least to this extent; they saw the uniform, not Riley Crane."

"Then maybe this isn't personal."

"It **feels** personal. Very personal. Very specific in terms of an attack. Like somebody figured out what makes me tick and deliberately aimed to take away all my defenses. Not just the spooky senses, but even my memories, my sense of self. Gordon, somebody has been getting inside my **head**."

"You sure about that, babe? I mean, no disrespect, but, fact is, your memory is shaky and the spooky senses are AWOL, so—"

"They aren't AWOL anymore, thanks to Ash. Not a hundred percent yet, but getting there." She sent Ash a quick smile when he reached over and took her hand.

"So what're they telling you?" Gordon asked.

"That I'm part of the puzzle. Maybe even the reason all this is happening. That somebody has been getting inside my head."

"And using black-occult energy to do it?"

"At least partly." Riley frowned. "I've been trying to think of a possible enemy with that sort of knowledge, because it really is specialized and not something you read about in a textbook. But I've only encountered two black-occult practitioners during investigations, and both of them are dead."

Ash said, "You only mentioned one when we talked at lunch. The last time you investigated supposed occult activity, a few months back, and found a serial killer operating."

She nodded. "He wasn't psychic but had learned how to channel dark energy pretty damn effectively nevertheless. At least to the extent of being able to . . . oh, cloud my senses, for want of a better phrase."

"Which is what this enemy seems able to do," Ash pointed out.

"Yeah, but aside from the fact that I was present when the guy was autopsied, his effect on my senses was very different from what I'm going through now."

"Maybe because he didn't Taser you first," Gordon suggested.

That possibility gave Riley pause. "Well . . . could be. If you start out with an artificial disruption of the electrical activity of the brain, any additional sort of attack is bound to have a more extreme result. On the other hand . . ."

"What?" Ash was watching her intently.

"I'm just wondering if the Taser **was** the initial attack. If whoever this is has the ability to channel dark energy, then maybe he was having an effect on me from the very beginning. Blocking me somehow, distracting me. Slowing my reaction time, even clouding my judgment. Maybe that was why I had the sense there was something wrong here, despite the lack of any real evidence of occult activity—before we found Tate's body, at least."

Gordon shook his head slightly, and said, "I've seen your spooky senses at work long enough not to easily doubt them, babe, but I got to wonder this time. If you've got an enemy deadly enough to set all this up as a lure to get you here and then spend weeks messing with your head and your life, how can you not know who he is?"

"I thought I did know," Riley admitted. "Especially when I found out about the serial the police are after in Charleston. But it can't be him, that's why I didn't mention him. He's dead." **Bishop said so, and I can trust that.**

"Who did you suspect?" Ash asked.

"The only other serial I've ever encountered who had an interest in the occult," Riley said. "John Henry Price."

She thought for an instant it was only her hand that had gone cold suddenly, but then she realized it was Ash, his hand, and when she looked at his face, the coldness went all the way to her bones.

"You knew him," she said.

"Still no luck?"

Leah looked up from her desk, surprised that the sheriff had come to her rather than summon her to his office. "The background checks? No, nothing new. We do have confirmation of Jenny Cole's marriage to Wesley Tate—and their divorce. Just as she said."

"Shit." Jake scowled. "There's gotta be something more."

"Sorry, but so far nada. None of the group was anywhere in the area when the arson took place, so we can't connect any of them to those crimes. So far, all the background checks are coming up clean, just like the preliminary ones did. A couple of watch groups that keep an eye on occult activities have these people on their lists, but nothing violent has ever been reported, much less proved."

Still scowling, Jake said, "What about the background check on Tate? Any reason somebody'd want to kill him?"

"Nothing's come up so far."

"Nothing **nothing,** or just nothing you consider motive enough?"

Leah blinked. "Sheriff, as far as we've been able to determine, Wesley Tate was respected in the business community of Charleston and well-liked. He didn't date much, there was no special woman in his life, and the women he had seen in the last year or so were available and without obvious jealous boyfriends, past or present. Everybody liked the guy. Everybody we've talked to seems genuinely shocked he's been killed—especially like that."

"No interest in the occult—despite his ex-wife's **lifestyle**?"

"He was a Baptist. A deacon of his church, and in the family pew every Sunday."

"Including the years they were married?"

"Yes. According to friends and family, he just said she 'wasn't religious' whenever anyone asked. Didn't seem to be a big deal to him, as far as anybody could tell."

"And his will?"

"Bequests to friends and family, most to charity."

"You're kidding."

"No. A half-dozen charities he gave to while he was alive pretty much split his estate now. And, before you ask, his ex-wife was not mentioned. At all. So it looks like Jenny Cole was wrong in believing he was still hoping for a reconciliation."

"Then why'd he invite them here? Come to think of it, why **here**? He didn't live in Castle, on Opal Island. Not a single realtor has him on the books as a previous tenant, right?"

"Right."

"So why here? Why invite them to a place he'd never been to himself?"

"He may have come here before as part of a group," Leah pointed out. "Just never had a previous rental in his name, is all."

Jake grunted. "Or maybe he used his version of your famous pin-in-a-map way of deciding his future."

Leah cleared her throat. "You weren't supposed to hear about that."

"I hear everything. What about Tate's phone records?"

"They back up what Steve Blanton told us. Tate called the house where the group was living outside Columbia."

"Did he call anybody here in Castle? On the island?"

"Not as far as we've been able to determine."

Jake swore, not exactly under his breath.

"Sorry, Sheriff, but it's a dead end. Pardon the pun."

He turned without another word and stalked back toward his office.

Not exactly beneath her own breath, Leah muttered, "Thanks so much, Deputy Wells, nice job. I'm sure talking to all those shocked people wasn't much fun but, hey, them's the breaks."

"I heard that!"

She winced and reached hastily for her phone, rolling her eyes when one of the other deputies in the bullpen grinned at her.

Riley drew her hand away from Ash's, repeating slowly, "You knew him."

"No. And yes."

She waited.

Ash glanced at Gordon, then returned his intent gaze to Riley's face. "I told you I left the Atlanta DA's office because I got tired of the politics."

A memory, wispy and incomplete, flitted through her mind, but Riley made no effort to catch it. She simply waited.

"That was only part of the truth. I also left

because I lost a case I should have won. Before he started his multistate crime spree, John Henry Price was indicted for one count of murder in Atlanta. He was guilty. I couldn't convince a jury."

This time, the memory surfaced clearly in Riley's mind. "I never saw your name. In the case file. Just the notation that Price was only caught once, in Atlanta, more than five years ago. That he stood trial and was acquitted."

His mouth twisting, Ash said, "Circumstantial evidence, not so unusual in a murder trial. But it was enough, I thought. It needed to be. Because I looked that man in the eye . . . and it was like looking into hell itself."

"I know," Riley said. "I tracked him for months. I stood over the hacked-up bodies of his victims. I even got inside his head. Or—he got inside mine. Whichever. By the time I caught up to him, I'm not sure I would have taken him alive even if I'd had the chance."

Ash drew a breath and let it out slowly. "I never saw your name either. Just the newspaper reports that he'd been shot and killed by a federal agent. After killing all those men. Men he never would have killed if I'd done my job."

"It wasn't your fault. He was smart. And he was careful."

"And a good prosecutor wouldn't have let him get away." Ash shrugged. "That's knowledge I live with every day."

After a long moment, Riley reached out and twined her fingers with his once again.

Gordon, who had watched and listened without a word, spoke up then to say slowly, "Am I the only one at this table who doesn't really believe in coincidence?"

Riley shook her head.

"Me either," Ash said. "But I don't see the point. I mean, if we're saying this has something to do with Price."

"He's dead," Riley said. "They never recovered the body, but he's dead." **But hunting him is one of the strongest memories in my mind. I keep reliving that time, like flashbacks. There must be a reason for that. There must be.**

Gordon rubbed his jaw briefly, then said, "You said he got in your head or you got in his. That couldn't still be, right?"

"No. I'd know if that were the case. The unit's had to deal with cases where disembodied energy—a soul, if you like—was able to inhabit and even control another individual."

"Possession?" Ash shook his head. "I didn't think that was possible."

"Stick with me and I'll take you to all the impossible places." Riley sighed. "Possession may be real enough, but I don't see it in this case. Tracking him like I did, whether he was in my head or I was in his, I got to know him very, very well. Price had a soul so black I don't see how it could . . . hide . . . inside another person. Not without giving himself away."

"The murders in Charleston?" Gordon wondered.

"A copycat, according to Bishop."

"And he'd know?"

"He'd know."

"Okay. So maybe you and Ash both having a connection to Price doesn't mean a thing."

"Yeah. And you also believe in the Easter bunny."

"Stranger things have happened," Gordon reminded her. "We've both seen 'em. You say Price is dead and isn't walking around wearing somebody else's body, and that's good enough for me."

"I wish," Riley said, "it was good enough for me."

2½ Years Previously

G ot you," Riley whispered, her eyes fixed on her quarry as he walked briskly along the buckled sidewalk. To call the area shabby would have been a considerable understatement; these dark streets close to the river had pretty much been abandoned long before, when a spring flood had turned this port into no more than an inlet far from the flow of traffic.

It was nearly dawn, the full moon low and bright in the sky, and Riley had been shadowing

Price all night. She had expected him to make a move long before now, but although he had been in and out of several different bars, he had left each one alone. And currently he was headed for what used to be a major dock but was now mostly a rickety wreck with a few small boats tied alongside it.

Riley was conscious of a prickle of unease, but she didn't allow it to cause her to hesitate. She had her weapon in hand and was dressed for tracking tonight in jeans and track shoes, and most importantly, she had John Henry Price in sight.

No way was she backing off just because of some nameless anxiety.

Except . . . after more than a week of glimpses, why had he been so visible tonight? Hell, why had he let himself be seen at all?

Let himself?

You're falling behind, little girl. Can't keep up?

Riley picked up her pace instinctively, pushing the doubts aside. She was **not** going to miss this opportunity.

But . . . why was he moving along the dock now, past the boats, toward the end where there was nothing except murky, slow-moving water?

Because it ends here, little girl.

She hadn't realized they were so close, less than ten yards apart, when he whirled suddenly to face her, his hand lifting, arm extending.

Fast as she was, Riley had barely begun to re-act when the gun bucked in his hand and she felt the bullet slam into her.

You don't get to win, you bastard. You don't get to win!

I've already won, little girl.

But even as she was falling, Riley was taking aim, driven by a determination stronger than anything she'd ever felt before to stop Price here and now. She shot twice as she was falling and three more times after she was on the ground.

And hit Price square in the chest.

His gun fell from his hand and he staggered back a step or two, teetered for a few eternal seconds at the end of the dock, and then went over backward into the sluggishly moving river.

Vaguely aware of the throbbing agony in her left shoulder, Riley lay on the ground and stared at the end of the dock, where Price had stood. Instinctively, she tried to open her mind, her senses, and even as she heard the distant sirens begin wailing, she could have sworn there was a final whisper in her mind.

Don't celebrate . . . just yet . . . little girl.

Present Day

"You didn't tell me the bastard shot you," Ash said.

"I'm telling you now." Riley shrugged. "Left shoulder, and missed anything that really mattered."

"You don't have a scar."

"I don't scar. Otherwise, I'd look like a freakin' road map."

Ash sent her a look. "Gordon wasn't kidding about you being a lightning rod for trouble."

"Not really, no. Consider yourself warned again."

"I consider myself warned." It was nearly four that afternoon when Ash pulled the Hummer into a parking place near the burned remains of the beachfront house apparently torched by an arsonist.

"What do you expect to find?" he asked Riley as they got out of the vehicle.

"I don't know. Probably nothing." She waited until they were ducking under the yellow CAU-

TION tape encircling what was left of the house to add, "Something's been nagging at me since I came here with Jake. I just can't figure out what it is."

Ash took her hand. "I'm sorry I didn't tell you about Price. About the truth of why I left Atlanta."

"You didn't know it would matter."

"That isn't the point."

"Okay. So why didn't you tell me?" She kept her gaze on the charred pilings and mounds of debris before them.

"It wasn't my finest hour, Riley."

"Hey, if you want to swap tales of frustration and failure, I've got a few of my own. We all have them, Ash."

"I doubt yours went on to butcher a score of innocent men."

"Don't be so sure. I was in the army, remember? An officer. Some of my choices and decisions were bound to cost lives." She shook her head. "We can only do the best we can do. And some things have to happen just the way they happen."

He looked at her curiously. "You really believe that."

"I really do."

"And you still believe you were lured here,

that someone has been pulling strings and influencing events?"

Riley nodded.

"Why? Why would someone go to all that trouble?"

"I don't know. Revenge. Payback. Grandstanding." As soon as she said the last word, she was conscious of its incongruity.

"Grandstanding? As in a competition? A contest of skills?"

She tried to focus on something in her own mind, some wispy fragment of knowledge or information she could . . . almost . . . see. There was a question she should have asked someone. A lead she should have followed—

"Riley?"

She blinked and looked up at Ash. "I've missed something. A connection."

"What sort of connection?"

"I'm not sure. Things? Places? People? Damn, why can't I make it come clear in my head?"

He frowned as he studied her. "Are things fuzzy again? Distant, the way they were before?"

"No. Yes. Dammit, I'm not sure. Fuzzy around the edges. I keep coming back to Price. Remembering the hunt for him. That's why I told you, because he's been on my mind the last few days. I can't help wondering . . ."

"Wondering what?"

"Wondering if I missed something. All those months I tracked him. Having his thoughts in my head by the end of it." She turned her gaze back to the burned building. "It became almost surreal. And unbelievably creepy. There was something almost . . . gleeful about him. As if he knew a secret, and knew it was something—"

. . . gleeful about him. As if he knew a secret, and knew it was something—

Riley blinked at the laptop's screen, conscious of a moment of sheer vertigo. Everything in her seemed to be whirling dizzily, time and space and reality tumbling.

She put her hands up to her face, rubbing hard until the whirling stopped, the dizziness faded, then opened her eyes cautiously to peer at the screen again.

Her report.

Report?

More reluctant than she wanted to admit to herself, she shifted her gaze to the lower right-hand corner of the screen, to the date and time.

Two A.M.

Friday morning.

"Oh, Christ," she whispered.

Riley pushed herself up from the table in her beach house, surprised to find that she was fully dressed but not so surprised that she felt shaky and disoriented.

It had been Thursday afternoon, and she'd been at one of the arson sites with Ash, she was sure of that. Looking for answers. They'd been talking, and—

A wave of dizziness swept over her, and she closed her eyes, holding on to the edge of the table, her fingers digging into—

Charred wood.

She stumbled back a step and stared at the debris visible in the glare of a security light. The acrid stench of burned wood stung her nostrils, and she could hear the surf on the other side of the dunes, rolling in close because it was high tide.

She held up her hands and stared at the blackened tips of her fingers for a moment, then looked at the piece of burned wood she had apparently been holding on to.

"Enough," she whispered. "Goddammit, **enough.**"

She didn't dare close her eyes, was almost afraid to blink for fear there'd be another insane shift through space and time.

Only that wasn't it, of course. That wasn't what was happening. It was all in her head.

She reached out slowly and touched the rough surface of the burned wood, testing its reality. It felt like solid wood, charred though it was. Real wood. Burned wood.

She kept her fingers on that hard, rough surface and looked slowly around her. The security light was painfully bright, so that it was difficult to see anything but darkness beyond it. But she thought she could make out the hulking shape of Ash's Hummer parked in what would have been the house's driveway.

Parked. Engine running.

Someone behind the wheel?

Riley didn't want to let go of the wood. Didn't want to move out of the glare of the light and into the darkness. She stood there listening to the surf pound the beach and asked herself with something she recognized as terror whether she would be able to bear it if the connection she had missed had been right in front of her the whole time.

With her.

In her bed.

She didn't think she would be able to bear it.

"No," she whispered. "It's not him. I trust him."

Then who is it, little girl?

The jolt of coldness went so deep Riley thought her very bones had turned to ice.

You can't face the truth. You could never face the truth.

"Stop." She forced herself to let go of the wood and walked steadily toward the vehicle. "You're dead."

Did you think you had killed me? Silly girl. Some things never die. Haven't you learned that by now?

"Everything dies. You died. I killed you."

Are you sure, little girl?

The Hummer loomed in darkness, its engine idling quietly as she approached it. She steeled herself, but when she opened the driver's-side door, it was to find the vehicle empty.

Oh, did you think he was here? No, little girl. It's just us. Just you and me.

Riley hesitated, then climbed up into the driver's seat.

Are you going to run back to him and hide from the truth? Or come to me and find it?

This time, she didn't hesitate. She put the truck in gear and backed out of the driveway.

Stupid. Of course it was stupid. She was unarmed. And listening to voices in her head.

What kind of sense did that make? No sense, no sense at all.

Because her thinking was fuzzy and she felt cold, and the only thing she was certain of was that this was a bad idea and she would surely regret it.

But you've always wondered, haven't you? Since that day at the river. You've always wondered whether you missed, after all.

"I never miss."

Always a first time, right? And you weren't thinking clearly, after all. He was in your head—

Ah.

"He. So you're someone else, after all."

Silence.

Riley heard a little laugh escape her and realized she knew where she was going, where she needed to be. "Don't tell me there was someone who actually cared about him? Someone who actually missed the miserable son of a bitch once he was gone?"

It's not going to work, little girl.

"You mean I can't make you mad? I'm betting I can. Sooner or later."

Want to bet your life on it?

She drove across the bridge to the mainland

and into Castle, heading for the park. The veil was back in her mind, distancing her from her senses, even herself. But this time, she made no attempt to fight her way through it.

This time, she knew a better way.

Conversationally, as though to someone in the passenger seat, Riley said, "What were you, the apprentice monster? Someone he was grooming to pick up wherever he happened to leave off?"

Don't try to work it all out, Riley. You'll just waste precious energy. Don't you realize you're going to need everything you can summon to fight me?

"Done toying with me, are you? After all these weeks of playing with me like a cat with a mouse. This—today—was all very sudden. Jarring. Almost as if you felt . . . rushed. I wonder why."

Silence.

"You saw the truth today, and it scared you, didn't it? You hadn't bargained on Ash. Oh, you delighted in taking away my memories of falling in love with him, but you didn't truly understand the connection between us. You had no idea it wasn't dependent on memories, that knowing I had trusted him would give me the anchor I needed. And you had no idea he could replenish the energy you were taking away."

He's not here, little girl. Just you. Just us.

Riley didn't let herself think about that, beyond the fleeting understanding that Gordon had been right, that she would always charge into things alone, convinced not so much of her own invincibility as of the responsibility she owed to others.

Those one loved were not put carelessly in harm's way.

Simple, that. A rule to live by.

Or maybe die by.

She parked the Hummer near the break in the fence that was no longer guarded. The path was lit only by what moonlight could filter through the trees, but it was a full moon, and very bright, so Riley could see well enough.

Not that it mattered, really. She was being drawn here, and this time she wasn't fighting it. Beneath the clouded surface of her mind, like a fogged mirror, she waited patiently to emerge. The fog protected her; now that she understood it, she could use it, wear it as she wore so many surfaces.

She allowed confused fragments of thought, seemingly random, to skitter across that misty barrier, while underneath, her mind was working with a clarity as bright and sharp as a knife.

Assembling the pieces of the puzzle.

Riley emerged into the clearing, her gaze going to the peculiarly ancient shape of the stone altar. Nothing hanging above it this time, but the circle had been re-created. She knew that, even though she couldn't see the salt, because there were candles placed at specific points.

Black candles.

Burning.

She took no more than two steps into the clearing and, preoccupied, failed to heed the prickle of warning on the back of her neck that came just seconds before he grabbed her from behind.

21

Riley could command a literal arsenal of hand-to-hand combat techniques, everything from exotic martial arts to down-and-dirty street fighting, and it was the latter instincts that guided her in this particular instance.

With lightning speed, she reached back and grabbed him, her hand squeezing with full strength and short nails digging into his testicles.

He howled in agony and let go of her, and as he fell she twisted expertly and ended up facing him—with his gun in her hands.

Curled on the ground clutching his bruised flesh, gagging and moaning, he was so wrapped up in his own suffering that Riley was reasonably sure he was blind and deaf to everything else around him for at least a couple of long minutes.

She waited him out, his own gun trained on him, and, when he showed signs of beginning to recover, spoke calmly.

"Nature gave you greater size, more muscle, more aggression. Your edge. She also gave you balls." Riley cocked the revolver she had taken from him. "My edge."

Jake didn't even try to get up, and wheezed a few times before he was able to say, "Jesus . . . you fight dirty."

"I fight to win," she told him. "Always."

He wheezed some more, finally getting out, "I figured . . . you'd use some . . . of that . . . martial . . . arts shit."

"Yeah, I could have. But this way was more fun." Even as the flippant words left her, Riley had a realization, and there was no humor in her voice when she added, "You shouldn't be here. Goddammit, Jake, what're you doing here?"

He made a halfhearted attempt to rise, then fell back with a groan. "Shit, Riley, you told me to meet you here. Said you had it all figured out, and—"

She lowered the gun but continued to hold it

in a practiced two-handed grip. "Then why did you grab me?"

"For the hell of it," he replied with another groan, this one more theatrical than real. "I thought you might try to throw me over your shoulder or something, but—Jesus Christ, Riley—"

Typical macho bullshit, she thought, not sparing the energy to even be indignant or disgusted by it. He'd been curious about her self-defense skills, and he'd wanted to get his hands on her.

Figured.

Some of her energy was focused on maintaining the deceptively foggy surface of her mind, but she spared a few tendrils to reach out and probe the clearing.

Absently, she said to Jake, "Stay down, understand? Don't even try to get up. I didn't call you myself, did I? Somebody passed on a message?"

"What're you talking about?"

"Who told you I wanted to meet you, Jake? Or can I guess?" She raised her voice. "You can come out, Leah."

There was a moment of silence, and then the tall redhead stepped into the clearing on the other side. And into the circle. She was definitely out of uniform, wearing a long black robe. The hood was down, allowing her long red hair to gleam in the bright moonlight.

"When did you know?" she asked calmly.

"Slow on the uptake, I'm afraid," Riley answered, matching the other woman's calm. "Today—or yesterday, rather—just before you started yanking my mind around. I figured out there was a connection I had missed. Gordon said it. That he didn't believe in coincidence. Ash and me both here, each with a past connection to John Henry Price, that was what he was thinking. Couldn't be coincidence. And wasn't. You wanted Ash in this. That's why it had to be here. In Castle. Because this is where you found Ash. Right?"

Leah smiled faintly. "I may have underestimated you."

Riley kept going. "Ash was here, and he wasn't going anywhere. He was the only one who had come close to putting Price behind bars where he belonged. And it didn't matter to you that he'd failed. It mattered to you that he had dared."

"He shouldn't have done that," Leah said. "It was . . . upsetting. The trial. All the watching eyes. We don't like watching eyes."

Riley resisted the temptation to follow that tangent. "So it had to be here. Where you'd make your stand and even all the scores. You'd already met Gordon. Probably in Charleston, when he was looking for his retirement spot. That was the question I forgot to ask him, you know, who it was suggested Opal Island as a nice place to retire. I had it backwards, thanks to that sweet little story you spun for me about picking Castle by sticking a pin in a map. I thought he was already here when you came. But it was the other way around, wasn't it, Leah?"

"I'm going to regret Gordon, I think," she replied. "He's been fun. And amazingly easy to handle. Most men are, I've found."

It was taking everything Riley had to split her focus, to keep her eyes on Leah, her voice even and calm as she talked, while another part of her consciousness was reaching out in another direction entirely.

Everything she had was—she hoped—just enough.

"You had already picked your group of satanists," she went on. "Thanks to Price and his interests, you knew the right people. Knew how to find what you were looking for. A tame group ready to relocate, a member with an ex-husband hoping to reconcile. It was, as you say, easy enough to manipulate Wesley Tate. Maybe you went out with him once or twice and found out about Jenny that way."

Leah shrugged, still smiling.

"You had almost all the players ready. Gordon was here. Ash was here. Tate was primed to get his ex-wife and her group here. I was next. To get me here, you needed to worry Gordon. So you did. By planting all those little signs of occult activity. I don't know, maybe you planted a bit more than signs. Maybe you planted the worry in Gordon, or strengthened it. So he'd contact me."

Riley took a half step to one side, coming around just a bit to face the other woman more squarely.

She didn't raise Jake's gun.

"And I came. All according to your plan. Or was it his plan? Does your father control you even from his grave, Leah?"

That surprised Leah, her smile fading and tension visible as she stiffened.

Riley nodded. "He really didn't like women, but he had tried to be what he believed was normal. No marriage on the books, no girlfriend we could ever find, so I'm betting your mother was a one-night stand. What was she, Leah, some hooker he paid to help him get it up?"

Leah's head moved slightly in an odd, twisted

way—and in the circle all the candles flared suddenly brighter.

The extra light allowed Riley to see what she had been afraid of seeing. In the center of the circle, lying limply across the flat altar stone, was Jenny.

Not dead yet: The long, curved blade of the knife Leah held was not yet bloodied. But the dark woman was clearly unconscious.

Riley was still trying to hide the part of her mind and senses that was reaching desperately for a connection, so she made her voice a bit slow and uncertain.

"I guess the darkest energy would come from the sacrifice of a priestess, wouldn't it? And you need the darkest energy tonight. A full moon, a satanic priestess. What else, Leah? Does Jenny have some of your blood in her stomach like Tate did?"

"So you figured that out, did you?"

"That it was your blood? Had to be, really. Whoever planned that sacrifice had saved and stored the blood. And you really couldn't afford to have another body turn up before your plan was under way. So it had to be your blood."

"My father's blood."

Riley didn't allow herself to be distracted. "I'm betting you were a teenager when he found you. Or you found him. Evil calling out to evil, I imagine. It does that, we've found. Anyway, he had his apprentice. His blood princess. And you were good, I'll give you that. The whole time I was tracking him, you were on me, weren't you? I was focused on him, so obsessed I was blind to you being right there. Watching me. Reporting back to him."

"He would have beaten you," Leah said suddenly, her voice changing, dropping and taking on a guttural edge. "That was the plan. To seem to be shot. To fall into the river. So we could stop running. So we could settle somewhere."

"What went wrong?"

"So stupid and senseless. The body armor he wore saved him from your bullets. But it was heavy. The current was stronger than we'd anticipated. And he was winded from the chase. He drowned."

"Pity," Riley said without remorse. "I was hoping he really suffered."

Again, Leah's head moved in that stiff, twisted way, and again the candles flared, this time as though the flames were fed by gas jets. The clearing was nearly as bright as day, the woods around them dark and shadowed.

From the corner of her eye, Riley made sure Jake was still. And he was. In shock, probably, she thought. Shock of the emotional kind. Or total bewilderment.

She said, "I guess you've been having a lot of fun messing with my head, huh?"

"You have no idea," Leah said. "You were a challenge at first. I was only able to cloak my mind without affecting yours very much. That's why I resorted to the Taser."

"Yeah, that plus all the dark energy you were channeling, especially from the sacrifice, was enough to get the job done. And I'll bet you really enjoyed butchering Wesley Tate. Chip off the old block, aren't you?"

"I am my father's daughter."

Riley thought she had never heard anything so chilling as that proud statement. She drew a breath and fought to keep her own voice even and steady.

"So it was all about payback. You took your time, set up the situation just as you wanted it. Used the satanists as window dressing, something to keep us distracted while you were performing all the black rites alone. Using fire. Using blood. Using death. Whatever it took to get the power you wanted, you needed. To destroy me. Not just kill me. Destroy me."

"You took away my father. You have to pay for that," Leah said reasonably.

"Your father was a sadistic bag of evil," Riley said in a matching tone. "The world needed to be rid of him. The sane world, at least."

Leah stiffened again but laughed, the sound like brittle sticks rattling together. "You don't seem to get it, little girl. I've already beaten you. I've stolen time from you. I've wrecked your memories. I've fixed it so you don't even remember falling in love. How sad is that?"

"Now, see, **that's** the one step too far. That's the one that's going to cost you, Leah. Because I understand the need for vengeance. Makes perfect sense to me. Even to avenge a sadistic bag of evil like Price. I get that. But the memory of finding my soul mate? I want that back. And you're going to give it to me."

This time Leah's laugh was a bit—just a bit—uncertain. "What you don't get is that you've lost. Your mind is so weak there's no way it can even fight me, much less take back what I stole from it."

"You're right. I'm not strong enough to beat you. Not alone. But that's what **you** don't get, Leah. I'm not alone." Riley reached back with one hand and felt Ash's fingers close around hers.

There was a frozen moment when Leah realized, understood. She lifted her knife and lunged toward Jenny's prone body.

Needing the sacrifice. The power.

Riley fired one shot, hitting Leah in the hand so that the knife fell from her suddenly useless fingers.

"No," she said hoarsely. "I won't let you—"

Riley had never tried to do anything even remotely like this before, yet somehow she knew exactly what to do. When Leah gathered her fury, all her emotions, and screamed, sending a visible, jagged spear of dark energy from the circle aimed at Riley, it didn't find its target as a weapon, but as a tool.

It was almost like the Taser attack that had really started everything, only this time Riley wasn't caught, wasn't trapped, and was a long, long way from defenseless. And this time she didn't discharge her strength into the earth but channeled the sheer energy flung at her, took from it what she was determined to have, and then sent what was left streaming back to its source.

But when it returned to Leah, it was white-hot and burning, and her second scream shattered the night even as the energy shattered her circle of power. There was an almost blinding burst of light, the scream was cut off as though by a knife, and then it was over.

The candles were gone. The salt scattered to

the winds. And clean moonlight shone down on the two women closest to the altar, one of them just beginning to stir and the other a crumpled form on the ground.

"Is she dead?" Ash asked.

"No," Riley answered. "But powerless now. Jenny was drugged, but she's coming out of it. She should be fine."

"With a stomach full of blood, she's going to be sick."

"Well, after that, she'll be fine. I don't know if she'll go back to being a satanist, but she'll live."

"Thanks to you."

She turned and looked at him, smiling. "Thanks to us. Hello. I remember you."

Ash was smiling as well. "Good."

Jake struggled to rise from the ground, his "What the bloody **hell** is all this?" several octaves higher than he, perhaps, would have preferred.

Riley glanced at him, and then said to her soul mate, "I have a feeling the debriefing is going to take some time."

"That's okay," Ash said, pulling her into his arms. "We have time."

EPILOGUE

Gordon admitted he'd been feeling uneasy about Leah for weeks before he called me," Riley said. "It was nothing he could put his finger on, just a feeling something wasn't right. When all the supposed evidence of occult activities began turning up, he thought maybe that was it, that somebody'd put a hex on her or something like that."

Ash raised his eyebrows. "A hex?"

"Hey, we've all seen weirder things, believe me. And Gordon's Louisiana roots run deep. Thing is, stories his grandmother told him clash with his Duke education, so he has a tendency to doubt his own instincts when it comes to the paranormal."

"Duke, huh? I guess that also explains why he's drawling one minute and talking like a college professor the next."

"Yeah, that explains it." Riley leaned against the deck railing and gazed down the beach, where a bonfire burned brightly—surrounded by a rather sober group of satanists. It was Friday night, and they were having their scheduled "marshmallow roast."

"I don't think they're having much fun," Ash noted.

"No. Too much to take in, probably. Even though they weren't involved, they got too close to the dark side for a while. The very dark side. That tends to give people pause."

"I can see how it would."

Riley smiled slightly, without looking at him. "But not you, right?"

"Any pausing I did was early on," he said. "Back when we were both cranky about falling in love. Once we fell, there really wasn't anything to be done about it. Except enjoy."

"Glad you added that last part."

"Probably a good thing I can. I mean, I'm hitching my fate to a clairvoyant ex-military FBI agent who specializes in the occult and has the power to yank me out of a sound sleep in the middle of the night and draw me miles to her side in order to help her defeat the evil spawn of a serial killer."

Riley chewed on her lower lip for a moment, and said, "Well, when you put it like that . . ."

"I'm a very brave man."

"Yes. You are." Riley turned and smiled at him in the bright moonlight. "Bishop's going to try to recruit you, you know." It wasn't quite a question.

"I had a feeling."

"Well, we'd make a hell of a team."

Ash pulled her into his arms. "We already do, love."

It was all the answer Riley needed.